Blu

My entire life is my music—and all the trappings that come with it. Sex, booze, and rock 'n' roll is all I ever wanted. Touring the world as the lead singer of Balefire, I have it all. Until on hiatus, I meet the girl next door.

Ashleigh Baker is nothing like the groupies and celebrities who usually have all my attention. In her cute floppy hat with her knees stained with dirt, she spends her days creating a flowering show piece from her rented yard. She's the most gorgeous woman I've ever met, and she acts like she doesn't want a damn thing to do with me. But from the moment I laid eyes on her, she's all I can think about.

Ashleigh

Growing up the only child of an Air Force Colonel, all I wanted was to stay in one place for more than a minute. When I score a pretty little house with a long-term lease, I just want to grow my flowers and my freelancing gig as a music reviewer. Then a loud Harley wakes me from a sound sleep and I discover my neighbor is Blu Connolly. Yeah, that Blu Connolly, lead singer for my favorite band Balefire. With his killer good looks and panty-melting voice, he's a walking temptation to sin. Though I do my best to avoid him, it seems Blu has other ideas. He's on a mission to wear me down, let him in, but what happens when he stops wanting to sing for me?

Other Books by Tam DeRudder Jackson

The Talisman Series
Talisman
Warrior
Prophetess
(novella)
Bard
Druid

The Balefire Series
Play For Me
Sing For Me

Sing For Me

Tam DeRudder Jackson

Editor: Nikki Busch Editing
Cover Design: Steamy Designs
Formatting: Damonza
Distribution and POD: IngramSpark

For all the musicians, roadies, drivers,
promoters and small live music venues who had to
take over a year off from live music:
your fans love you, we missed you,
and we can't wait to see your live shows again.

Chapter One

Blu

WITH A TALL pretty blonde tucked under my left arm and a gorgeous bronze-skinned brunette under my right, my fingers loosely holding the neck of a bottle of beer, I surveyed the action. Music pounded a decibel-ripping beat. A rainbow of lights pulsed across the ceiling and along the walls of the ballroom. Raucous laughter punctuated loud conversation. Buffet tables groaning beneath a feast of regional food lined one wall while bars flowing with alcohol lined two others. People gyrated on the dance floor in the middle of the room, and something resembling a mosh pit writhed in front of the dais where a local band thumped furiously to impress the crowd. Oh yeah, this after-party was ending the Australian leg of our tour in epic style.

Spotting the monk, I carried my half-empty bottle of Australia's finest beer with me while I walked the girls over to where he sat in front of one of the bars.

"Hey Jack. Look what I've got." I grinned. "You know I like to party with multiple ladies at once, but I'm up for sharing if you're interested. Blonde or brunette, which do you prefer?"

Jack Whitehorse, Balefire's drummer, saluted me with his beer, took a pull, and said, "Wouldn't want to horn in on your fun, Blu my man. You enjoy yourself." He smirked at me before turning his attention to the ladies in my arms. "I have no doubt you two beauties will enjoy yourselves."

He took another swig of beer and gave me a pointed look to shove off. I stared back at him for a long moment, daring him with a smirk to do something.

Jack joined Balefire a couple of years back when our old drummer decided he couldn't stay sober and tour with us. Though it drove our lead guitarist Dakota Perri nuts, Jack preferred to keep to himself, and not once had I ever seen him wander off with a woman while we were on tour. One time, Jack overheard Dakota and me talking about his preferences, and he burst out laughing, so I guess he likes girls after all. You wouldn't know one way or the other from his behavior.

I leaned in and spoke directly into his ear. "It's the last night of our Asian tour, Jackie-boy. You haven't indulged in any of the first-class exotic pussy on offer anywhere we've been. You're worrying me, man."

Jack pulled a face and sat back. "We discussed this on the jet, Blu. I've got someone special waiting for me back home." Addressing the girls, he added, "Thanks for the offer."

Dakota and Adam Tron, our bassist, said Jack hooked up with a hottie last summer after we played a show back home at Red Rocks, but I think they might have been jerking my chain. From where I stood, Jack had earned his nickname "the monk."

When I'd offered him one of the girls with me, I already knew his answer. The standing joke between us involved me offering whatever candy I scored during or after a show and Jack politely declining. Dakota liked to steal his phone and program it with a wake-up call featuring a prerecorded come-on from whichever girl he took to his room after a show. The joke had worn pretty thin with Jack these days. The two of them had almost come to blows over it more than once, so I might have been walking on thin ice making my offer tonight.

Still, with it being our last night on tour for a while and all, I thought Jack could use a good time. The two pretty sheilas I had my arms around could be exactly what he needed to pull him out of the dark mood he'd crawled into at the end of last fall. Couldn't say his refusal surprised me though.

I poked the bear anyway. "If you change your mind, buddy, here's the spare key card to my room." I let go of blondie long enough to fish the card from my back pocket and hand it to him. "Don't bother to knock. Just let yourself in. We'll welcome you right into the party, won't we girls?"

"Sure, Blu. Anything you say."

"Whatever you want, Blu. We just want to be with you tonight."

Jack laughed and took the card. "Ain't gonna happen. But thanks again for the offer. You all have a nice time."

"I'm sure we will."

I noticed he pocketed the card before taking another pull off his beer. Interesting.

Dakota and I often shared girls when we were on tour. Sex, drugs—in our case booze—and rock 'n' roll were big draws when we started Balefire back in high school. Tron had never been into sharing women, and apparently, Jack favored Tron in that department. Unlike Jack though, Tron did entertain his fair share of the ladies whenever we hit the road on tour.

After ten years together, Dakota, Tron, and I remained best friends and committed to the life. Changing drummers three years ago, though, amped up the music, and none of us could deny how much our new drummer improved our sound. Not only was Jack Whitehorse a virtuoso drummer, he was also a damn fine songwriter. On this tour alone we'd written like ten or twenty new songs. As much as I enjoyed touring, I couldn't wait to go home, relax my vocal cords a bit, and hit the studio to record our new material.

The giggling of the girls pasted to my sides brought me out of my reverie, and I smiled at each of them in turn. "Looks like you're going to have me to yourselves tonight, ladies. You do know how to share, don't you?"

More giggling answered my question.

I walked the girls down the bar and signaled the bartender. "Hey buddy. Snag me a couple of bottles of champagne, would ya? And three glasses."

Speaking to each girl in turn, I asked, "Champagne all right with you?"

"We love champagne," brunette said.

"Whatever you want, Blu," blondie added.

Something about the girls' unconditional willingness to do whatever I suggested irritated the back of my conscience, but I finished off my beer, set the empty on the bar, and pushed the nebulous thought from my mind before it crystallized into something I had to deal with. I grabbed the bottles of champagne the bartender set in front of us and gestured to the girls to snag the champagne flutes before I escorted them from the after-party to a different kind of party up in my suite.

Ashleigh

"I swear I have never seen a young person who loved her flowers as much as you do, Ashleigh Baker," Diane Connolly commented from her side of the fence separating our yards. "You're renting your place, aren't you, darlin'?"

I leaned back on my heels from my hands-and-knees position in front of the roses I was planting. "Diane, I moved into this place because my landlady said she'd subtract some rent if I indulged my hobby. Win-win." I grinned.

The last Saturday in May found me in my favorite place— my backyard garden. My part-time job as a substitute teacher surprisingly limited the time I had to spend in my garden since finding my rental earlier in the spring. I wanted to complete my long list of tasks while I still had the time. Plus, the weather in Denver cooperated so beautifully with my gardening plans that nothing could have kept me indoors.

"Are you at a point in your planting that you could take a break and join me on my patio for lunch?"

"Is it lunchtime?"

A quick glance at the sun high overhead and a rather embarrassing rumble from my stomach confirmed I'd lost myself in my yard again.

Diane laughed. "Why don't you ditch your gardening gloves and come over for a bite to eat? I made chicken and avocado sandwiches and a lovely fruit salad with strawberries and feta cheese. And I have a gallon of fresh-brewed sun tea to wash it all down. It's on my table waiting for us."

I stood and brushed dirt and mulch off my bare knees. "You're absolutely the nicest neighbor anyone could ever have. Let me go inside and wash my hands, and I'll be right over."

"See you in a few," she said with a smile.

After living in a tiny apartment for years while I finished college, I'd become claustrophobic. All the noise and lack of privacy and space wore on me, something I mentioned one day at one of the schools where I worked. One thing led to another, and a teacher friend suggested I check out a sweet little house she'd heard had come up for rent. Something with a yard. Next thing I knew, I was living next door to Diane Connolly.

Yes, *that* Diane Connolly, mother of Blu Connolly, lead singer of my all-time favorite band Balefire. I'd skipped lattes for a month to save money for a ticket to their show at Red Rocks last summer. It was worth every penny and more. I'd fallen half in love with Blu Connolly merely listening to his voice on the Balefire station on my music streaming app. Seeing him perform in person with all that raw energy radiating excitement and fun and sex—did I mention the guy's moves as he projected his stadium-sized voice to the world?—completely blew my mind.

Almost as much as discovering I'd moved next door to his childhood home, the home where his mom still lived. The amazing part? Diane turned out to be the most normal, down-to-earth, open, and sweet person I'd ever met. She also seemed lonely. Ever since I'd moved in, whenever she invited me to lunch most Saturdays or the occasional Sunday, I accepted.

Ancient elm and willow trees shaded her backyard and patio, a welcome respite from the blazing sun I'd worked under all morning. I seated myself at her table and downed a cooling swallow of iced tea.

"This looks delicious. You must have spent the whole morning cooking, Diane," I gushed as I surveyed the feast in front of me—a feast she served on fine china with cloth napkins and fancy silver flatware. The woman knew how to entertain, even if the only person I knew she entertained was me. It seemed no one else ever came to her door.

"It's nothing, really," she demurred. "I saw this recipe for California chicken sandwiches on one of the cooking shows I enjoy and thought I'd give it a try. Go on, dig in."

With her avidly watching me, obviously eager for my response to her offering, I cut my sandwich in half and took a bite. Closing my eyes, I groaned in pure ecstasy as a symphony of flavors reverberated over my palate. Smooth, rich avocado, spicy chicken, something sweet yet tangy—the dressing maybe?—and the full-bodied flavor of sun-ripened tomatoes flowed over my taste buds, all bookended with warm buttery homemade bread.

Opening my eyes, I said, "Diane, are you married? 'Cause if you're not, I might ask you to marry me." I savored another bite. "I've never had the pleasure of enjoying a gourmet sandwich before, but I think I could get used to it if given the chance."

At the mention of marriage, a cloud briefly passed over her face before she banished it with a smile. "I'm so glad you like it. Honestly, I wasn't sure about the dressing. It's sometimes a challenge deciding whether certain flavors will work together, like Dijon mustard, fennel, and poppy seed."

"Ah. That's the secret dressing." I grinned and took another bite of sandwich heaven.

"There are one or two additional ingredients, but putting those three together worried me a little. I'm so glad you like it." At last, she cut into her sandwich and took a delicate bite.

"Like it? It's borderline orgasmic." I licked sauce from the corner of my mouth before being polite and using my napkin. After watching Diane with her sandwich, I tried for a more ladylike bite. "I need to eat this slowly, savor it, but it's so good, I'm not sure I'm disciplined enough to slow down."

She beamed and took another dainty bite of her sandwich.

For a few minutes, we ate quietly, enjoying the food and the lovely early summer day.

Diane broke the silence. "What are your plans when school finishes this week? Do you have a summer job lined up?"

"I've been hitting the local bars on the weekends to listen to the bands playing them and writing reviews for a couple of online newspapers and a blog. The writing doesn't pay much, but it keeps my name and, more importantly, my work in front of editors." Setting my sandwich down, I sipped some tea and continued. "I'm hoping someone at one of those outlets will give me the chance to write for them full-time. After all, that's what I went to college for."

"Well, I've read some of your reviews in the local paper, and I think you're a very talented writer. As you can probably guess, I enjoy my son's music, but one of your reviews of some bluegrass band had me tapping my feet as I read it and thinking I might catch that band the next time they're in the area."

"You're sweet to say that. Thanks."

"Speaking of bands, Bu's Asian tour wrapped up yesterday. I

expect him home early next week. If you don't have any plans, I'd like to have you over for a meal, introduce you to my son."

She extended the invitation so casually, so matter-of-factly. Like she didn't have a clue about her son's fame. Of course she had no clue about my private love affair with his incredible voice. Good thing we were eating alfresco since I splattered the sip of tea I'd taken all over her patio.

"Ashleigh! Are you all right?"

I choked and coughed for another minute before trying ineffectually to wipe up tea from the patio's flagstones.

"Fine, Diane. Really." I cleared my throat. "Sorry about that." My face felt like it was trying to mimic the color of the tomatoes on my sandwich.

She laughed so hard that tears ran down her pretty face. The woman damn sure didn't look old enough to have a son who was nearing thirty. Her good humor at my expense was infectious, and before long I found myself laughing with her.

"If you could have seen your face when I told you Blu will be in town next week," she gasped.

I sobered up at last. "You do realize that normal people don't just drop that sort of information into a casual conversation, right?"

"He's my son, Ashleigh. I brought him into the world and changed his diapers and listened to his teachers love his charm and despair of his wildness. That was something I despaired of even more than they did. Forgive me for forgetting for a minute how famous he is."

The visual of Diane changing Blu Connolly's diapers momentarily sidetracked me as I tried to get a handle on it. "I guess I have a hard time thinking about the guy I saw strutting all over the stage at Red Rocks last summer as someone's little boy. Especially *your* little boy."

At the look she shot me, I hastily added, "Only because he has a reputation as a wild man and you're so sweet and normal. You live in a modest house on a quiet street in the suburbs of Denver. You don't drive a fancy car or flaunt a lot of money." She cocked a brow, and I rushed on. "Plus, with your trim figure and smooth skin and that thick blond braid you favor, you look more like Blu's older sister than his mom. How old were you when you had him? Seven?"

"You're a sweetheart, Ashleigh," Diane said, and there was genuine warmth in her voice. "I can't wait for you to meet my son. I think you two are going to hit it off so well."

CHAPTER TWO

Ashleigh

"WHAT ARE YOU doing this summer, Ash?" my friend Jaime Hughes asked as I helped her pack up her classroom on the last day of school.

"I put my name in to sub for summer school, and I'll continue to review bands at the local bars for the regional papers. Likely, I'll have to find something else too. I doubt I'll have as many subbing jobs in the summer as I do during the regular school year." I ran the packing tape over the seam of the box I'd filled with books and walked it over to a growing stack in the corner of her classroom.

"If you'd like a sidekick to tag along with you on your band reviews, count me in," she offered as she marked a box with her Sharpie and carried it to the stack.

"I'm taking you up on that, especially for road trips when I venture up to Fort Collins or over to Telluride." I grinned.

She grinned back at me. "That sounds like a ton of fun. I'm all over that."

"Maybe you'd be all over coming with me when I meet Blu Connolly from Balefire too," I said casually.

Jaime nearly dropped the box she'd picked up. "*What?* What did you say? You're meeting Blu Connolly? When?"

Grabbing an empty box, I started filling it with books she'd left piled on students' desks. "I don't exactly know. Turns out, his mom is my neighbor. Didn't I mention that?"

Jaime planted her hands on her hips and shook her head, the look on her face expressing rather eloquently what she thought of my little omission.

"Anyway, he's coming home soon, and she wants me to meet him. Honestly, I can't decide if I'm excited, terrified, or worried about meeting him."

"Excited. Definitely excited. And terrified." She laughed. "But why would you be worried?"

Tipping my head to the side, I went brows up and stared her down.

"You can't believe everything you read in the supermarket tabloids, Ash. Everyone knows that."

"Still, you know what they say: where there's smoke, there's fire. Balefire actively encourages women to toss their bras and panties onstage." I added a box to the growing stacks on the side of the room. "Plus, every photo ever taken of Blu offstage shows him with his arms around two or three or more girls. Blu Connolly could be the poster boy for the term *fuckboy*."

Jaime's eyes danced as she handed me yet another box of supplies to put in the corner. "As hot as he is and with the way he can sing, who could resist him? I doubt I could." She waggled her brows. "But I'd love to test that out by meeting him."

"You'd think with all his money, he could at least buy his mom a nicer house though. The one she lives in next door to me is a mirror image of my rental." I took a swig from my water bottle. "The patio in her backyard is an improvement, and she has new carpet and a state-of-the-art kitchen with stainless steel appliances, granite countertops, and beautiful blond oak cabinetry." I took another drink, capped my water bottle, and set it on a nearby desk. "But the house itself is something right out of 1965. Besides the kitchen, there's a modest living room, tiny bathroom, an average-sized master bedroom downstairs, and two small bedrooms and a bathroom on the second floor. As houses go, it's not much."

"Maybe she likes it there," Jaime said as she filled another box with reference texts that lived on her desk during the school year.

"How could she? All the neighbors are in their sixties and seventies, easily twenty years older than she is. Plus, there's no excitement at all in our neighborhood. Zero. Zip." I curled my fingers into zeroes to emphasize my point. Honestly, I was sure I lived on the quietest street in Denver. "She leaves her house maybe two or three days a week, but most of the time, all her lights are on at home where she spends her time alone as far as I can tell."

"You live in the neighborhood too. So it can't be that bad." Jaime's eyes danced.

"I live there because the rent is cheap, and I have a yard I can putter around in. Diane offers me lunch every weekend practically, yet I never see anyone else visit her." I held a couple of dioramas in my hands, student projects from the looks of them. "Where do you want these?"

"Put them on the top shelf in the closet, please."

I arched a brow in question.

"They're excellent examples to show other students for that assignment next year."

With a shrug, I headed over to the closet at the back of Jaime's room. "I think she's lonely. If Blu were any kind of a son, he'd use some of his vast wealth to help out his mom is all I'm saying."

"If she invites you to lunch while he's in town, guess you'll find out if he's a fuckboy, a selfish bastard, or a regular guy with a badass reputation."

"Guess you're right."

Blu

On some latent adult level I usually tried to suppress, I knew racing my Harley up Mom's quiet street at eleven o'clock on a Wednesday night wasn't cool. Then again, irritating her annoyingly uptight neighbors had been one of my favorite pastimes since I could remember.

When I pulled into Mom's driveway, I revved the engine a couple of extra times for old times' sake and to alert Mom that I'd made it home. Cutting the engine, I didn't bother to hold back a grin when all the lights flipped on in the house next door. Mission accomplished. Old Man Smith would be out any second to tell me off and Mom would come out to apologize to him and pretend to scold me. He'd grumble and go back inside his house while Mom wrapped me in a breath-squeezing hug, and I'd know I was home.

Imagine my surprise when a gorgeous spitfire in a short silk pearl-gray robe stood in the halo of the porch light next door glaring at me. "Who the hell do you think you are roaring up this quiet street at this hour of the night?" she hissed. "Do you have any manners at all?"

She planted her fists firmly on her hips, and my hands itched to join them there. One fuzzy slippered foot pushed in front of the other, while her rich brown hair fell in soft waves over her shoulders and down over her full breasts. *Da-amn.*

I was about to pop off with some smart-ass comment about how mannerly I could be when Mom appeared out of nowhere beside me.

"Blu, baby! You're home! I'm so glad to see you." She wrapped her arms around me in one of her signature tight hugs. I'd probably be ninety, and the woman would still hug me like she was trying to absorb me into her skin. I had to admit though, I'd missed these Mom hugs.

When she pulled away at last, she addressed her neighbor from inside the circle of my arms. "Ashleigh, I'm sorry I didn't warn you.

The rest of the neighborhood is not surprised that Blu announced his return the way he did." She slanted me a look. "I'm not sure they're used to it, but they're definitely not surprised." It was as close to scolding as Mom ever came. "Ashleigh Baker, this is my son, Blu Connolly. Blu, this is my new neighbor Ashleigh," Mom said, a big smile on her face.

"Of course you are," Ashleigh drawled. She didn't sound neighborly at all. Which meant I'd need to turn on the charm since I wanted to explore the hot woman beneath that cool exterior. Those fuzzy slippers made me think she wasn't as aloof as she tried to sound.

I couldn't see her face well in the shadows of her porch light, but the rest of her put my dick on high alert. Her long legs, slender arms, nipped-in waist, and exceptionally nice rack grabbed my full attention and refused to let go, even with my mom plastered tightly to my side.

"It's late, Blu," Mom said. "Why don't you come inside and settle in? You can tell me all about your latest tour."

"Sure Mom," I said, my eyes never leaving Ashleigh Baker who didn't make a move to go back inside her house.

"We'll have Ashleigh over for lunch tomorrow, and you two can meet properly. Will lunch tomorrow work for you, Ashleigh sweetheart?"

She didn't respond right away, and I wondered what was going through her mind. At last she replied, "Sure Diane. Let me know what time. Good night."

Was it just me, or did she sound less than enthusiastic about the idea?

Jetlag must have fucked up my brain more than usual. I hadn't even formed a come-on in my head before Ashleigh spun around and walked back inside her house, letting the door slam behind her. I had the distinct impression the woman didn't like me.

Huh.

Challenge accepted.

♪

I forgot how much the day change messed with me when I returned home from a Pacific tour. Mom and I sat up and talked until nearly three o'clock in the morning the night I returned home. After going to bed, I didn't wake up until the middle of Friday morning. Which meant I still hadn't met Mom's new neighbor properly. Something Mom—and I admit I—meant to remedy at lunch this afternoon.

Mom noticed Ashleigh working in her backyard garden, which I gathered the woman did every day, and asked if I wouldn't mind walking over and inviting her to our place. When I followed Mom's eyes out her kitchen window, I saw beneath a floppy straw hat a long brown braid pointing the way to a very sweet ass as she knelt over her flowers. Mom didn't need to ask me a second time to make a trip over to the neighbor's.

"Hey beautiful!" I called out before casually vaulting the fence separating the two yards.

No response.

"Hey gorgeous!" I called a little louder as I walked across the grass.

No response.

"Pretty woman, whatcha doin'?"

Still no response.

So I walked over and stood in front of her. When she didn't look up, I squatted down and pushed her hat up a bit off her forehead and looked into her breath-stoppingly stunning face.

I stared for several seconds before I pulled myself back together, but sweet Jesus, she was incredible.

"You have your earbuds in or something, sweetheart?" I asked with a grin.

"No."

I sat back on my heels. "Why didn't you acknowledge me when I was talking to you then?" I asked.

"I didn't realize you were talking to me."

"Who else would I be talking to?"

"Hard to say."

What the fuck? Kinda hostile, this one.

Giving her my best sexy smile, I said, "You're the only pretty woman in this yard."

She stared at me, the sapphire-blue gems of her eyes clear and emotionless, and said nothing.

"What?" Now she was downright irritating. Women did not respond to me the way Ashleigh Baker responded to me.

Ever.

"I'm digging little holes for my flowers with a trowel. *You* are digging a giant hole for yourself with an excavator." She cocked her head and gave me a smug smile beneath raised eyebrows, like she expected something special from me.

Damned if I knew what. "Come again?"

"Beautiful, gorgeous, pretty woman, sweetheart—why bother learning the names of the women who can't wait to get naked with you or even just drop to their knees to wrap their lips around your dick in the back of your tour bus? I bet you didn't even hear my name when your mom introduced us the other night." She rested her gloved hands on her thighs, drawing my attention to her smooth, tanned skin. "That's kind of a bummer for you because I don't answer to anything else."

I racked my brain trying to remember what I'd said or done the other night to piss this woman off so much. Aside from my usual antics on my bike, I couldn't come up with one damned thing. She stared at me for a long minute while I tried to figure it out. Then she went back to planting her flowers.

This one might be beautiful—scratch that—Ashleigh Baker was fucking gorgeous. But she had attitude to give away, and I wasn't in the market for it. Without thinking, I reached out and put my hand on hers, stilling her in her work. Even through her thick gardening gloves, I could feel her vibrancy, one of the few people I'd ever met who was passionately, wildly alive. My hand on hers shot heat straight through me to my dick, but I ignored it.

"Ashleigh Baker, my mom would like you to come over to her place for lunch. That is, if you're not too busy planting flowers or digging up assumptions about the neighbors."

I stood and jogged across her yard back to the fence, vaulted it again, and walked back into Mom's house.

"You two were talking for quite a while out there. I knew you'd hit it off," Mom said, beaming, when I strode through the back door into her kitchen. "Did Ashleigh accept our invitation?"

"I assume so, but I just remembered I have something I need to do. I'll grab some lunch when I'm done, so don't worry about saving any for me." I kept moving right through the house into the living room and up the stairs to my old room.

Mom started to say something, but I took the stairs two at a time and didn't catch it.

Deliberately.

As I dressed in my leathers, Ashleigh's words echoed in my brain. And I didn't like how close to the mark she'd hit. I'd thought about her several times after I woke up this morning, not only what she looked like the night we met, but also how she acted in my dreams as I slept off my jetlag. I hated to admit to myself that my plans had included charming her right out of her clothes, and yes, maybe even enjoying those plump pink lips of hers wrapped sweetly around my dick, dammit.

Who the fuck does she think she is calling me out like that? I jerked on my heavy riding boots with a scowl. What royally pissed me off was in that one short conversation, Ashleigh had gone and cranked up the volume on that nagging little voice in the back of my mind, the one that had been pushing to be heard throughout most of our last tour. The one that kept trying to remind me that I wasn't always an asshole who never bothered to learn a tenth of the names of the women I fucked. They each got as much—or more—out of the experience as I did. After all, they could go home and brag to all their girlfriends that they'd done a rock star.

Why did a stranger's observations make me feel like a douche? What was it about Ashleigh in particular? After all, she was just another pretty face. Though I suspected she possessed a smokin' hot body, I had yet to see it all clearly, with or without clothes.

I stomped down the stairs and out the front door, ignoring Mom's questions and that annoying little voice trying to gain some traction in my head. A ride would clear away those thoughts before they turned into something I'd have to face honestly.

Yeah, and I might have given in too much to the asshole as I revved my bike loud and long before I tore out of Mom's driveway.

CHAPTER THREE

Ashleigh

ALTHOUGH BLU ACTED like the entitled playboy the press reported him to be, I couldn't ignore the jolt of electricity that shot up my arm when he placed his hand over mine in my garden. His heat radiated through my suede gardening gloves, and for a second there, I irrationally worried he could feel my heart race beneath his long fingers.

Frustrated with myself and my talent for leaping to conclusions, I sighed again. Blu putting me in my place with his quiet invitation to lunch showed me he wasn't the only one who knew how to bury himself under a mountain of the wrong words. Still, who could blame me for thinking he didn't know or care to know my name after his initial come-on?

And why did Blu Connolly have to be even more devastatingly handsome in person than on the cover of a magazine? The playfulness in those changeable hazel eyes of his could tempt a nun to sin. Plus, most women would kill to have even half the length of his long dark lashes. Then there were his deep dimples when he grinned at me, dimples that would add character to his face as he aged, keeping him handsomely young his entire life.

The loose-limbed grace of his movements initially distracted me from his size, but when he squatted down in front of me, his broad chest and shoulders took up my entire line of sight. When I turned my head to watch him lope away from me after I stuck my foot firmly in my mouth, I noticed how impossibly tall the man was. At five feet six, I'm not a short woman, but the way Blu basically stepped over the four-foot-high fence separating Diane's property from mine told me he stood well over six feet.

That gorgeous package contained a voice from heaven inside it. During our brief conversation, his rich baritone vibrated through me even more than the almost haunting half-step higher quality of his singing voice, which I listened to regularly. No wonder women threw their panties at him whenever he performed live.

Apparently, I'd spent a little too much time thinking and showering and dithering over what to wear to lunch at Diane's because right as I stepped out my back door en route to her patio, I heard Blu's Harley roar angrily to life. After several loud surly revs of the engine, I heard him kick the bike into gear and tear out of Diane's driveway. Huh. Perhaps the sunny yellow halter dress I'd toned down with demur brown espadrilles would impress his mom?

Or maybe she forgot some exotic ingredient, and Blu tore off in a hurry to retrieve it so we wouldn't have to delay lunch?

Doubt it.

Pasting a bright smile on my face, I let myself through the gate between Diane's yard and mine and walked purposefully over to her patio. I'd splurged on a bottle of good white wine as a gift to her for having me over for lunch so often. And maybe to impress her son a little. Like he would have noticed anyway.

"Hello? Diane?" I sang out. "Am I too late for lunch?"

Plates and flatware lay stacked in the middle of her patio table like they couldn't decide if they were coming or going. The tablecloth fluttered absently in the breeze. The scene resembled one of those movies where the family disappears into a sudden vortex or is kidnapped by aliens, leaving behind their dinner to spoil in the sun.

"Diane? Are you here?"

Maybe Blu convinced her to skip lunch with me, and they headed off together on his Harley to eat at some exclusive restaurant. That would be a treat he owed his mom, in my opinion.

As that thought crossed my mind, Diane bustled out the back door, her smile appearing the tiniest bit forced.

"I'm sorry, Ashleigh. I'm afraid it will be only the two of us for lunch today. Blu remembered he had something to do downtown, so he won't be joining us."

"No worries, Diane. Ever since I moved here, lunching with you has become the highlight of my week." I handed her the bottle of wine. "Here. A little something to say thank you for all the wonderful meals you've shared with me." When she looked like she might try to decline, I added, "Is there anything I can help you with?"

She stared at me for several seconds before collecting herself. "It's unfortunate Blu isn't here to see you looking so pretty. Your dress is absolutely darling." Something distracted her before she returned her attention to me. "Well, it can't be helped." She sighed. Though she seemed to be referring to Blu's absence from lunch, I couldn't help but pick up on the idea she meant something else. What, I couldn't imagine.

Pulling in a long breath and letting it out slowly, she seemed to come to a decision. Standing a little taller, she said, "How 'bout you set the table while I decant this wine and let it breathe. I'll be out with lunch in a few minutes."

I set the table for two and stood beside it wondering what to do with the spare plate and utensils, my thoughts wandering to the man Diane had intended to use them for. Where could he have gone? Did my skeptical response to him turn him off? Or did he find me and my big mouth so unattractive he'd rather not eat with me?

Diane rescued me from my morose thoughts.

"I'll take those, sweetheart. How 'bout you arrange the bread and the salad and come inside for the wineglasses and the napkins. Thanks so much."

Sweetheart. One of the words Blu used to address me. Come to think about it, Diane often called me sweetheart or honey or darlin'. Maybe Blu hadn't been coming on to me in my yard after all. Maybe he talked the way he'd been raised. *Shit.*

Jaime's voice echoed in my head—*Don't believe everything you read in the press. Give Blu Connolly a chance.*

So far, I'd blown that. I'd yelled at him when he first arrived home on Wednesday night and stereotyped him to his face in my backyard this afternoon. The count was 2-0 with nobody on base. In the game of first impressions, it appeared I had one last chance to make a good one whenever I met Blu again.

Blu

Whenever Balefire was on tour, what I missed most about home was Mom and her incredible cooking. A close second was riding my bike. When I returned to her house after three solid hours of attitude adjustment on the open road, I wished I hadn't told her not to save me leftovers from lunch. Although Ashleigh didn't appear big enough to eat her share and mine, she'd been working in her yard for most of the morning, so she might have had an appetite. Or Mom might have sent the leftovers home with her to spite me for being a prick. And I'd deserve it.

As I swung off my bike, I glanced up to see Ashleigh backing out of her one-car garage. Her ride—a red four-door compact that had seen better days—begged for a tune-up as it clattered out of her driveway. She didn't even spare me a glance as she checked to be sure the street remained empty while she backed into it. *Damn.*

The good mood I'd ridden myself into threatened to cloud over as I watched one of the most stunning women I'd ever met drive away. Her attitude still pissed me off, but Mom sure seemed taken with her, so maybe I'd met her on a bad day.

Letting myself in through the front door, I called out, "Hi Mom! I'm home!" Receiving no response, I ran up the stairs and divested myself of my gear. The heat of the day left my T-shirt wet and stinky beneath my leathers. Same with my socks in my boots. Leaving them on the floor in my bedroom, I jogged back downstairs in jeans and nothing else.

"Mom? You here?" I asked the air in the kitchen.

"Back here, son," she called from the patio.

I found her swinging in her hammock, her hand cradling a glass of something on her stomach.

"How was your ride? Did you work out whatever was bothering you?"

Her question caught me off guard and reminded me of all the times growing up when I thought she must be psychic. She always seemed to know exactly what was going on inside my head.

"Some. How was lunch?" I bent down to kiss her cheek.

"Lovely. I saw a recipe for stuffed shrimp and salad on one of my cooking shows, and it turned out great. We had this delicious wine that paired perfectly with the fish. I think I might have left a taste of it in the bottle on the table if you're interested."

"I'm kinda interested in stuffed shrimp, actually."

"Oh, I thought you said you were going somewhere for lunch, so I sent the leftovers with Ashleigh. She gushed about the food, and I know she doesn't make much money, so I thought she might enjoy it again later. Sorry."

Mom's tone didn't say sorry. Her tone said I got what I deserved. Since I'd reached the same conclusion earlier, I had to laugh. "Well then, guess I'll drink my snack."

The wine in question turned out to be a damn fine California chardonnay, and I wished the two of them hadn't enjoyed most of it too. Or maybe Mom had enjoyed most of it judging from her mellow mood.

"Since you won't let me move you into something bigger and modern in a nicer neighborhood," I began, and she huffed out a sigh at the mention of our ongoing argument, "I'm glad you spend some of the money I send you on good wine."

I sat back on a lawn chair near her on the patio, tipping my head back to catch some rays.

"Oh, I didn't buy it. Ashleigh brought that over when she joined me for lunch. I tried to stop her since I know she pinches every penny, but she insisted. I think she wanted to impress you."

"Really?" My tone dripped sarcasm. The way the woman spoke to me in her yard and ignored me as she left her place a few minutes earlier made it pretty clear she wanted nothing to do with me. "What makes you say that?"

I casually took another swig of excellent wine and tried to pretend Mom's answer didn't matter.

"Well, most of the time, she brings me small gifts like flowers or berries from her garden. Today, she came with that gorgeous wine. She wore a darling little halter dress and brushed out her braid. Usually, she only washes her hands and comes over in her shorts and T-shirt."

"Huh."

"That bottle of wine probably cost her a half-day's pay on her salary, so it is a gift. That's why I decided to finish it off after she went home."

"It's mellowed you out . . . for the most part." I grinned.

Mom lasered me with her eyes, and I barked out a laugh. Baiting my mother—another thing I'd missed.

"What does Ashleigh do, exactly?"

"She's a substitute teacher at your old high school and she writes articles and submits them to all sorts of publications."

"Yeah? What does she write about? Gardening?"

I might have laughed at the idea yesterday, but after seeing her sweet ass up in the air as she bent over the row of flowers she planted this morning, I had a sudden appreciation for gardening.

"She writes about music. Does a darn fine job of it too. She's reviewed several local bands as well as some big ones. She even wrote a review of your show at Red Rocks last summer for some little blog. Her description of Dakota's guitar and your voice specifically could have made Balefire a household name had you needed the boost. Her writing is that good." Mom took a nonchalant sip of her wine, but I caught the look she shot me. "Or maybe I'm biased since she complimented my boy so flatteringly."

"Yeah, well, maybe I should sing to her next time 'cause she sure didn't flatter me today when I invited her to lunch."

The conversation led me right back to that dark place it had taken me three hours of hard riding to escape. Ashleigh's wine soured in my mouth as I heard her accusations in my head again.

Mom ignored my comment and my sudden bad mood. "You slept away most of the first two days you've been home. What are your plans for this evening?"

"Haven't thought about it much. Maybe head down to the Dollar, see if anyone from the old days is still around, shoot some pool. After you feed me dinner," I added with a sly smirk.

Truly, I should have offered to take Mom out to eat, but the woman could outcook any chef in the state. After months on the road, I craved her home cooking.

She smiled back at me, reading my mind again. "Your favorite dinner is thawing on the counter right now. I baked it last weekend for when you came home."

"Yeah?" I asked carelessly before I bounced up out of my chair and raced into the kitchen. Sure enough, a huge pan of lasagna sat on the counter. Jesus, did I love that woman.

The tangible evidence of my mom's love for me put a giant smile on my face as I headed to the bathroom to shower off the road grime and sweat from my ride. Though it was early June, the temperature insisted on summer, and I could smell myself when I walked back into the house.

When I finished cleaning up, I found Mom in the kitchen singing some pop tune softly as she busied herself with dinner. Her taste in music ran to mellow, and I had to laugh as I walked into the kitchen. As our biggest supporter early on, she attended almost every one of our shows and smiled and danced all the way through them. We'd been playing professionally for three or four years when I discovered the earplugs. To this day I have no idea what she heard in her head as we played, but it wasn't us. Still, she'd had a good time and inspired others around her to join her in that, which improved the vibe of our early shows.

Thoughts of those long-ago shows led me back to Mom's comment about Ashleigh's articles. After dinner, I googled her to see what she'd said about us. Not that it mattered. The woman appeared pretty hostile to me during our first two meetings. Then I read an article she wrote for *Rocky Mountain High*, an online arts and entertainment blog.

> The Balefire concert at Red Rocks last weekend blasted all expectations of what a rock show is or should be. The band's musicianship, sound quality, pyrotechnics, and light show exceeded anything offered at Red Rocks in recent memory. From Jack Whitehorse's opening drum solo pounding through the collective chest of the crowd to Dakota Perri's blistering guitar licks revving the audience into a frenzy to Adam Tron's driving bass forcing people to jump out of their seats and dance, the band grabbed the audience by the throat and refused to let go for two solid hours of nonstop, over-the-top thrill ride.
>
> However, Balefire's signature sound lies in the incredible vocal range of the band's lead singer, Blu Connolly. From

his primal screams on "Out of My Head" to his smooth baritone rumblings on "You're the One" to his pitch-perfect harmonies with Whitehorse on their new song "Missing You," Connolly's voice is the heart and soul of the band. No wonder during a Balefire concert, women toss their underwear at the stage with wild abandon. The man has the ability to make panties drop every time he steps up to a microphone.

Huh. So Ashleigh liked the show at Red Rocks. More than that, she loves my voice, at least when I'm using it to sing.

Mom was right about Ashleigh's ability to review music too. Her words made me think back on that show, one of our best. Her article reminded me why I absolutely fucking love what I do for a living even when a tour wrings me out. Panty-dropping voice. Her description made me smile. Sobering, I pondered what it would take to tempt the delectable yet prickly Ashleigh Baker to drop her panties for me.

CHAPTER FOUR

Ashleigh

WHILE JAIME DROVE us to the Dollar, I sat in the passenger seat of my little car and finished taking notes about the set we'd just listened to. What the band lacked in musicianship they made up for in enthusiasm and volume. As much as I didn't enjoy their set, the lead singer's propensity to wander through the crowd using his wireless mic and sing to people up close and personal certainly kept the crowd engaged. I'd interviewed several followers of the band who said the lead singer's personality was the main draw. Maybe the guy should consider a career change to game show host or something. Or maybe his brand of raw screaming vocals on the same note at maximum decibels was an acquired taste that grew on people with repeated exposure.

At any rate, their show wore me out, and I looked forward to relaxing with a glass of cheap white wine and maybe a round of pool before we called it a night. The Dollar offered both. The house band played hard rock covers passably well and had no aspirations beyond making beer money on Saturday nights, so I felt no pressing desire to dissect their sound whenever we stopped in for a drink.

We'd settled in at two open stools in front of the bar when Jaime nearly aspirated her drink into her lungs.

"That's Blu Connolly!" she gasped staring straight ahead at the huge mirror behind the bar.

I glanced up, and sure enough, there he stood. Blu leaned on his pool cue watching another man's shot as he played a round of pool with a guy I recognized as a regular. The low light of the bar did nothing to hide his mouthwatering good looks. I couldn't help but key on his sharp cheekbones and the sexy stubble covering his square jaw or the way his full lips parted to reveal his perfect smile when he laughed at something his friend said. His tight T-shirt showed off his defined chest and shoulders, the sleeves straining to contain both beautiful biceps. When he shifted, his sleeve hitched up enough to show the bottom of what looked like a tribal tattoo. As I continued to gaze at him, he moved to take a shot, and I noticed how his jeans hugged his perfect ass and accentuated his long legs.

"You said you'd introduce me," Jaime reminded me as I continued to watch Blu surreptitiously in our reflections.

Blowing out a breath of frustration at my belly-tightening response to finding him in my new favorite bar, I turned away from staring at him to look at Jaime's profile. Her expression told me she wouldn't be able to have enough of Blu Connolly no matter how many endearments he used instead of her name.

"Yeah, I did promise you that. You want to interrupt his game or give him a chance to finish it?"

"You don't sound too enthusiastic about introducing us." Jaime smirked. "Are you trying to keep the man all to yourself?"

"Not at all," I said trying to sound cool and nonchalant while butterflies practiced the cha-cha in my belly.

Mentally jerking up my big girl panties, I slid off the stool, grabbed my glass of wine, and nodded at Jaime to follow me.

"Oh my God, you're seriously going to introduce me to Blu

Connolly." For a moment, her luminous green eyes flashed panic before she gathered herself and slid off the stool to join me.

The guy playing pool with Blu noticed us before he did. "Hell-oooo pretty ladies. You here to pick up a few pointers, or to challenge us to a game?"

The guy stood at least six feet six with shoulders nearly as wide. His sleeveless vest showed off the sleeves tattooed over his enormous arms. If one were so inclined, it might take her into the next morning to determine each tattoo he'd had inked over his muscular arms. His wide friendly smile, however, compensated for his imposing stature.

"Depends on the stakes." Jaime parked a hand on her hip. "Low enough, we might be inclined to challenge you. High enough, we might need some pointers."

I gaped stupidly at my friend before I realized how uncouth I must have looked and shut my mouth with an audible snap. Catching her eye, I mouthed at her, "Where did that come from?"

My normally sedate high school English teacher friend shrugged and ghosted a smile before returning her attention to tall, built, and inked.

"That does pose a dilemma. What would constitute low and high stakes to you?" he drawled, his dark coffee-colored eyes dancing.

Tilting her head and putting a finger to her lips, Jaime put on a show of considering the question. "Hmm, let me think," she began. "Low stakes would be a drink. High stakes would be a date."

My eyes nearly bugged out of my head when she dropped that one. From the other side of the table, Blu burst out laughing, and I finally looked over to see his laughter directed at my response. "You didn't talk that over with your friend before you offered it, did you, darlin'?" he purred in that too-rich-for-my-own-good baritone voice of his.

"No, but to be honest, I was too busy bugging Ashleigh to introduce me to you to notice your hot friend," Jaime said before she returned her attention to shorty. "I'm Jaime, and you are?"

"Delighted." He grinned. "This is a first, Blu old man," he added with a smirk in Blu's direction before he turned back to Jaime. "My name is Vaughn. And I'm very pleased to meet you, Jaime."

He stuck out his hand, which swallowed Jaime's when she took it, but I don't think she noticed. At last, they let go of each other, so I had a chance to do what Jaime had demanded of me in the first place.

I couldn't believe her. With his size and charming smile and dancing eyes, Vaughn certainly grabbed a woman's attention, yet I couldn't see how my friend preferred him to Blu. Vaughn's size intimidated me while Blu's long, lean frame, all sinewy muscle and grace, made my lady parts pulse with interest. Where Vaughn cut his dark hair short all over, Blu wore his hair short on the sides and back and longer on top, just enough for thick, soft, golden-brown curls to form. Vaughn's full mustache and goatee gave him kind of a pirate air. Blu's sexy stubble made me think of all the interesting ways I would enjoy it against my skin.

A not-so-subtle throat clearing jarred me from my private observations, and I tried to cover my lapse with an eye roll and a sip of my wine. Then I did the honors.

"Jaime, this is Blu Connolly. Blu, Jaime Hughes."

"Pleasure to meet you Jaime. Ashleigh Baker, Vaughn Hamilton," Blu said, returning the favor.

"Now that we have introductions out of the way, what's the bet again?" Vaughn asked, mischief in his eyes.

"Drinks," I said.

"Dates," Jaime said at the same time.

"Glad that's settled." Blu laughed.

"Dates it is." Vaughn waggled his eyebrows and aimed a lopsided smile at Jaime.

I set my wine on the edge of a nearby table before grabbing a pool cue from the rack behind me and chalking it up. Maybe this was my chance to make a better impression on Blu Connolly. Especially since he remembered my name when he introduced me to his friend. Though I didn't delude myself into thinking I could actually go out on a date with the guy. A player like Blu Connolly served only one purpose—to be a heartbreaker, and I liked mine intact thankyouverymuch.

"The added stakes for the bet include pointers for the game. You look like you know a little something about what to do with a pool cue, Miss Baker. Let's have a look at your shot," Blu said, a challenge in his unusual and arresting hazel eyes.

"We're not starting the game yet?" I asked, stalling.

"We'll let you ladies practice on the balls we still have on the table," Blu said. "Line up a shot, Ashleigh. Let's see what you got."

I set the cue ball behind the line and aimed for an easy shot since the ten teetered on the edge of the side pocket near me. Right as I popped my wrist forward to execute the shot, Blu subtly brushed my arm. A ghost of skin sliding over skin, but I shanked the cue and missed the shot so wide even I, who knew I came down to the Dollar a couple of times a month to shoot pool, would have thought I'd never held a pool cue before.

"Oops. A little bobble there, Ash. Let me help you," Blu said, his expression one of concern.

"You did that, Blu," I accused, indignation in my tone.

Opening his eyes wide, all innocence and confusion, he said, "I have no idea what you're talking about. Here, let me help you line up the next shot."

He stood behind me, reached his arms around me, placed his hands over mine on the pool cue, and short-circuited every synapse in my brain. I breathed in his scent, something woodsy with a hint of citrus, the faint smell of yeasty beer on his breath. My body tightened in anticipation of feeling his body against me. The nerve endings along my extended arm, down my side, and over my back and ass fired all at once as Blu's body made contact with mine. My nipples tightened and my skin pebbled as our bodies came together. For several seconds, all I could do was absorb how good, how perfectly his hard body fit mine.

My breath caught, and I'm not sure I could have moved at all let alone execute a perfect shot had Blu not taken charge of my body's motion.

"See. With the correct positioning, a little thrust, the ball drops perfectly into the pocket."

Did he really go there?

The laughter dancing in his eyes as he looked down at me dared me to call him out on his innuendo.

"Thanks. I'll try to remember that."

The hardness, the warmth of his body still touching mine, his scent, the smooth cadence of his voice, the laughter in his eyes combined to render me motionless. Like I couldn't muster the will to escape his magnetic pull, I simply stared at him as he imprinted himself on me.

"Your turn, Jaime. Let's see how well you handle a pool cue," Vaughn said, the interruption of his voice cutting off Blu's singular hold over me at last.

I stepped to the side to make room for Jaime and snagged my wineglass, gulping my wine to cool me off and calm me down. Responding to him the way I did nerved me up. I knew better than to believe any of the promises Blu made to me with his body as he touched me. Too bad my traitorous body insisted on believing every last one of them. He was a rock star, a player in every sense of the word. He thrived on the adoration of women, made promises to them all the time, promises he had no intentions of keeping. But when he turned on the charm, turned on the flirt, it became hard to remember it was only a rock 'n' roll show, nothing more.

Blu

When Jaime distracted the others as she chalked up her pool cue, I discreetly adjusted myself, grabbed my beer, and finished it in one long swallow. In the space of a couple of minutes, Ashleigh Baker ratcheted me up to warp speed, and we both were still fully dressed. I couldn't remember the last time a woman affected me the way she had . . . if one had *ever* affected me that way. My hands already itched to touch the silky waves of her dark chocolate hair before she tucked a stray lock behind her ear as she leaned over to take her shot. I couldn't resist stealing a touch right as she let her shot go. Her reaction to that tiny move told me all her bravado in her backyard this afternoon was a bluff. I did affect her after all.

Of course, I had to have some fun with that. Yet now the joke was on me. As I leaned over her to *help* her with her shot, her soft pliant body molded to mine like she'd been made for me. The light scent of her perfume, something fresh that reminded me of her summer garden, wafted into my nostrils, and it was all I could do not to nuzzle my nose in her neck and suck in a lungful of her smell as I adjusted our hands on the stick.

And that ass. Its beautiful tight roundness had been my first sight of her after I vaulted the fence into her backyard this morning. When I leaned over her to line up the shot, I couldn't help but enjoy how perfectly her ass fit against my groin. A picture of that sweet ass all bare and waiting for me flashed into my head, and it had taken all my self-control not to start dry-humping her right there.

Good thing Vaughn interrupted when he did, or I might have done something stupid, like kiss that gorgeous mouth of hers when she turned her face to stare at me. After our little conversation in her backyard this morning, I wouldn't have thought she'd like me stealing a kiss. In public no less. But when she'd held her breath following the shot, I wondered exactly what crossed her mind right then. Like I wondered what she was thinking when I noticed her studying me in the mirror's reflection above the bar before she finally came over to our table. After she jumped away from me, the wine in her glass disappeared fast. Obviously, I wasn't the only one to sense something flash between us when I touched her that first time this morning.

Vaughn, being Vaughn, had Jaime in his arms before she could even chalk her pool cue. A thought seemed to occur to him, and he changed the angle of the shot he helped her with, causing the ball to drop neatly into the pocket and bounce the cue ball over to line up the next shot exactly.

"There, like that. You're a quick study, Jaime Hughes," he said, even though he'd done all the work.

"Are we ready to play, then?" Jaime asked, a twinkle in her eye.

"Almost. Just so we're clear, what are the stakes again?"

"We win, you take us out on a very fine date," Jaime reminded Vaughn.

"And we win, you ladies are treating us guys? Is that it?" he asked.

"Yes."

"Either way, we're going on a date. The stakes are a matter of who's buying."

"Exactly."

I surreptitiously glanced at Ashleigh to gauge her response to this exchange and wondered at the stiff way she held herself. She tossed back the last of her wine and signaled the waitress for another. Neither of which indicated she wanted anything to do with a date with me. A thought ran through my head as I observed her. Maybe the problem was she and Jaime both wanted the same guy, but Jaime had the inside track on him. And wouldn't that be a kick in the ass.

When the waitress arrived with Ashleigh's refill, I stepped in. "I've got this. Bring me two beers when you come back with drinks for my other friends as well, please."

"You don't have to buy me a drink," Ashleigh began before I cut her off.

"I'm aware. Enjoy that, would you?" Nodding toward the table, I added, "You're up."

She shot me "the look," chalked her pool cue again, and stepped forward to determine her shot. Vaughn had broken and done the job damn poorly. He popped the balls so well that he didn't drop a single one but left the table wide open for the ladies to pocket nearly everything, no matter how badly they played. The sly devil. Taking a pull from my beer, I hid a grin at his tactics.

Ashleigh made short work of half the balls on the table before she finally missed one. Then I was up. Acknowledging Vaughn's game, I made an easy shot. It grazed the cue ball against the ball Ashleigh had left teetering in a corner pocket. I couldn't make another good shot though, because she'd slid the cue ball along the edge. Instead, all I could do was bank it. Which, of course, left a perfect not-to-be-missed shot for Jaime, who obliged effortlessly. She dropped four more balls after that, leaving only the fifteen and the eight. Vaughn did his job and dropped the fifteen into a side pocket and left a foolproof line for Ashleigh to finish off the game by dropping the eight into a corner pocket.

She glared at Jaime who returned a noncommittal look, and I barely restrained my laughter until she successfully ended the game.

"Good thing they let us win since we know at least one of these guys is loaded," Ashleigh said, throwing me a sardonic look.

I didn't even try to wipe the grin off my face as I returned her stare. "All right." I placed a handful of quarters on the table. "Best two out of three."

"Come on, darlin'," Vaughn began before I cut him off.

"Since you won that one, you break this time."

Ashleigh didn't break with quite the pop Vaughn did, but she managed to drop three balls and leave a shitty shot for me. Shitty that is for achieving our goal. I had to hand it to her; she could play pool. So could her friend, though it appeared from her play that Jaime would be perfectly willing to take us boys out on a date. Or Vaughn at least. Staring Ashleigh down, I chugged one beer and took a healthy swig from the second before chalking my pool cue and gauging my shot.

"Way to set me up, Ash. You're not even trying to win."

She rolled her eyes at my obvious antics, and I laughed again as I dutifully pocketed two balls before missing the next shot.

Jaime dropped four more balls and gave the table back to Vaughn, who messed around with a trick shot he couldn't—or rather didn't—want to pull off, and the game rotated back to Ashleigh.

I don't think she meant to show off her impressive rack when she huffed out a breath and took her shot. But she showed it off all the same. I tried to be a gentleman enough to drag my eyes away from her. Yeah, I'm such a gentleman. Dainty lace lined the scooped neck of her white cotton button-up blouse. When she bent over the table to take her shot, she gave me a mouthwatering view of her tits. Then her gorgeous thick hair fell forward, obscuring the hint of lacy white bra I caught, and I had to take another long pull off my beer to cool down.

Her whole package tied me in knots. I couldn't ignore the way she filled out her blouse and jeans and all that shimmering chocolate-colored hair falling in layers and curls halfway down her back. Then there were those gorgeous blue eyes. Her scent filled my nostrils even when I didn't have the opportunity to deliberately stand next to her. And baiting her? That was a bonus.

"Nice job there, Ash. You going to leave anything on the table for me?"

I think she growled at me before she pocketed everything on the table.

"Guess not. Game over or should we play another one for funsies?" I asked and waggled my eyebrows at her.

"There are still quarters on the table, so I vote we keep playing. What do you say, Jaime?" Vaughn asked.

"Oh, I think we should give the guys another chance to try to prove they can play with the big kids, don't you, Ashleigh?"

She sighed exaggeratedly. "I've been outvoted all night. You break this time, Jaime, since we won—twice." Her glare said one thing, but her light blush said another.

Vaughn and I exchanged a grin, his eyes dancing as Jaime racked the balls and proceeded to break. By tacit agreement, we decided to play one for real. Since we'd already established that there would be a date, and Vaughn and I would be paying for it, it seemed only right that we show the women we could hold our own at a pool table. But it appeared they'd played us as much as we'd played them. After Vaughn pocketed most of the balls until one finally evaded him, Ashleigh didn't give me a chance to even get into the game before she ran what was left of the table.

She raised one dainty eyebrow over an enigmatic smile, challenging me.

"After three in a row, I think it's time we even the score a bit. This time we call balls. I'll break," I replied to her dare.

I dropped eight balls before turning the table over to Jaime who only managed two after Vaughn turned on the serious flirt. Vaughn finished the game.

"Impressive," Ashleigh drawled from where she leaned against a nearby table. "You two had mad skills that only came out after you had us on the hook for dinner."

"You have to admit, Ashleigh, no matter what, we win," Jaime said. "We played some fun pool with two sizzling hot guys, and they're taking us to dinner." She laughed and turned to Vaughn. "What are our dinner plans, by the way?"

"Sizzling hot, huh? That merits a really nice place. What do you say, Blu? You up for taking the ladies to the Bull's Ass?"

"Are you serious? The Bovine Behind? I've always wanted to try that place," Jaime gushed.

Vaughn laid it on thick. "Why haven't you then, darlin'?"

"Not on what I make," she said, a rueful look on her face.

"That goes double for me," Ashleigh added.

"As you've already stated, Ash, I'm loaded. Of course, Vaughn's buyin', so the Bull's Ass it is," I said laughing at my buddy's double take.

"Yeah, yeah. You 'starving musicians,'" he said with air quotes, "are always jonesing for a free meal on an engineer."

"Damn straight." I smirked.

Jaime stared at Vaughn before blurting, "You're an engineer?"

"Yeah. What did you think I do for a living?"

"Careful how you answer that. Remember, we want him to cover the tab," I warned.

"Wow. Hot and smart. What are you driving, Vaughn?" Jaime asked as she slipped her hand into the crook of his elbow.

"Right answer." I laughed and turned to look at Ashleigh who glared at her friend. *What the fuck? She wants Vaughn too?* The thought wiped the smile right off my face.

"I'll follow you guys," Ashleigh said.

"You can ride with me," I offered.

"No thanks. I'd rather not ride on the back of a bike driven by a half-drunk man." I swear she stuck her nose up with a tiny sniff, but maybe it was a trick of the light.

"You're right. I probably shouldn't ride my bike. Tell you what, Ashleigh. I'll ride with you instead."

Jaime beamed at me. "Great idea. We'll all meet up at the restaurant."

She cuddled up to Vaughn as they led us out of the bar, a none-too-happy Ashleigh walking beside me and not touching me at all.

♪

"You know, gorgeous, if you invited me in to your place, I bet we'd have a great time together," I said, giving her my best sexy grin, the one that worked on every girl every time.

"Sure. Just like every other night you've spent with 'gorgeous,'" she said sarcastically and exited her car.

Tipping my head back against the headrest, I closed my eyes in disgust. She'd finally thawed out enough to flirt with me through dinner. That was why I pretended to be drunker than I was. Though the buzz I had on probably would have gotten me into trouble on my bike. Then I blew it with her. Again.

I watched as Ashleigh unconsciously made my dick rock hard with the sexy sway of her very fine ass as she strode up the sidewalk to Mom's front door. After she rang the bell, she put her hand up in front of her face to shield her eyes from the glare of the porch light Mom flipped on before opening the door.

Deciding the game was up, I exited Ashleigh's rattletrap of a car and made my way to the porch.

"Evening, Ma. Ashleigh here was nice enough to give me a ride home." Turning to Ashleigh, I asked, "You sure you wouldn't like some company tonight?"

I mean, what the hell? She was thoroughly pissed at me already.

She pretended to ignore me, but I caught the way her breath hitched at my suggestion. She closed her eyes for a second and opened them, addressing Mom. "He's all yours, Diane." Turning to me, she added, "Thanks for dinner, Blu."

Without another word, she walked away. Her thick, long hair bounced against the middle of her back as she beat a hasty retreat on those impossibly long legs. Legs made even longer by her choice of skinny jeans and sky-high sandals. Legs I could think of a much better use for than speed walking away from me. I watched her all the way to her front porch and for a few seconds after she retreated into her house. With a sigh, I stepped up to the door where Mom gave me a probing look up and down.

"Dinner?" she asked.

"Vaughn and I might have purposely lost a pool game or three. The stakes were dinner. And yes, Mom, I think your new neighbor is hot."

I kissed her cheek as I slid past her and into the house where I spent a restless night trying not to think about all the ways I wanted to know Ashleigh Baker.

CHAPTER FIVE

Ashleigh

AFTER MY LONG night of band reviewing, pool playing, and flirting with Blu over dinner until I regained my mind, I'd over-slept. Though I should have been on the road to Fort Collins fifteen minutes earlier, instead I was rushing out to my teeny single-car garage. Unlocking the side door, I stepped inside and stopped dead in my tracks. Someone sang softly as he lay beneath my car, someone with long legs who liked to sing half a register up from his sexy deep speaking voice. Someone who had no business in my garage.

"Blu, what do you think you're doing?"

"Good morning to you too, Ashleigh." He slid out from under my car.

I blew out a breath. "How did you get into my garage? And what are you doing under my car?"

"The lock on your garage door is a joke. I'll fix it when I finish tuning up your car. When was the last time you had the oil changed in this thing, anyway?" His severe expression brought heat to my cheeks. "Also, your carburetor needs an adjustment."

Planting my hands on my hips, I tried to recover some control of the situation. "Why are you doing this?"

"I think the correct response is 'Thank you, Blu, for working on my car.'" He grinned.

My hands slid off my hips. "I'm sorry. I guess my manners ditched me along with the time. At the risk of sounding even ruder, are you finished with whatever you thought my car needed?" He jacked a brow. "Because I need to be in Fort Collins to listen to a band I'm assigned to review, and I'm already fifteen minutes late."

"Sorry Ash, but I just dropped the plug out of the oil pan. It's gonna take a while for the oil to drain before I can refill it."

"You don't understand, Blu," I began, my panic rising at warp speed. "This is my job. If I miss this band, I'll probably lose any chance of finding a permanent position writing for the Colorado Music Works blog." I paced beside my apparently inoperable car. "During the summer, freelancing for them is my main source of income. If I screw up this gig, I might not be making rent next month."

"You got any leather pants?" he asked.

I gaped at his non sequitur before blurting, "What the hell does that have to do with my present crisis?"

"If you don't own a pair of leather pants, a pair of jeans will do and boots if you have any." He pulled a rag from his back pocket and wiped grease off his hands.

"What?"

"Your car won't be ready in time for you to do what you need to do, so I'll take you to this gig on my bike. If you start moving, I might even deliver you there on time," he finished with a smirk.

Go for a ride on Blu Connolly's Harley? With Blu Connolly? Whose absolute gorgeousness and sexy-as-sin voice were already lethal to my common sense? I'd tossed and turned half the night thinking about his come-on when we arrived home last night, another contributor to my imminent lateness. Now I was seriously contemplating letting him take me to Fort Collins?

"Well?" he prompted me from my wayward thoughts.

"I have jeans and boots. I'll be out in two minutes."

Before I could think better of it, I whirled around and hustled back into my house. Stripping out of the breezy sundress I'd slipped on earlier, I jerked on a pair of jeans and a turquoise T-shirt. I pulled on black suede ankle boots, grabbed my purse, and raced back out of my house, locking the door behind me.

"Two minutes exactly. Impressive," Blu said when I crossed the strip of grass separating Diane's property from my rental.

"I thought you might not have one of these, so you can borrow mine. This helmet too." He held up a badass-looking black helmet with one hand and handed me a leather jacket with the other.

As I shrugged into the jacket, the scent of his woodsy citrus cologne enveloped me, and I couldn't resist sneaking a full inhale before I zipped myself into it.

"You fill that out a little differently than I do." The corner of his mouth turned up. "I like it."

"Can we get going?" I cringed inwardly at the edge in my voice. "As we've already established, I'm going to be late."

"You're cute when you're bossy, Ash."

I rolled my eyes and pulled the helmet over my head.

"There's a switch on the side here. Let me turn it on."

He reached up and fiddled with something on the side of my helmet. Then I heard a sound inside it and realized his helmets contained an internal speaker system.

He slid his helmet over his head and swung a long leg over the bike. "Now we can talk to each other as we ride. Hop on, Ash. Let's get this show on the road."

Carefully, I climbed up behind him and tried to figure out where to put my hands, at last deciding to settle them on the tops of my thighs. His familiarity with shortening my name, making himself helpful with my car, and offering me a ride threw me enough. Now that I sat on the back of his bike, the proximity of our bodies did weird things to my insides.

"You'll need to hold onto me, Ashleigh, if we're going to make your venue on time," Blu's voice commanded through my helmet's speakers.

Blowing out a breath, I leaned forward a little and slid my hands around his waist along his belt line. The move brought my whole front, from my core to my collarbone, in contact with his ass and the muscular length of his back. I tried to tell myself not to respond, but my body had other plans. My nipples pebbled inside my shirt and my pussy pulsed against my panties and jeans where I'd settled flush with Blu's backside. Like he knew exactly how my body responded to him, he subtly cradled his ass back even farther into the V of my thighs, causing them to join the full-contact party happening on his bike.

I was grateful to be wearing a helmet. That way he couldn't watch my face as I tried to deal with the intimate physical contact. He turned the key, kicked the starter, and the bike roared to life. As I'd discovered he liked to do, Blu revved it up before he put it in gear and headed us down his mom's driveway.

When he turned onto the street, I attempted to distract myself from so much of his body rubbing against mine. "Why are you doing this?" I asked.

"Because you needed me to."

"I wouldn't have needed you to take me anywhere if you hadn't torn my car apart."

He chuckled. "You needed me to do that for you too."

"Really," I drawled. "I'm not helpless, you know. I can take my car to a shop to have it serviced."

"Uh-huh. So why didn't you? When you started it last night, the engine sounded like it might knock itself out." He slowed for the stop sign at the end of the block, checked the traffic, and thrilled me with the way he smoothly executed a left turn into traffic.

"It isn't that bad," I hedged.

"You didn't answer my question."

Even though I knew he couldn't see me, my cheeks flamed with humiliation. Admitting to multimillionaire rock star Blu Connolly that I didn't have the money to have my car serviced this month—or last month for that matter—would be giving him too much information and might make him think I was a gold digger—or worse.

"Juggling multiple jobs doesn't make for a regular schedule. I haven't had time."

All the previous humor in his voice evaporated. "If you want to keep driving your little ride, you need to make time."

"Are you always this nosy and bossy with the neighbors?"

"Only the ones my mom likes."

I could hear the smile in his tone and started to smile too until a rather unpleasant thought entered my head. "How many women have lived next door to your mom over the years?"

"Counting you? One."

"What?"

Blu snickered. "The grouchy old guy who lived in that house while I was growing up and even after I went on the road was one of my favorite targets for every prank I could imagine and some I couldn't—but my friends could." He braked a little hard for the stop sign at the end of the next block, forcing me to tighten my hold on him. Either he didn't notice, or he pretended not to. "One time Dakota climbed up on the roof of your house with a bucket of rocks that were painted bright red. Old Man Smith was home, so Dakota had to be very quiet as he spelled out 'Old Man Smith sucks' across the street side of the roof. It stayed up there for two days before Smith saw it." He turned his head to watch for traffic to clear. "Of course, he blamed me, but I'd been out of town on a choir trip, so it couldn't have been me." Another laugh erupted from him as he navigated the corner. "It wasn't necessary to mention that I'd painted all the rocks Dakota used."

"That's certainly more creative and daring than tossing toilet paper around the shrubbery in the yard," I said with a giggle. "Is that why you deliberately revved the engine on this bike when you pulled in to your mom's the other night? Because you were goading Mr. Smith?"

"Maybe." He stretched the word out. "Turns out he moved away to live with his daughter and let the place out for rent. To a gorgeous—"

"Humph."

"Woman whose car is in desperate need of a tune-up." He guided the bike out onto a main thoroughfare and gunned the engine up to speed. "Who are we going to see in Fort Collins?"

I noted his deliberate change of subject and let it go. At some point, I'd make him explain the real reason I found him working on my car this morning. "It's a bluegrass band called Lightning Strikes. They've created quite a buzz in the music scene up there, so I thought I'd check them out, see what the fuss is about—if anything."

"What's that supposed to mean? If anything?"

"Oh, you know. Some bands like to start their own rumors, create an artificial buzz about themselves. Fake it till you make it and all that. It's my job to figure out who's for real and who's dreaming and report on it for the blog."

Blu leaned his body into a long turn as we merged onto I-25, and I had no choice but to move with him, our bodies in sync as the big bike ate up the road. "You're a music critic? That's your job?"

"One of my jobs. I'm a freelance writer."

"What else do you do?"

"Substitute teach, which is how I met Jaime. It's a good gig that leaves the weekends free for checking out bands. I actually caught a Balefire show at Red Rocks last summer. That was quite a production." Hoping my voice sounded even instead of breathy, I tried to downplay my enthusiasm. No doubt he heard gushing fans all the time. Judging from the way he insisted on flirting with me last night, he already expected me to be all impressed.

"Yeah? You liked it? Did you write a review of it?"

For some reason, I didn't want him to know that I'd written a pretty glowing review of the show for a local paper. Balefire put on a spectacular production with lights and pyrotechnics to complement the driving sound of the rock 'n' roll party calling itself a band. Since I loved their music, I probably wasn't the most objective of critics. Still, a show like theirs could only garner rave reviews.

"I liked it a lot, but I was only a fan. The big boys whose names appear in the bylines of the blog wrote the review. Your promoter gave them the free passes to the show and the after-party. Your sound and light show reached out to the whole amphitheater though, so even fifty rows back from the stage, my seat was still good."

"Guess we'll have to do better by you when we play here again. Let you see what it's like up close and personal," Blu said.

Traffic picked up as we neared the city center, and we remained quiet while Blu concentrated on the road. The lull in conversation was a relief. Listening to that voice through the intimate speakers of the helmet felt like I already had that up close and personal concert seat. Yet without conversation to distract me, my attention wandered back to how much of him touched me and where, making me sweat in the cocoon of his leather jacket. I was up close and personal all right.

Out of nowhere, he shot to hell all my resolve to resist him. As we left the traffic of Denver behind, he began to sing. There I rode, snuggled up to the hottest singer in the country on the back of his bike as he sang me my own private concert. I'm not sure I breathed as I listened to him start with "Resurrection," smoothly segue into "Outta My Head," then treat me to the vocals for an acoustic version of "Missing You."

After the third song, he chuckled. "You still with me, Ashleigh?"

Finally, I inhaled, trying to calm down enough to speak without giving myself away. "I'm here, Blu."

"Yeah? You said you saw the show at Red Rocks last summer, so you must like our music."

"I do. Balefire is one of my favorite bands." Admitting that, I knew, risked inflating his already huge ego, but that impromptu concert compelled my honesty.

"Then why aren't you singing along? Don'tcha know the words?" he teased.

I know the words to every single Balefire song.

"I don't think anyone would confuse what I do vocally with singing, Blu. Which is why I leave singing to the pros."

"What's your favorite song?"

"Are you fishing for a compliment?"

"Nope. I thought you might sing along if I sang your favorite."

"You already sang my favorite. 'Missing You' is such a great tune."

"You like that one?" I could hear the smile in his tone. "Jackie-boy will like hearing that since that one's his. What's another one you like?"

"Well, when I need to fire myself up for some event, cranking 'Hotter Than Hell' does it for me."

"Now we're talkin'. I wrote that one when we were on tour in California a couple years ago. Good to know you like what I write too." He patted the outside of my thigh and returned his hand to the handlebars.

Before I could call him out on needing his fragile ego stroked, he launched into the song. When he reached the chorus, he demanded, "Join me Ashleigh. We can scream this part together."

I shook my head and laughed. "When I'm alone in my house, my singing and dancing theatrics remain my own private embarrassment. There's a difference between your primal scream and my caterwauling screech, something that could get me arrested for disturbing the peace if I made it public."

"Come on, Ash. It can't possibly be that bad."

"You have no idea how it really is that bad."

Before he could badger me again to join him, the car in front of us suddenly swerved, and Blu's tone leaped from playful to deadly in a nanosecond. "Hold onto me Ashleigh. Tight."

I'd instinctively tightened my hold on him with the first word of his command. As the rest rumbled through my brain, I closed my eyes to avoid seeing the end when it came. My burr-like hold on Blu's body meant I moved with him as he rocked the bike to the side while simultaneously pushing the throttle hard. Whatever caused the disturbance in the traffic flow shot behind us as Blu wove his bike between cars and down the painted line between the lanes.

"Okay, babe. You can relax now."

As I pulled my head away from the broad expanse of his back between his shoulder blades, I opened my eyes and saw that we were now alone on the road with the next nearest car at least a quarter mile ahead of us. Too afraid of sending us off-balance if I turned my head to see behind us, I asked, "What happened back there?"

"Looked like someone left part of their car in the middle of the lane. I don't think the guy in front of us was paying much attention till he nearly ran it over. He didn't see us until we shot past the front of his car. Good thing you were already holding on tight to me."

I could hear the smirk in his voice, and it made me want to smack him. Which I might have done if I could have pried my hands apart from where one gripped the other around his waist. He took his hand off the handlebar long enough to rub the back of mine, sending a jolt of electrical energy through my hand and up my arm.

Instead of comforting me, he tripped my heart rate into triple time. "Hey, shouldn't you keep both hands on the bike?" I asked. I might have even sounded as tough as I'd intended if my voice hadn't come out all breathy, much to my disgust. The last thing I needed was for Blu to catch on that, like every other woman he'd ever met, I couldn't deny my attraction to him.

There should have been a law against Blu Connolly's bad-boy sexiness.

CHAPTER SIX

Blu

THOUGH SHE WOULDN'T give in and sing with me, I enjoyed the way Ashleigh hugged herself to me from Denver to Fort Collins. For a second there I worried I might have to lay the bike down when that idiot swerved to miss the debris in the road. On the upside, Ashleigh tightened her hold on me and didn't let go until we parked the bike on a side street a couple of blocks off Old Town.

Having her sweet body pressed to mine kept me semihard for the whole ride. Good thing she took a few minutes composing herself after she slid off my bike. It gave me time to adjust myself and get my hard-on back under control. As skittish as she'd acted around me so far, I didn't need to add to her poor opinion of me by giving her any more ammo.

Yeah, I'd caught on to that. I also caught on to the idea that maybe she liked me more than she wanted to admit. After all, we had miles to go after the incident with the car parts scattered over the road, but she didn't even offer to loosen her grip on me. When I sang to her on the bike, she went all breathy, which made me think

I might have a chance with her even though we didn't start out on the right foot.

"Where are we headed?" I asked as I locked the helmets to the bike.

"There's a venue near Old Town called Avogadro's Number that features local bands. This afternoon, Lightning Strikes is playing there," Ashleigh said while she drove me crazy unplaiting the thick braid she'd wound her hair into before riding the bike.

My hands flexed as I watched her lift her arms and fluff all that gorgeous hair of hers. With her arms raised, her pretty tits lifted even higher than they already were, and I couldn't decide where I wanted to put my hands first—plunge them into that silky mane of hers or palm and plump her luscious breasts. She tilted her head and shot me a quizzical look, making me glad for my mirrored shades so she couldn't see where I was looking or what I had going on in my head.

"Ready?"

"Lead the way, babe."

Though she didn't comment, she scowled at the endearment and blew past me. Damn. I needed to remember that.

As I watched her sexy ass undulate in that truly sexy way only some women have, I forgot my good intentions. Ashleigh moved with an unstudied grace that left me discreetly adjusting myself again as I trailed along behind her.

We reached the bar with barely a minute to spare as the band's lead singer stepped up to the mic and introduced their first song. Fascinated, I watched as Ashleigh whipped out her phone, opened a blank page on the screen, and started making notes. Since it was obvious she took her job seriously, I looked around for a place to sit. The bar was packed for a Sunday afternoon, but I finally found an open table over in a corner.

"Come on, Ash. I found us a table."

She glanced up with a kind of absent look on her face before she registered what I'd said and followed me as I wove through the crowd to the table I'd spotted.

"No wonder this one was open," she said. "You can't see anything from here. Maybe this can be home base if you're willing to stay here."

"You need to see them to review the band?" I nearly had to shout to be heard over the band and their rowdy crowd of followers.

She slanted me a look like she was talking to an imbecile. "I review the whole show, not only the music."

"Right. We'll make our way toward the stage," I said into her ear before I stepped in front of her to break a trail to the front of the room.

It took two more songs before I finally had us positioned in the front and a little to the left of the stage. I pulled my ball cap around to the front of my head and tugged the bill down to shield my face before I took off my sunglasses and settled them over the brim of my cap. Somehow, I knew Ashleigh wouldn't appreciate her review of a bluegrass band interrupted by some Balefire fan recognizing me in the crowd. Plus, I kind of liked being just another guy out with his girl.

I stood behind her and tried a couple of times to sneak a peek at her notes, but she held her hand over her phone as she traced the screen with her stylus, denying me my goal. Finally, I resigned myself to working to keep my hands off her and paying attention to the talent she came to see.

The band's boring name understated their sound. The two acoustic guitarists, the upright bassist, the mandolin player, and the fiddler had played together for a long time judging from the tightness of their instrumental harmonies. The upright bass player was entertaining as hell to watch as his facial expressions seemed to pinch and pull, slip and slide with every note he plucked from the strings. He threw his entire body into his performance like he and his instrument danced an intimate tango that drove the band's sound. I pulled my phone from my jeans pocket, videoed a bit of his play, and sent a text to Tron.

Between them, Tron and Jack drove our sound. But ever-steady Tron kept his cool as he played. I couldn't help but have some fun with him when I sent the text: *Hey Tron. Maybe if you sprang for a prettier bass, you could play it like a lover. You might even attract some extra lacy panties from the ladies if you make love to your bass like this guy—ha, ha.*

Tron must have had his phone on him, 'cause only a couple of seconds passed before he shot back: *Sure, Blu. I'll fuck a big-ass bass like that if you'll sing like someone stole your nuts.*

I barked out a laugh, startling Ashleigh. She shot me a look, her eyebrow raised in question or skepticism, I couldn't tell. Still grinning at Tron's assessment of the lead singer's skills, I shrugged and waited for the fallout.

Instead, she returned her attention to the band and her notes, which for some reason disappointed me. Oh, hell. I knew exactly what pissed me off. I wanted to go a round with her. After our first meeting in her garden yesterday and the *date* last night, I'd discovered a few things about Ashleigh Baker.

One, without question, she was attracted to me. Two, she didn't want to feel that attraction. Three, she hid her emotions by calling people out on their bullshit. Though I didn't like that last one much, I had to admit the reason had more to do with my conscience calling me out on my bullshit than on Ashleigh drawing attention to it.

The fact she deliberately ignored me after my outburst only made it more obvious that I got to her, which made me feel a little better since the woman grabbed all of my attention. The bass player's antics kept me entertained even as the lead singer's voice grated on my nerves. The band played an hour-long set before breaking. By then I was parched.

"I need a beer. What can I get you, Ashleigh?"

She scribbled something else down before looking up at me.

"Should you be having a beer if you're going to drive us back to Denver on your bike?"

"Seriously, Ash? It's one beer. Besides, if we stay for the entire show, we're going to be here for at least another hour."

She blew out a breath. "Fine. I'll have whatever you're having."

I grinned at her. "Stay here. I'll be right back."

Even elbowing my way through the crowd, it took me ten minutes to reach the bar and another ten minutes to snag the attention of one of the overworked bartenders. By the time I'd bought three beers—two for me, one for Ashleigh—the band had launched into its next set.

Two songs later, I finally reached her, only to find some dude trying to chat her up. I couldn't have that, especially when I noticed she'd put away her phone and her damned notes.

"Hey babe. Sorry it took me so long. The bar was packed," I greeted her as I deliberately stepped between her and the dumbass who thought he had a shot at her.

"That was rude. We were talking," she said, glaring at me when I handed her a beer.

"Yeah? I thought you were reviewing the band." I nodded at the stage as I took a pull from my second beer.

"I was. I am."

"So, how is my handing you a beer rude then? Wait, were you flirting with that guy? 'Cause I kinda had the impression we came here together."

Her eyes rounded, and she blinked at me several times before pointedly returning her attention to the stage and taking a long drink from her beer. I watched, fascinated as she exposed her long slim neck when she tipped the bottle back, my fingers itching to trace her soft skin as she swallowed.

About then, dumbass managed to step around me and grab Ashleigh's attention again. Right as I figured out what he had in mind, she handed me her beer.

"Would you mind holding this while I dance? Thanks."

The guy was wearing a plaid button-down shirt and khakis, for fuck's sake. He looked like a banker or something. Too tame for a woman as passionate as my Ashleigh.

He led her to a spot directly in front of the stage where people had cleared out enough to dance during the second set. I couldn't, wouldn't take my eyes off the two of them as banker-boy tried to impress my girl with his fancy spin moves and dips, anything to have his hands all over her. By the time the band finished the song, I'd finished my beer and the rest of hers, but I didn't feel the least bit mellow. When it looked like banker-boy might try to keep her out there away from me, I made my move.

Yeah, I sing lead in a big-time rock band, but I'm no pussy. I work out religiously, whether or not I'm on the road. All the guys in Balefire do. So I can move, and I can move other people out of my way when the mood strikes me. I moved several people, some of them even kinda gently, as I stalked over to Ashleigh and stepped between her and dumbass.

"You don't mind if I take over now, do you?" I growled *politely* at her partner and turned my attention to her. "I didn't know you liked to dance, babe. I thought you were only here to review the band. You should have said something."

I took her in my arms and started moving. Her eyes widened in surprise—at my claiming her or at my awesome dance moves, I didn't know. It didn't matter. Holding her in my arms erased all the anger gathering inside me from watching her dance with someone else.

She glared up at me. "Just because you're a celebrity rock star doesn't give you the right to be rude. Chad was trying to talk to me."

"Chad huh? Figures banker-boy would have a name like Chad."

"Banker-boy?"

"Yeah. But I'd rather not talk about him when I'm dancing with you."

I spun her out away from me in perfect rhythm with the music, but I kept a tight hold on her hand before I spun her back into me, hauling her up close against the length of my body. Not sure that was such a good idea in a public place, but I couldn't let her go. Which should have made me nervous. I didn't do commitment. I didn't do jealousy over a woman. Neither of which seemed to matter where Ashleigh Baker was concerned. Not when she felt so good, so right in my arms.

Judging from the way she gasped when our bodies molded together like two halves of the same whole, she noticed what a good fit we were too. She clamped her lips shut, drawing my attention to their rosy plumpness, tempting me to lean in for a kiss. She shot daggers at me with her eyes, warning me not to go there, and damned if that wasn't a dare if I didn't know one. But the song abruptly ended, and she stepped neatly out of my arms to stalk off the dance floor.

I caught up with her a couple of seconds later, right on time for her to round on me.

"Where the *hell* do you get off pulling a stunt like that, Blu? Just because you're a celebrity doesn't give you the right to expect anything from me," she bit out, her gorgeous chest heaving. She didn't appear out of breath from dancing, so it must have been something else.

Oh, yeah. She was pissed. But the way she leaned toward me, the way she flipped her hair, the way her pretty little tongue darted out to make a pass over her upper lip told me maybe the real problem had nothing to do with me horning in on banker-boy and everything to do with not taking her dare on the dance floor.

I was about to remedy that little oversight when banker-boy interrupted—again. The dude materialized out of thin air and came perilously close to stepping on my last nerve.

"Blu? Did she call you Blu? Are you Blu Connolly who sings for Balefire? You are, aren't you? I thought you looked familiar. Sorry I tried to move in on your girl, man. I didn't realize. No hard feelings?"

He stuck out his hand, and I hesitated, let him think I might leave him hanging.

"No hard feelings so long as you remember she's with me."

"Hey, I know you're out for the day enjoying yourself sort of incognito, but would you mind letting me have a selfie with you? I want to prove to my buddies at the office that I saw you here."

Great. Banker-boy was a fan. Likely with an active Facebook page.

"Sure."

Whipping out his phone, he leaned into my shoulder. I tipped my cap up enough for his camera to show my face. He snapped the photo and slapped me on the back. "Thanks man. That is so cool of you. My buddies and I are huge fans. You guys totally rocked Red Rocks last summer. You playing anywhere nearby this year?"

"Not to be rude. Chad, is it?"

He nodded enthusiastically.

"Not to be rude, Chad, but I'm here with a hot girl who wants to listen to the band. Enjoy yourself."

I turned to find Ashleigh glaring at me, and this time there was no dare whatsoever involved.

"You had to go there, didn't you?" she shouted to be heard above the noise of the band and the crowd.

"What?"

"Look around. People are staring, pointing. In thirty seconds, you're going to be mobbed by Balefire fans, and the band I came to see won't be finished with their show. I need to review the whole thing, not just the part where you kept yourself to yourself."

"At the risk of making you even more pissed off, you started this by shouting my name." I raised a brow. "Just sayin'."

I couldn't help the smirk that accompanied my words. She looked so damn cute all riled up.

The lead singer interrupted our spat with an announcement sure to send Ashleigh's snit into the stratosphere.

"It's come to our attention that we have someone else in the house who sings lead in a band. We'd like to invite him onstage to join us as we wrap up our show. What do you say, Blu Connolly? You up for singin' a little bluegrass?"

The lead singer stared me down, giving me no choice but to take up his offer even though I knew full well Ashleigh wouldn't like it. It wouldn't take much to know what she was going to think of my next stunt.

I hopped up onto the stage directly in front of the lead singer's mic and shook the dude's hand before looking out over the now screaming audience and tipping my cap to them. After I leaned in to whisper in the singer's ear, he turned to the rest of the band to give them the cue.

The band launched into Alison Krauss's "The Lucky One," and the lead singer did a credible job of harmonizing with my voice. For an impromptu number, it didn't suck. Of course, our impromptu duet brought down the house, but the best part was the stunned look on Ashleigh's face as she realized I wasn't the one-dimensional rock 'n' roll star she'd pegged me for.

I stepped toward the back of the stage and let the lead singer end the show. When the crowd chanted for an encore with me, I mentioned "The Lucky One" was the only country or bluegrass song I knew, and thanks for coming out to support Lightning Strikes. However, I stepped to the back of the stage where I wouldn't be mobbed.

Sliding over to one of the guitar players, I said, "Hey man, would you mind doing me a favor?"

He bobbed his head, "After the way you singlehandedly elevated our set? Name it."

"See that gorgeous brunette in the turquoise T-shirt in front of the stage?" I nodded in Ashleigh's direction.

"Yeah?"

"Could you tell her to meet me outside behind the stage door, please? She's my date, but if I step off this stage, she's not coming anywhere near me for a while, which won't make either of us happy."

"No problem. Geez, I'd like to score something that hot."

The white-hot anger that flashed through me at his comment stunned me. I sucked in air through my nose, which seemed to signal the guitar player to shut his mouth and do me the favor. He hot-footed over to the side of the stage and pointed at her to gain her attention. Subtle, this guy.

When I saw her nod at him, I turned to the bassist and said, "You're an interesting dude to watch. Enjoyed your show."

I stepped behind him and his huge instrument as I spoke to him, putting the two of them between the crowd and me. Then I slipped through the backstage door and out into a mostly deserted alley behind the bar.

As it crossed my mind that I might need to chance going back in to gather her up, Ashleigh came striding down the alley from the direction of the street.

"Without going up onstage, I couldn't follow you outside, so I had to walk around. You want to tell me what the hell that was in there?"

Again with the heaving chest, and I didn't think it was because she had to walk around the building to meet me. Maybe it made me a jerk, but I enjoyed pissing off Ashleigh Baker when it meant watching her pretty blue eyes flash and her cheeks flush and her chest rise and fall like that.

Might as well go all out since I already had her on a roll. "What was what, babe?"

"Don't you 'babe' me, mister. You know what—singing with the band. Now I have to mention it in my review, and that's going to be a big deal to explain to my editor when she asks what else I know about you being in the audience for a Lightning Strikes show." She shoved her fingers into her hair and walked in a tight circle. "Jesus, what a cluster."

With her hand on her hip, she stomped her foot then paced in front of me.

"Slow down, Ash, before you wear yourself out. It was one song, so what difference will it make with your review?"

She stopped to stare at me like I was the dumbass now. Shaking her head, she said, "You really don't know? Lightning Strikes has great instrumentation, but you singing with them proved their lead singer needs to be a backup, which isn't going to go over well in the review if that's what I write."

"So don't write it. Just review the rest of the show."

"Too many people in the audience read the blog. That's why I scored the gig because the crowd at Avogadro's Number is the blog's target demographic. If I don't mention your cameo, someone is going to write in to ask why, which would imply I didn't stay for the whole show. The editor recently fired another reviewer for not staying for the entire show."

She waved her hand through the air and headed up the alley away from the bar. "Ugh! I'll figure it out. Can you take me home now, please?"

CHAPTER SEVEN

Ashleigh

AT LEAST THE ride back to Denver passed uneventfully. I made sure to hold onto the sides of Blu's jacket only and to keep a little space between our bodies when I could. The seat configuration on his bike ensured our thighs would touch for the entire ride, but without road hazards for Blu to swerve around, I didn't have to remain plastered to his muscular back. Judging from the hardness of his back and the contours of his chest and shoulders and biceps, which his tight T-shirt showed off to perfection, the guy spent serious time in a gym. Which didn't jibe with the playboy persona he expressed onstage and in the press.

The way he seemed sort of territorial about me at the bar didn't jibe with that persona either, now that I thought about it. He'd given me a ride since he'd torn apart my car. It wasn't like we were on a date or something. Perhaps he had a fragile ego. Besides, it wasn't like he would actually date a regular girl like me, not when he could have his pick of celebrities of every style and color.

I sighed and tried not to think about how perfect his body felt against mine when he held me in his arms as we danced. Or how much I wanted him to kiss me when I caught him staring at my lips. That sort of nonsense would only lead to trouble, and I didn't need more of that. Not after the way Blu interrupted my review. At least I could be thankful no one threw underwear on the stage after his performance.

The man in question interrupted my thoughts when the rock radio station he played through the speakers on our helmets segued into an old Balefire tune from about five years ago.

"This is a blast from the past. Do you know this one, Ash?"

"Yes."

"You going to sing along with me then?"

"We're back to this? No, Blu. I'll leave the singing up to you."

"I don't think you do know this song. You probably don't know any of our songs. That's why you won't sing along," he challenged, but I could hear the grin in his voice.

"Exactly. So I should be quiet and listen, maybe catch the words, huh?"

"You know, Ashleigh, you don't play very nice."

"Oh, I play very nicely when I choose to."

"But not with me?"

There was something in his voice—a dare? A plea? Both? Any of which was too scary to contemplate.

"It's almost over. Sing your song, Blu."

"So you *do* know it. And you know I wrote it. Maybe you're a fan after all," he teased.

In an instant, he upended my world—again—with his gorgeous, sexy voice. I nearly melted over him as he harmonized with himself on the radio. The next song up was an oldie by Hinder, another of my favorite bands, and Blu surprised me by singing along to all the words, harmonizing perfectly with Austin Winkler's lead vocals. The following tune was by Nickelback, one Blu helped Chad Kroeger sing as it played on the radio. By then I had to say something.

"Are there any songs on this station you don't know?"

"Probably not."

"Wow."

"You say that like it's a bad thing. I'm a musician. I like music, especially rock music. But I've been known to sing a little bluegrass now and then."

I could hear the smirk in his voice, and it took everything I had not to growl at him or maybe throw a punch. The first choice would only play into his joke and make him happy. The second would likely land us in a heap on the side of the road. So I settled for blowing out a breath and rolling my eyes, neither of which satisfied me or affected him in the least.

♪

It was early evening when we returned to my place. Instead of pulling into Diane's driveway, Blu pulled into mine and cut the engine on his bike. I slid off the back and tugged the helmet off my head. By that time, he'd already set his helmet on the gas tank between his legs.

"You going to invite me in to dinner? Seems the least you could do after I drove you all the way to Fort Collins and back today. Entertaining you the whole way, too, I might add," he said with a grin, damn the man. He was entirely too sexy for my own good.

"You'll be disappointed, I'm afraid. I'm not a gourmet cook like your mom."

"I've had three beers all day, and I'm starving. At this point, I'd be perfectly happy with macaroni and cheese."

He popped the kickstand down on his bike and slid off, taking the helmet from my hands and securing it to the back of the bike before turning back to me.

"Well?"

"Glad you're happy with macaroni and cheese," I said as I led the way into my house.

Seriously? Was I losing my mind? Inviting Blu Connolly inside my house after the way I'd responded to him all day?

"Huh. The layout of Old Man Smith's place is the same as Mom's. I had no idea." He looked around my living room and kitchen area. "Only it's flipped with the tiny garages between them."

"Your mom's place does have that state-of-the-art kitchen in it while this one is still Formica countertops and orange linoleum straight out of 1975. But other than that, yeah, they're the same."

"She does enjoy that kitchen. And her patio." He smiled. "Don't forget the fancy patio I installed in her backyard."

His comment caused my curiosity to override my good manners—or good sense—and before I could censor myself, I asked, "Why did you stop there? Why didn't you buy or build her a nice new house in an upscale neighborhood?"

Blu's face clouded over, and I wondered if I would be dining alone after all as he replied in a clipped tone, "You'll have to ask her that."

"Oh."

Oh wow. Oh wow, wow, wow.

Oops.

"Sorry. Didn't mean to poke a sore spot."

Like flipping a switch, his face lit back up into a smile. "You cooking dinner or what?"

I shook my head to right my thoughts after he changed emotions at light speed. Stepping past him into the kitchen, I started boiling water for pasta. After gathering mozzarella, smoked Gouda, and Parmesan cheese from the fridge, I pulled a bowl from the cupboard and my cheese grater from a nearby drawer and started grating the cheeses together.

Blu leaned nonchalantly against the counter beside me, his arms crossed over his sculpted chest, his feet crossed at the ankles as he watched me cook.

"I don't know, Ash. Looks to me like I'm in for a gourmet meal here too."

Not sure about his angle, I slanted him a look.

"Plus, the hot cook is fun to watch."

The cheeky grin accompanying his words let me know he enjoyed pushing my buttons. I rolled my eyes and tried hard to ignore him. Like that was possible.

When the water boiled, I added the pasta, setting the timer on my stove for five minutes. While the pasta cooked, I tore fresh basil over top of the cheese, added a couple of twists of pepper from my hand grinder, splashed some white wine into the mixture, and tried to pretend the sexiest man I'd ever met, a man I'd secretly dreamed about for years, wasn't standing right next to me in my kitchen, waiting for me to respond to him in some way.

After I drained the water off the pasta and poured it into a baking dish, I folded the cheese mixture in and topped it off with a sprinkle of Italian bread crumbs. Next, I slid the dish into the oven to melt the cheese and crisp the top of the bread crumbs. While dinner baked, I pulled ingredients for a simple green salad from the fridge and said, "You just going to watch the show, or are you going to help?"

"I don't know. The show's been pretty entertaining so far, what with the stimulating conversation and all."

With a snort, I handed him a bag of lettuce. "Maybe you could tear these up and put them in this bowl, please?"

"Sure, provided you tell me one thing about yourself that doesn't include writing, teaching, or playing pool since I know those things about you already."

With a sigh, I said, "Honestly, I can't sing. No musical talent whatsoever. In fact, I'm pretty sure my piano teacher so despaired of me that she paid my mom to stop my lessons when I was nine."

When he stared back at me, a look of disbelief on his beautiful features, I pointedly nodded toward the lettuce in his hands, and he started tearing it into bite-sized pieces.

"Your turn. And it can't be something about touring or playing with Balefire since I already know that. Plus, I already know Dakota, Tron, and you grew up together."

"Been researching me, huh?" He cocked his head, a grin dancing in his eyes.

"That's all in the reviews of the last two albums Balefire released after Jack Whitehorse replaced Dave Brubaker. I write reviews, remember? It's smart to read them too."

"You kinda enjoy busting my balls, don't you, babe?"

"And we're back to meaningless endearments." I sighed. "Yet you still haven't taken your turn."

He gave me a look and seemed to come to a decision. "My dad left us when I was five. About that same time, I met Dakota. His mom left him and his dad when we were eight. It messes with your head when the people who should be there for you forever up and disappear from your life without a backward glance."

"Wow, Blu. I didn't know. I'm sorry I—"

"Don't be. We landed on our feet." The timer on the oven shrilled loudly in the void left by his revelations. "You gonna get that?"

"Could you add the tomatoes and peppers to the lettuce while I rescue dinner from the oven, please?"

I set the hot baking dish on a wooden cutting board in the middle of my tiny kitchen table. While the pasta rested, I set the table with my mismatched stoneware, garage sale flatware, and embroidered cloth napkins I'd picked up at a secondhand store. After what Blu had revealed to me about the way he'd grown up, I thought he might not care too much that I couldn't set a fancy table.

"Beer or wine? I've got IPA and stout and a bottle of chardonnay in here," I said as I opened the door to the fridge and perused my beverage selection.

"IPA and gourmet mac and cheese. Sounds like my kind of dinner." Blu seated himself at my table. "Your turn, Ash. Something more substantial than your 'terrible' singing, which I've yet to hear, so I'm not sure I believe you about that anyway." He helped himself to a heaping serving of pasta.

I blew out a breath and busied myself with putting salad on my plate as I debated what to tell him. "I'm an only child too. My dad's a colonel in the Air Force. He's finishing out his service as an instructor at the Air Force Academy, which is how I ended up in Colorado. I've lived in Germany, Italy, California, Washington, Montana, and Texas. I was born on base in San Diego, so I don't remember much of that. We lived off base when Dad did his second stint there."

"An Air Force brat. Does that mean you've always been kind of a vagabond?"

"Pretty much. The last seven years that I've lived in Colorado are the longest I've stayed in one state ever. But in Colorado, I've lived in Colorado Springs and now Denver."

"Is that why you like to garden? As a way of putting down roots?"

What the hell?

"I thought your job was fronting a rock band. You practice pop psychology on the side?"

I was going for flippant, but the way Blu scowled at me said I'd completely missed the mark. Then he executed that swift about-face in emotion again. "I gotta tell ya, Ash, this is by far the best mac and cheese I've ever tasted. Mind if I have seconds?"

He reached for the serving spoon even as he asked the question while I tried to catch up from his lightning-quick mood change.

"I like to grow things. When I lived in my apartment, I kept an indoor garden. Mr. Smith's daughter rented this place to me at a discounted rate if I kept up the yard and revived the flowerbeds. Win-win."

"Was that so hard?" Blu asked, the grin softening the sarcasm in his tone.

"Your turn."

"Mom's a waitress because she chooses to be. I've offered to move her into a nicer place, set her up with her own business, even bring her along on tour with us. She wants to stay here."

He cocked an eyebrow, daring me to comment. Jesus, I'd clearly revealed much more about my personal prejudices and attitude about rock 'n' roll singers—or at least one rock 'n' roll singer in particular—than I thought.

"She invites me to lunch almost every Saturday. It's the highlight of my week. Adding the wine to the mac and cheese is her invention, by the way. Her secret ingredient. That's why it's good."

He nodded and ate another bite of his dinner. "What's your favorite music?"

"Fishing for a compliment, are you? I already told you I saw Balefire last summer at Red Rocks."

"Loving Balefire goes without saying, Ash." He slanted me a look. "What about in general? Is rock your favorite?"

"In my job, I listen to all kinds of stuff, but yeah, when given a choice, I listen to rock. I get a kick out of catching local bands, up and coming or wannabes who will never be. Reviewing music is all an adventure." I smiled at him, and he stopped a bite of pasta midway to his mouth for a second before continuing.

Although that was weird, I was catching on that Blu Connolly ran so much deeper than his bad-ass rock 'n' roll singer persona.

We finished dinner, and he surprised me again by stepping up to the sink for dish detail without me even suggesting it. In short order, we had dinner cleaned up and put away.

After drying his hands, he pulled another beer from the fridge, clearly signaling his intention to continue our conversation. He twisted off the cap and took a sip before heading over to sit on my couch where he terrified me by looking completely at home.

Wow. I never would have envisioned this scene in a million years: the most famous lead singer in the country seated comfortably on my secondhand couch in my tiny rental and looking for all the world like he belonged right there.

"You joining me or what, Ash?"

His smirk told me all my emotions were once again flashing over my face like a neon sign. Good thing I'd never had an interest in gambling—aside from inviting Blu into my home. After grabbing a beer from the fridge, I joined him on the far side of the couch, turning and placing my knee on the cushion between us.

"Judging from the shape your car's in, you don't have a boyfriend."

"That's a rather personal observation."

"True, though, isn't it?"

"I don't see what having a boyfriend has to do with my car," I huffed before taking a couple of swallows from my beer.

"If you had a boyfriend, and the guy was worth a shit, your car would have had regular maintenance long before now. So what's the deal? You're gorgeous, educated, fun when you loosen up." He swallowed a mouthful of his beer. "Why aren't you seeing anyone?"

"I don't see how my dating life is any business of yours."

"Are you telling me you're not into guys? 'Cause that would be a real shame for every red-blooded man with a pulse."

"I'm straight, Blu. But don't feel obligated to hit on me because I fed you dinner. That was for driving me to Fort Collins today. Thanks again for the ride, by the way."

"It was my pleasure. All of it."

He set his beer on the table beside the couch before leaning forward and taking my beer from my hand and setting it beside his. I watched in deer-in-the-headlights fascination as he slid his hand along the back of the couch until he reached my shoulder. For a couple of seconds he traced circles with one finger over my T-shirt before he lifted his hand and ran his calloused fingers down my cheek then slipped them into my hair, cupping the side of my face with his big hand.

"Your skin and your hair are as soft as they look," he murmured as he stared at my cheek and my hair. The hunger I saw in his golden-green eyes was intense enough to make my breath catch.

It took me several seconds to catch on that his other hand had slid up my thigh and gently pushed against it to encourage me to drop my knee from the defensive position in which I sat. Of their own volition, my knee and foot moved off the couch, giving Blu the opening he sought to slide closer to me.

"If you don't want this, Ash, now is a real good time to let me know. Otherwise, I'm going to kiss that luscious mouth of yours that's been tempting me all day."

I blinked at him, stunned. Blu Connolly had spent the day entertaining thoughts of kissing me?

Obviously, I'd lost my mind when he touched me because I nodded yes in answer to his question. He leaned in and brushed his lips over mine. I couldn't help it. I gasped at the electricity that slight contact shot through me, and Blu didn't hesitate. He gathered me into his arms, and my nipples puckered instantly at the contact they made with the hard wall of his chest. Entranced at the fierce way he stared at my lips, I couldn't have moved even if I'd wanted to. Which I didn't. Finding myself in this man's arms didn't just thrill me—it felt exactly right in a way I could never explain.

He kissed me like a starving man at a feast. His mouth devoured mine, his lips pressing hard against mine, his tongue demanding a mating with my own, a mating my body compelled me to give. My whole being sparked, electricity leaping from his skin to mine, fizzing through my veins.

My fingers scraped the short hair at the base of his neck. The spiky texture of his hair contrasted with the resilient muscle beneath his smooth skin amped through my senses. Between the sensations coming through my fingertips and those Blu elicited with his fingers in my hair while his free hand roamed the length of my back, my skin erupted in goose bumps everywhere.

The apex of my thighs heated and pulsed, my core tightening even as I felt a surge of wetness when my body answered the summons Blu demanded with his talented mouth. Our tongues mated and danced, sliding over, under, twining around each other before we explored teeth and the insides of lips and cheeks. The kiss was hotter than anything I'd ever experienced but still not enough. I needed to be even closer to him.

He must have agreed because the next thing I knew, I found

myself straddling his thighs. One of his big hands still held my head right where he could plunder my mouth while the other explored my back down to my ass. When he cupped me, I heard myself whimper and discovered the hard evidence of his desire where I rocked my heated center into him. He groaned as he surged against me, holding me in place with his hand on my ass. We ground together, our clothes adding to the delicious friction of the wild electric experience that was Blu Connolly's kiss.

All too soon, he tore his mouth from mine and gasped out, "Jesus, Ash. Give me a minute," implying I'd started this thing between us.

As his words penetrated the lust-induced fog of my brain, it hit me that Blu probably considered me another groupie, yet another woman who wanted a piece of the rock 'n' roll star action. Which meant, of course, that he expected me to join the parade of other forgettable one-night stands left in the wake of his life. The realization humiliated me in an instant, and I jumped off his lap, heading toward the middle of my living room and as far away from him as my small space would allow.

"What the fuck?" His confusion at my behavior might have been understandable. After all, I'm sure no sane woman had ever said no to him, rock god that he was, but I wasn't a groupie, not even for a night of what I'm sure would be pure bliss with Blu Connolly.

"I'm sorry, Blu. I know I've given you completely the wrong impression. But I don't do one-night stands. I'm not wired that way."

"I don't recall asking you for sex. Which is why I needed to slow down for a minute. Come on back here." He patted his thigh and smiled a slow sexy smile that nearly crumbled my resolve. But the distance I'd put between us served to cool me down, make me think about where we were, and I couldn't imagine resisting his advances if I ended up in his arms again.

"I think maybe you should go now."

His tone turned from playful to serious. "Hey, Ashleigh, you were into that kiss every bit as much as I was. What's different all of a sudden?"

"Look. You're a big-time celebrity. You're on the road most of the year, and no one expects you to settle down. Women throw themselves at you knowing full well they're not going to have any more of you than a roll in the sheets and a kiss goodbye."

He scowled at me, but I hurried on. "Which is fine. You don't promise more than you plan to deliver. It's only that I'm one of those people who need monogamy, fidelity. I guess because we moved around so much, my parents only had each other, so they're a team, a unit, and they raised me to expect that too." The weird look on his face told me I'd probably insulted him, so I decided to cut my losses all at once. "I don't sleep with anyone unless I'm in a relationship with him. So you and I need to walk away from this."

Blu shuttered his gaze as he folded his arms across his chest.

Trying to explain, trying to make him see how I wasn't criticizing him, I continued. "You couldn't know where I came from because it didn't come up in our question-and-answer session. Knowing how I am, I should have never let you kiss me." I crossed my arms over my chest. "Again, I'm sorry I led you to believe otherwise, but I'm not having sex with you tonight." I swallowed because saying no to Blu Connolly was so much harder than I could have ever imagined, especially after I'd kissed him. "Or any night. You'll go back out on the road and forget all about me, which will be for the best, I'm sure."

"You have it all figured out, don't ya, Ashleigh? You know everything about me from spending almost one whole day with me."

The look he shot me as he stood from the couch and stalked toward me was equal parts anger and pain, neither of which made any sense.

"You're right of course. It's for the best that we forget all about tonight. That we forget all about how this feels—for both of us."

Taking my face in both of his big hands, he kissed me again, a fierce deep claiming that turned my knees to jelly. When he let me go, I staggered before righting myself and staring after his broad back, which he'd turned on me the second he ended the kiss.

He slammed out my front door, and seconds later, his Harley roared angrily to life. He revved it loudly in my driveway for a long minute before I heard him turn it around, the deep rumble of the engine giving way to a bellowing howl as he raced out of the neighborhood—and probably out of my life.

CHAPTER EIGHT

Ashleigh

THE NEXT MORNING, I woke up groggy and out of sorts. Having spent the better part of the night replaying my evening with Blu on an endless loop, even in my dreams, my sorry state came as no surprise. His voice seduced me the first time I heard a Balefire song on the radio. When I saw him perform live last summer, I'd spent many nights afterward dreaming dreams someone with common sense didn't dream. Then there he was in my house, on my couch, kissing me like he could never get enough, and I nearly gave in to the fantasy.

No doubt, thousands of women the world over fantasized about having sex with Blu Connolly. Those women, however, didn't live next door to his mom, didn't have to risk seeing him with someone else after they'd enjoyed their turn, didn't have to know for a fact that the fantasy would never extend past a one-night stand. The reality of my situation made me think twice about doing something completely out of character for me when I had the chance. Now I'd have to be careful to maintain my distance from him.

Or not.

After the way he tore out of my house last night, maybe that little problem had taken care of itself.

With my thoughts in a jumble, I headed out to my car to drive to the store. When I started to unlock my garage, I remembered Blu had torn my car apart to service it yesterday. Sighing, I realized I'd have to make two trips to the grocery store on my bicycle. Afterward, I'd have to find someone to finish whatever Blu had started on my car.

When I stepped through the side door to the garage, I nearly jumped a mile in the air as Blu stood up from the floor on the other side of my car.

"What are you doing here?" I demanded, willing my heart to slow down.

"Finishing the tune-up I started on your car. From the looks of it, you forgot about that." He pointed to my purse. "Going somewhere?"

Impatient with myself for my ridiculous happiness at finding him in my garage and also for forgetting the state of my car, I said rather more tartly than I intended, "Yes. It seems I'm low on groceries. And I did remember the state of my car. I was going to ride my bike to the store."

"Uh-huh." He crossed his arms over his chest and smirked. "In a dress."

"Um, well, no. Excuse me. I have to change."

I turned for the door when Blu interrupted me. "Wait. I need to test drive your car to be sure everything I did works the way it's supposed to. Let me wash up, and I'll ride with you."

"Why are you helping me?"

"Like I said yesterday, because you need it. Besides, I like working with my hands. I'm good at it."

Desire flared in his eyes as he looked me up and down, and though I pretended to ignore his innuendo, my body didn't, heating up at the promise in his eyes. His pupils dilated so big as to leave the barest ring of gold around them. Involuntarily, I sucked in air, and

Blu smiled wickedly at me. When I lowered my lashes and caught a glimpse of my chest, I knew why.

Crossing my arms over the evidence of my arousal, I said, "Are you trying to start something here?" I aimed for commanding, but my words came out all breathy, much to my utter disgust and embarrassment. I did *not* want to feel anything for Blu Connolly.

"That's exactly what I'm trying to do, babe," he drawled, and with a wink, he threw me completely off-balance.

"Why? Why me?"

"Now who's fishing for compliments?" He laughed as he pushed the garage door opener and disappeared out the big door and across the yard into Diane's house.

Sputtering at his parting shot, I barely had time to debate whether to drive my car without him and take a chance before he returned in a clean T-shirt and jeans.

"Ready?" he asked.

Seriously? The man wore his clothes tight, showing off the contours of his long lean muscles and full chest. *He must work out—a lot.* My face must have advertised my thoughts: either that or the drool gave me away because he grinned and said, "You gonna stand there ogling me all day, or are you going to hand over the keys so we can get this show on the road?"

Trying to cover my embarrassment at being caught out openly staring at the man, I dug in my purse, located my keys, and tossed them nonchalantly at him. I didn't look to see if he caught them before I opened the passenger door and slid into the front seat. Busying myself with my seatbelt, I ignored Blu's chuckle as he slid into the car beside me.

"I usually shop at the Safeway off of Broadway. Do you know it?" I asked.

"Every single aisle."

I slanted him a look.

He checked the rearview and the side mirrors as he backed into the street from my driveway. "My mom sent me there on my bicycle when I was a kid. She made me put a basket on the back of my bike to carry her groceries. I hated it." His voice vibrated with a mix of exasperation and humor. "Everyone at school made fun of me for being 'basket boy.' Finally, I talked her into buying me a backpack with a frame, and I carried her groceries in it. Much cooler." He chuckled at the memory.

As I tried to reconcile the idea of ubercool Blu Connolly riding around the neighborhood on a bicycle with a basket on it, I struggled to admit that the rock god I'd idolized from afar for five years was a regular guy. Yet, so far, the evidence pointed to him being exactly that. Except for the way the man could kiss. There was nothing regular about that. The reality of Blu Connolly was proving to be so much better than the fantasy. Dammit.

Heat suffused my body at the thought of his kisses, and I was glad my sunglasses shielded my eyes from more than the sun. At least he couldn't discern my thoughts from my expression.

"Basket boy, huh? That's tame compared to some things I hear kids say to each other when I sub."

"Vaughn and I discussed that when you and Jaime excused yourselves to the ladies' room the other night."

"The bad nicknames kids give each other these days?" I asked in confusion.

We'd reached the intersection with a main thoroughfare onto Broadway. Blu signaled and made the turn as a laugh rumbled out of him. "No, the fact we never had teachers as hot as you two when we were in school, and what the fuck was up with that?"

The man was an inveterate flirt. Still, I understood that as Diane's single next-door neighbor, I was attractive to Blu because of my proximity to him during his hiatus from Balefire. Nothing more.

"Jaime and Vaughn hit it off the other night, didn't they? Honestly, that surprised the heck out of me after the way she badgered me for an introduction to you."

"Yeah? Jaime wanted an introduction? I'll make sure to tell Vaughn next time I see him." He slid a sideways smile at me, reminding me how much he liked all the girls' attention all the time.

I needed to remember that.

When we arrived at the grocery store, he surprised me again by knowing and acknowledging several of the locals, even stopping to chat for a few minutes with Scotty, the produce manager, asking him about his kids. Like a regular guy. Which is also how people in the store treated him. The more time I spent with him, the more normal he seemed.

Which was so not good for my resolve to stay away from him.

Blu as a celebrity was far less dangerous to my emotions than Blu as a regular human. It took me a while, but at last, I noticed he'd been surreptitiously adding items to my cart.

"What, exactly, are you doing?"

He gifted me with a look of supreme boyish innocence, one I'd seen countless times when I'd caught out a student who clearly had nefarious intentions. "Shopping?"

"For who? Jalapenos are definitely not on my list."

"They're on mine."

"So get your own cart."

"That's silly when we're shopping together."

Planting my hands on my hips, I said, "We are *not* shopping together."

"You implied before we left the house that I'd eaten up your food last night, so I thought shopping with you meant I'd replace it. Since I'm doing that, I wanted to add one or two things I like that I noticed you didn't have."

The way he imparted that information implied we had something going between us, and his words in the garage came back to me.

"Blu, we are not starting something here."

"You're right. We aren't starting something—" He dragged out the word. "We already started it the other night at the pool table in the bar." Grinning, he took the cart to push it down another aisle of the store.

For several seconds, I stood in the middle of the aisle and stared after his broad back.

Glancing over his shoulder at me, he said, "Come on, Ashleigh. We need to finish up here so I can stop at the hardware store." He sounded like we were any other couple out shopping together.

Without making a scene, I had no choice but to follow him through the store as he added several items to my cart. When we reached the checkout, I started dividing the cart between the items on my list and those he added, intending to pay for my own food and bagging it separately from his. As we'd walked through the store, I'd determined to make sure he went home to Diane's with his purchases.

There would be no repeat performances of last night at my house.

Like he'd read my mind or something, he unloaded the cart at nearly superhuman speed, preempting my plan. I tried to add up my share in my head, and I thought I came pretty close, but as I reached for my wallet, he handed the cashier his credit card, and she rang up the sale as one purchase.

"I have cash. I'll pay you when we get back to the car."

The look he gave me could have withered a cactus. "I got it. Do not make a scene about this, Ashleigh."

In silence, we unloaded the groceries into the trunk of my car. When we were both buckled in, I stated, quite calmly I thought, "Blu, you do not need to buy me groceries. It was macaroni and cheese, for crying out loud. Besides, I owed you dinner at least for fixing my car. I know how much my share was—"

"Shhh. I need to listen to the car for a minute."

Fearing something was wrong with my ride, I shut up. It took me some time to realize the radio played softly—and Blu had played me.

We stopped at a hardware store on the drive back to my place.

He spent only a couple of minutes inside while I fretted in the car, trying to figure out how I was going to deal with him and with my wayward emotions.

I spent the rest of the trip back to my house churning over my responses to the infuriatingly sexy man, trying to devise a polite way to send him packing before he had a chance to slip under my skin. Oblivious to my inner turmoil, and adding to it by the verse, Blu sang along to the radio the whole drive back to my place.

By the time we arrived home, I still hadn't figured anything out. We unloaded my car and carried bags of groceries into my house like we'd repeated this chore together weekly. As I unloaded the bags and put away the items on my list, I was careful to separate Blu's purchases and rebag them. He caught me, though.

"It's all staying here, Ashleigh. As my mom likes to say, find a home for all of it."

"Blu, I don't think—"

"I'm going out to the garage to do something about that candy-ass lock Old Man Smith put on the door to pretend to keep the place secure. While I'm fixing that, make me a sandwich, woman." He smirked at his clichéd sexist joke, which he punctuated by smacking me soundly on the ass, nearly lifting me off my feet. The way he cupped his hand as he executed his button-pushing move meant he made a lot of noise but didn't actually cause me any pain. In fact, he even managed to cop a feel with his maneuver.

"You did *not* just go there," I sputtered.

"I sure did, darlin'." His laughter rang through my kitchen.

"Really, Blu Connolly, who the hell do you think you are?" I folded my arms across my chest.

"The guy you can't stop thinking about. Lucky me." He winked. Turning on his heel, he called out as he headed back out the door, "I like jalapenos on my ham-and-cheese sandwich. Tomatoes and lettuce would be good too."

The wicked laughter I heard as the back door slammed shut

behind him punctuated the fact he was on a mission to push every last one of my buttons.

So far, he was succeeding.

"Ugghh! Men!" I stomped my foot and glared at the empty space where he'd been standing a couple of seconds ago.

With a snort, I busied myself with putting away the food and making sandwiches, my growling stomach telling me we'd shopped through lunchtime. As I worked, I thought about the morning. When my mind wandered to all the innuendos and winks and concerted efforts to have his way, I couldn't help but smile. The man could be devastating when he put his mind to it.

Remembering the stories I'd seen in the celebrity press and on TMZ concerning Balefire and, particularly, Blu and his buddy Dakota Perri, I sobered. Blu's antics with me fell squarely in line with his celebrity persona. One event stood out in my memory, a red carpet stunt Balefire pulled at the Grammys three years ago when Dave Brubaker still drummed for them.

In my mind's eye, I could visualize the stretch Hummer rolling up to the red carpet and disgorging the band and a half-dozen groupies they sicced on Drake and Justin Bieber. Balefire said they were making a statement about the real men who play rock 'n' roll. Of course, the fire-engine red tuxes each of the guys wore with matching bow ties and cummerbunds but no shirts certainly gave the impression of manly men. Another part of the joke. The stunt still came up from time to time when a new story about the band broke in the news.

Teasing me with that stereotypical chauvinist move only proved him to be the joker the tabloids and the band's Grammy antics implied. Which of course posed another problem for my crumbling resolve to resist him. Dammit some more.

Determined not to give Blu a chance to repeat last night's near miss on my couch, I carried our lunch outside to my tiny patio. It wasn't really a patio. I had a sidewalk with an awning over it, wide enough for two chairs situated side by side with a small table between them. It was nothing like the luxurious patio taking up a fair portion of Diane Connolly's backyard. I set our two plates on the table and went back inside for the iced teas I'd poured, carrying the two glasses and a bag of chips I'd snagged with one finger out to the table. As I set the glasses down, Blu banged through the garage door to join me.

"Looks good enough to eat," he deadpanned as he peered over my shoulder at the simple fare on the table.

"Again, you're not having the gourmet meal that's probably waiting for you at your mom's," I said as I chose my chair and sat down.

"She's at work, so lunch would have been up to me. Believe me, anything you've made will be more palatable. Thanks for making me lunch. Did you put sugar in my tea, by chance?"

Appreciative yet casual. Diane raised Blu with good manners. Why did she have to go and *do* that? I adored men with nice manners. Now Blu Connolly had inadvertently found another way to sneak through my defenses.

"Ash? Sugar?"

I blinked.

"For the tea."

"Oh. I'm sorry. I didn't realize you took yours that way. Be right back."

I hustled into the house and stuck my face in the freezer for several seconds to cool myself down from embarrassment at being caught thinking about the man while he sat right there. After taking several deep, frigid, calming breaths, I thought I might be back under control enough to return to lunch. I was about to step out the back door when I remembered the sugar. Then I had to go back for a spoon. For crying out loud, when did I turn into such a hot mess?

"Here you go," I said, setting the sugar on the now-crowded table. "Do you need anything else while I'm up?"

"Nope. This sandwich is delicious. I noticed you put jalapenos on yours too."

"Thought I'd try it," I said nonchalantly as I seated myself in my cheap lawn chair. I'd deliberately chosen it to give Blu the one good one my dad's crazy aunt had gifted me for my college graduation. Honestly, who gives someone one deck chair? Oh, yeah, someone who traveled the world alone and never married. Apparently, she sensed a kindred spirit or something. At least my mismatched chairs complemented my mismatched stoneware.

"Mom tells me Old Man Smith's daughter gives you a break on your rent for doing the gardening here. Does she cover the cost of those fancy roses you planted in this bed beside your patio?"

"That's why I don't have to pay full rent because I handle the upkeep of the yard, including paying for the plants and flowers. But I got a deal on those." I indicated with my sandwich before I took a bite, chewed, and swallowed "Someone at the nursery ordered more than a local landscaper specified, and I happened to be there when the shipment came in. Rather than take the wrath of his boss, the clerk gave me the flowers for cost if I'd take them immediately without his boss seeing me. I felt like I was stealing them or something. It was kind of fun." I grinned, and he grinned back.

"Ashleigh Baker, rose thief. Who knew?"

"There you are, Blu!" Diane called from her yard next door.

"Hi Mom. You're home early." He put down his sandwich and stood up to greet her.

Diane let herself through the gate in the fence between our yards and strolled over to my patio.

"I'd thought to make you lunch, but I see Ashleigh beat me to it," she said with a warm smile after she stepped back from hugging him.

"I told you having lunch over here would mean missing out on your mom's gourmet cooking." I shot Blu a look from beneath my lashes. "All the sandwich fixin's are still on my kitchen table since I didn't think one sandwich would be enough for this guy. Please, have a seat and I'll make you one."

I stood from my chair and gestured for Diane to take it.

"That is lovely of you, Ashleigh. Thank you," she said.

She seemed to melt into the chair, and I wondered for the thousandth time why she insisted on waitressing when she didn't have to. Something Blu said about asking her why she did it niggled at the back of my mind, but before I could follow the thought, I was back in my kitchen with Blu directly behind me.

"You left out the food so I could have seconds? See, you *do* like me, Ash. While you make me another sandwich, is it all right if I take one of your kitchen chairs out onto the patio since you only have two deck chairs?"

He already had a chair in his hands as he asked, and I nodded. As the first part of his question registered, I rolled my eyes. Ugghh! The man might have nice manners, but he certainly wasn't above expecting a woman to take care of him.

I carried fresh sandwiches and a glass of tea for Diane out to the table where I found the two of them in what seemed like a heated conversation.

"Oh, sorry. I didn't mean to interrupt," I said, standing there awkwardly with Diane's lunch in my hands.

"It's nothing, dear. As you may have noticed, Blu likes to get his way. When he doesn't, he keeps the argument going anyway." She directed the last bit at her son who stared mulishly back at her. "That looks lovely. Thank you," she added, as she relieved me of the plate of sandwiches in my hand.

I set the tea glass down beside her on the table before handing Blu another sandwich while she balanced her plate on the last spare space on the table.

"Blu tells me the two of you attended a bluegrass concert yesterday," she said, changing the subject. "He said he had a great time. Did you enjoy it?"

"Mostly."

She raised a brow and stared pointedly at her son.

"What?" he asked in all innocence.

"It was great until the end when Blu sang with the band."

"You're not still mad about that, are you Ashleigh?" The grin he flashed I'm sure worked on every woman he'd ever met, including his mother.

Too bad I knew my editor at the blog as well as I did. I'd written and submitted my review this morning before I went out to my garage to find Blu still working on my car. I had no doubt the fallout from our excursion yesterday would be awaiting me in my in-box when I logged in. It wasn't something I looked forward to.

"You sang with the band? For a show Ashleigh needed to review? Oh, son," Diane lamented.

"Not you too, Mom. Honestly, it wasn't that big a deal." He sat back in his chair, arms crossed over his chest.

"Yeah. That's why I can hardly wait to check my email this afternoon."

"You already submitted the review?" Blu asked.

"This morning. That's my job." I swallowed a cooling sip of iced tea. "Or hopefully after my editor reads my review, it's still my job."

CHAPTER NINE

Blu

OVER THE NEXT week, odd jobs at both Mom's and Ashleigh's places kept me busy. Usually, I spent the afternoons—and if I could stretch a job out—the evenings at Ashleigh's. Doors needed the hinges adjusted or had to be rehung, carpets needed stretching, bathroom faucet and shower leaks needed fixing. The irony of me fixing up Old Man Smith's place didn't escape me. Dakota would roll in hysterics if he knew. But it was worth it to have time alone with her.

I couldn't understand it. The more time I spent with her, the more time I wanted to spend with her, which was fucking weird considering we hadn't even had sex yet. Pictures of those sapphire-blue eyes that could sparkle or sizzle depending on how outrageous I decided to act flitted through my head, giving me a clue why I stuck around. When she narrowed them at me, it took everything I had not to laugh out loud. Nobody did indignant as cute as Ashleigh Baker. The fact she kept her distance but couldn't stop looking at me told me she wasn't immune to me either.

What I stopped trying to analyze was why I tried so hard to

win her over. It wasn't like I couldn't have any other woman. Hell, they threw themselves at me on the street sometimes and on nearly every occasion when Vaughn and I met over a beer at the bar after he got off work. Some women even threw themselves at me before they realized my identity. Since meeting Ashleigh though, I'd walked away from every offer, which was something I stopped trying to make sense of too.

Of course, I'd taken to touching Ashleigh whenever the opportunity presented itself. Since we are talking me here, that meant an opportunity came up every time I dropped by her house. *Casually* brushing my chest against her back as I reached over her to grab a glass from a cupboard before settling my arm against hers while I ran the tap and she washed vegetables for lunch. *Accidentally* reaching for the pepper at the exact moment she did so my fingers smoothed over the silky skin of her hand. *Coincidentally* wanting the trowel or the potted plant she also wanted as I helped her in her yard—yeah, those were all completely innocent moves.

She never said anything, but she sucked in a lot of air, and I noticed her skin pebbled beneath my fingertips often whenever I sneaked a chance to touch her.

It also didn't escape me during that first ride we took together on my bike that she liked my singing voice. Her response as I sang to her on the trip to Fort Collins told me all about it before I jumped at the chance to show off for her on the stage that afternoon. Now, I sang to her every chance I could.

My showing off that day, though, came back to bite me in the ass. To make sure I didn't jeopardize Ashleigh's job with the music blog, I'd agreed to give her editor an interview—in person. Guess she wasn't kidding about my antics causing her problems at work. Who knew?

Having worked in the business for going on ten years, I understood how to play the game. So I insisted Ashleigh be included in the interview before I agreed to give it. I wanted her to have the chance at least to share the byline after her editor nixed my original idea of Ashleigh doing the interview herself.

Seeing her struggle in the music business reminded me of how much the guys and I gave up initially to land our first big record contract. Which was the reason Dakota took online classes and earned a degree in business management on the side while I took enough online classes in accounting to have a clue about how to negotiate with the assholes when the time came after we broke big. When Jack joined the band, he proved to be almost excessively vigilant with the fine print on any contract we signed, which was another asset for us. Our manager did his job, but the business end of our music would always be the band's livelihood, so we paid attention to it too.

Yeah, there was no need for anyone to change their impressions, get the wrong idea about us as a party band. Our reputation gave us far too many perks and advantages to mess with the image. It wasn't something I planned on sharing with the blogger, but maybe Ashleigh would let me help her.

When I wasn't with Ashleigh, I studied her, reading her reviews online, casually asking Mom about her. Well, maybe not so casually since Mom had invited her over to dinner two nights this week already. Each time, I walked her back to her place afterward, and each time it had been all I could do not to wrap her in my arms and kiss her senseless. The moonlight silvered her hair and shadowed the secret places of her body I longed to touch. Her floral scent called to me over the night smells of fresh-cut grass and green leaves that I'd always loved whenever I visited home.

She'd made it clear my reputation was an obstacle, no matter how bad I wanted her. Still, the awkwardness when we left each other on those nights cheered me. Like last night. The conversation tugged a smile from my lips as I replayed it in my head.

"Tell your mom, thanks again for dinner."

"You did that, Ash. I think she believes you appreciated it."

"Um, sure." She laughed nervously.

"You still think you don't like me much, don't you?"

"It's not that I don't like you. I do like you."

"So what's the problem?" I stared at her full lips, remembering how soft they felt beneath mine. The thought had me crowding her, and she sucked in a breath before she took half a step back.

"You're a player, Blu, in every sense of the word. Getting involved with you would be a very bad idea for me."

"Have you ever walked even a short distance on the wild side, Ash?"

"N-no," she stammered, and it was so damn cute. I nearly said to hell with it and took a chance on pulling her into my arms and kissing those plump lips of hers.

Instead, I reached out and brushed a finger down the satin of her cheek. "Maybe you should give it a try."

I don't think she even realized she'd leaned into my touch before I reluctantly lowered my hand from her face, and she nearly fell forward.

"Oh!"

Even in the moonlight, I could see color bloom on her cheeks, and I smiled at her.

"Tell your mom thanks. Oh, dear. I mean, good night. I'll see you later," she gushed while she tried to turn and run simultaneously. She nearly tripped over her feet as she raced into her house, and I couldn't suppress the chuckle that escaped my lips.

Whether she wanted to or not, Ashleigh harbored an interest in me, one that had nothing to do with me being the lead singer for Balefire.

Which was good since I'd spent too much time in the shower jacking off to fantasies of Ashleigh Baker every day since I'd met her. 'Course, it didn't help me at all to know exactly how sweet her pretty mouth tasted, how silky her skin felt beneath my fingertips, the heavenly way her gorgeous tits pillowed against my chest, how an aroused Ashleigh's pussy could scorch the front of my jeans. One glorious evening on her couch taught me a whole bunch about what I was missing with her because she didn't believe in my very real interest in her. Wonder what she'd think if I shared some of my fantasies with her?

I'd have to save those thoughts for another time, though. No way would I further jeopardize Ashleigh's job by making her late for the interview. Dressed in my usual uniform of T-shirt, jeans, and leather boots, I pulled a ball cap over my head, slid my sunglasses on, and headed over to her place. She met me at her back door wearing a form-fitting yellow sundress with—surprise—enormous bright pink and orange flowers printed all over it. The halter hinted at her pretty cleavage, making my mouth water. I stepped back to admire the whole picture, enjoying the way the dress hugged her curves and stopped above her knees, tantalizing me with the perfect way it clung to her delectable body. She'd left her hair loose, letting it fall in waves over her shoulders, pure chocolate silk I longed to muss and pull and play with. As her floral scent washed over me, it was all I could do not to reach for her.

When she frowned at me, she broke the spell she unknowingly cast over me. "Judging from the fact you're wearing your boots, you thought to impress my editor with your badass biker persona, but I'm driving, Blu. This interview has to be perfectly professional." Softly, she added, "Please."

That did it. Her imperious tone put me in the mood to piss her off by insisting on doing as I damn well pleased and roaring up to the interview as I'd planned—to hell with her tight dress that wouldn't straddle my bike well. Then she ruined those plans with that quiet, sincere plea.

Still, I determined to remain in control of my man card. "Fine. We'll take your car, but I'm driving."

Laughing, she closed and locked the door to her house before leading me to her garage. So caught up in the way her perfect little ass swayed as she navigated her sidewalk in the tall wedge heels she wore, I almost forgot to ask her what was so funny.

As she handed me her car keys, she said, "You in the driver's seat of my compact car is not going to project the same badass rock 'n' roll singer persona you were aiming for on your bike. You sure you want to drive?"

"Depends on the way I drive your car, Ash. Don'tcha know it's all in the presentation?"

I slid into the driver's seat and fired up the engine. It didn't sound nearly as cool as my Harley, but thanks to my tune-up, her little ride didn't sound like it might be on its way to a scrap yard, either.

"Don't you even think about burning rubber in this car, Blu Connolly."

Again with the narrowed eyes. Damn, she could make me hard when I pissed her off. After I backed down the driveway, I popped the clutch when I put the car in gear, and we ripped down the street, leaving a trail of tire smoke behind us.

"Blu!"

"Whoops. Guess I'm a little overeager for this interview," I said, smiling apologetically as I smoothly shifted gears and slowed the car almost to the speed limit.

"That must be it. Remember that when I send you the bill for a new set of tires for my car."

She directed me to a coffee shop not too far from the diner where Mom worked. When I realized the location, it was my turn to slant her a look.

"Did you choose this place on purpose, Ashleigh? 'Cause you know I keep my mom away from the press. She's none of their damn business."

"I didn't choose this place. Camille did. Without giving your mom away, I couldn't object. But for the record, I did suggest the bar you and Vaughn like instead. Camille said she didn't want the distraction of a bar."

"She brings up my mom, the interview is over."

"Keep the car keys," Ashleigh replied.

I nodded at her and relaxed a fraction. Ashleigh wasn't messing with me at least.

Preceding me into the coffee shop, she treated me to yet another view of her delectable ass and long tanned legs. Her pretty heart-shaped calves told me she spent some time away from her garden working out. Watching the play of her muscles reminded me of my favorite fantasy of us together, the one where her delicate ankles rested on my shoulders, my hands palming those perfect calves as I drove into her so deep, hitting her G-spot over and over as she cried my name.

Down, boy, I reminded myself as I inhaled a deep coffee-scented breath and forced my mind to the task at hand—making Ashleigh look good in front of her boss.

The utilitarian décor created a subdued and focused vibe in the coffee shop. My idea of a coffee shop was a place to relax, have a casual conversation, maybe write a song on the community guitar the owner kept on a stand beside a comfy couch. This place was all square tables and hard wooden chairs resting on a polished cement floor. Framed photos of flowers couldn't soften the futuristic atmosphere accentuated by the exposed ducting on the ceiling and the corrugated metal walls.

Ashleigh scanned the room for a second before focusing on a table directly opposite the front door. Absorbed in her phone, a tall coffee in a go cup in front of her on the table, sat a bottle blonde. From beneath the brim of my ball cap, I checked out the other customers in the shop as we wove our way around tables to where the blonde sat. The shop's clientele this morning tended to business types busily working over their laptops and a couple of young moms whose toddlers played on the floor beneath their table as they visited. For a while, at least, I could be reasonably sure of not being recognized here.

When we reached her boss's table, Ashleigh stopped and waited for the woman to look up and acknowledge her.

"Oh, hello, Ashleigh. Punctual as always. I like a person who understands a deadline," the woman drawled. Then she caught sight of me and stood up. "Oh my gosh. You're really here. I'm really meeting Blu Connolly." Her imperious boss demeanor did a one-eighty to starstruck fan in three seconds flat.

Impressive.

"Camille Watson, Blu Connolly," Ashleigh said, introducing us.

The woman extended her hand, giving me one of those limp-wristed handshakes some women use to let a man know she could use his strength. I'd rather take confidence any day. *Bet Ashleigh gives everyone she meets a firm handshake.* Not that I'd know—when we met, she gave me a dressing down, something I probably deserved. Still, I'd take Ashleigh's initial response to me over this woman's any day. The thought made me smile, something Camille apparently misunderstood as she beamed up at me.

Ash took the seat next to Camille, leaving the seat across from her open. I didn't miss the nasty glare her boss gave her when she made that seating choice. Then Camille seemed to recover herself as she made a little show of sitting back down.

"So, you crashed a bluegrass gig. How was it you came to be there, and how is it you know Ashleigh?" She set her phone on the table between us and started recording.

With mind-blowing speed, the fan took a backseat to the journalist.

"Miss Baker and I met at a bar. I noticed her car sounded a bit unreliable, so I offered her a ride to the show. Someone in the audience recognized me and told the band, and they invited me to join them onstage. That's about it."

Ashleigh's eyes widened at my modified version of events, but otherwise, she gave nothing away. Camille's expression, however, implied she didn't quite believe my version of the story.

Before Camille could ask another question, a waitress sauntered over to our table for our drink order.

Ashleigh ordered first. "I'll have a tall Americano with half-and-half."

"Make that two," I added.

The woman appeared to be in her forties, but she gave me a quizzical look, like she might recognize me, so I dipped my head and glanced across the table at Ashleigh. The barista barely walked away to take care of our order before Camille picked up where she left off.

"That was quite convenient. Are you sure Ashleigh didn't track you down and invite you along for that review?"

"What are you implying, Miss Watson?"

Turning to Ashleigh, she said, "You were awfully eager to attend the Balefire concert at Red Rocks last summer. You even reviewed the show for another media outlet. Is this the way you get back at us for not giving you the VIP passes our blog received?"

"N-no," Ashleigh stammered.

"It's not Ashleigh's fault the band you sent her to review needs a lead singer. Her review was spot-on."

The incredulous look on Ashleigh's face was almost comical. "You read my review?"

"Of course." Because I didn't want her boss to get the wrong—or rather the right idea about us, I added, "I wanted to see what you had to say about a rock singer knowing some bluegrass."

The smirk I gave her was pure smart-ass, but before she could react, Camille was at it again.

"Seriously, how do you two know each other?"

"Like Blu said, we met in a bar over a game of pool. Purely an accident. I'm sorry if my review set off fireworks in the bluegrass section of the blog, but the lead singer does need to rethink his talent."

"I noticed the two of you arrived together, which implies a closer relationship between you two than you're trying to let on."

"I'm not sure where you're going with this, but I thought we were here because you wanted a Balefire exclusive." I tried to keep my tone light, but the woman and her insinuations were starting to wear on my nerves.

Camille seemed to compose herself. "Right. How long is the band going to be on hiatus, and when can the fans expect the next album?"

I remembered her phone on the table, the red light loudly proclaiming the interview was being recorded. I'd have to tread lightly so as not to piss off the other guys in the band.

"We've been touring almost nonstop since Jack joined the band two years ago. Right now, we're taking it easy, playing it by ear. We wrote a lot of music on our last tour, so we have enough material for a couple of albums. We'll probably go back into the studio sometime late in the summer."

"That means the rumors of a breakup aren't true?"

"You make it sound like the four of us are dating or something," I countered with a smirk. The rumors started dogging us when our former drummer, Dave Brubaker, left the band and they hadn't stopped since. After a while, answering the same tired questions wore on me.

However, my smart-ass comment created the opening for the one question Camille wanted to ask. "Are any of you dating? You, specifically. Are you seeing anyone?"

I might have given in to being a jackass about answering since she chose that moment to run her naked foot up the inside of my calf. No subtlety whatsoever with this one.

Turning sideways in my chair, I brought my leg up to rest my ankle on my knee, denying her the prize she sought and making it clear I had no interest in her. Ashleigh questioned my move with her eyes but said nothing.

"Not officially." I didn't want to lie, and I didn't want to give away my intentions with Ashleigh before I'd had a chance to act on them.

Ashleigh nearly choked on the sip of coffee she'd just taken as I answered.

"Miss Baker's response indicates otherwise."

Ignoring Camille, I asked, "You okay, Ashleigh? Coffee go down the wrong way?"

"Yeah. Sorry."

"Right. What do you know that Blu doesn't want to reveal to the media, Ashleigh? As a journalist, you have an obligation to share the news with your readers." No one within earshot could mistake the venom in the woman's voice, a voice that had grated on me in its high-pitched breathiness from the first words out of her mouth.

Preempting the ugliness I could see coming in this farce of an interview, I drawled, "We're musicians, Miss Watson. We play music people like to listen to. Women especially, judging from all the lingerie they throw at us. Enjoying the ladies is one of the perks of our job."

I smiled at her. "Next question?"

"Are any of the other band members involved with anyone special?"

"Did you not hear what I just said? Balefire likes the ladies."

"The band has a reputation for throwing wild after-parties following certain shows. Which shows will host those parties on the next tour?"

"Without knowing quite where we're going to tour next, I can't answer that question. Tell me, Miss Watson, are you angling for a date with a band member or an invite to one of our parties? It's tough to tell."

Ashleigh glared at me, but I ignored her. Her boss crossed the line into insufferable the minute she insisted on conducting an interview that had nothing to do with Balefire or our music and everything to do with meeting the band and scoring with one, or several, of us.

Camille fluttered a petulant look at me from beneath her lashes. "I would have thought I wouldn't have to hint," she said. "Inviting journalists backstage only increases the band's exposure to the fans who want to know everything about you."

"Yeah, well, I don't have control over that. If you want backstage invites, you'll have to contact our manager or the promoter. Did you have anything else you wanted to ask?"

The barista had barely delivered our coffees when Camille bared her teeth.

"You grew up nearby, didn't you? Your mom still works at a diner a few blocks away from this coffee shop. Why is that?"

"I hope you don't have to spend much face time with this barracuda, Ash." I pushed away from the table, not caring how the harsh grating sound of wood on cement disturbed the other customers in the place. "I'm outta here."

I grabbed my coffee and headed for the door. Behind me, I heard Ashleigh start to apologize for my behavior, so I stopped and spun around. "No, I'm not sorry for what I said." Pointing at Camille, I growled, "You're not interested in our music in the least. In fact, it's clear from your 'questions'"—I air-quoted the word—"that you only want two things: to get laid by someone in the band and to dish dirt about us in your blog. You're a piece of work, lady."

Pivoting on my heel, I didn't stop moving until I was on the street outside the coffee shop. Chucking my mostly full coffee into a nearby trashcan, I stomped toward Ashleigh's car.

"Blu! Wait up!" Ashleigh panted, out of breath when she caught up to me beside her car. "I'm sorry for what happened in there. I swear I had no idea what Camille's angle was. She made it clear that if I wanted to keep my job with the blog, I needed to get her an interview with you."

Her eyes mirrored the agony in her voice, and I let out a breath.

"Listen, there's a great coffee shop, not a warehouse masquerading as one, not too far from here. How 'bout I take you there, and I can give *you* a Balefire interview."

"Camille will never publish it on the blog."

"Sure she will. It'll just have her byline on it. Unless you shop it to another site," I added slyly. When that woman brought up my mom in a way that implied things she couldn't possibly know much less understand, I'd figured out Ashleigh's days reviewing for the Colorado Music Works blog were numbered even if she didn't know it yet.

"I don't know. I feel like I've taken advantage of our friendship enough as it is."

Friendship, huh? I'm making progress.

"Get in, Ash. We'll talk about it on the drive."

I'd spotted Camille making her way down the street toward Ashleigh's car, and the last thing I wanted was to continue any conversation with the woman. Thankfully, Ashleigh opened her door and slid into the passenger seat without arguing, denying Camille even the photo I noticed her trying to take with her phone. With my ball cap and dark glasses on, coupled with me entering Ashleigh's nondescript car, I was reasonably sure no one would ever believe Camille had taken a photo of me. When I pulled Ashleigh's car into the street, I didn't lay rubber, but I came damn close.

CHAPTER TEN

Ashleigh

TRUE TO HIS word, Blu gave me an exclusive interview, one where he told me about the band starting back up in the recording studio in a couple of weeks. They had forty or fifty songs to choose from for the ten or twelve tracks that would make up their next album. If things went the way they had in the past when the band returned to the studio, the guys would likely write five or six additional songs inspired by events during their hiatus or by the sound of something else they were working on. Knowing how much work it took me to find the exact right words to describe a band's sound and show, I was in awe of Balefire's prolific creativity.

In the end, I didn't even have the chance to lose my piece on Blu and Balefire to my boss. When I opened my email the next day, I discovered she'd given me my notice. Using the pretext that I'd misled her about my relationship with Blu Connolly, Camille determined that my review of Lightning Strikes was biased. She planned to include that particular insight in the retraction for my review she was posting on the blog. Vindictive bitch. It wasn't enough that she fired me from my steady part-time job, but she also planned to sabotage my career too? Shit. Now what would I do?

A sharp rap on the window of my back door alerted me that the man in question had arrived early to help me with my flowers today. Unfolding myself from my couch, I set my laptop on the coffee table and padded barefoot across my kitchen to the door.

"Hey Ash—"

"Now is not a good time." I tried to close the door, but Blu wasn't having it, sticking his foot in the way. Not wanting him to see my face, I turned my back and headed to the couch.

He danced around me, ducking his head, trying to catch my eyes. "What's wrong? You don't look happy to see me at all, which kinda hurts my feelings since I just had a load of that special dirt you like delivered to your backyard."

I slumped down on the sofa and pulled my computer onto my legs. Silently, I turned the screen toward him, and he sat beside me to read it.

"Son of a bitch! Jesus, Ashleigh."

The look of concern in those mesmerizing golden-green eyes nearly did me in.

"I'm so sorry. I only wanted to show off for you a little bit that day." He ran a hand through his hair and replaced his ball cap on his head, spinning the bill around to the back. "Getting you fired wasn't my intention at all."

His sincerity came through in his voice and the way he leaned toward me without crowding me. But I already knew he'd meant no harm with his antics at the bluegrass show.

"It's not your fault, Blu. I should have been more complimentary of the band's instrumental talents and left out the singing altogether. I could have made the point about the lead singer by not discussing the vocals except for how well he harmonized with a certain celebrity guest." Hindsight truly could be a jerk. I blew out a breath. "Then none of this—that awful interview with Camille, losing my job at the blog, her threat to end my career before I even really have a chance to start it—none of it would have happened." I tried to sound brave, but the thought of paying my bills on my now-diminished writing income left a wobble in my voice he couldn't help but notice.

Mentally dragging up my big girl panties, I slapped my laptop closed and stood. Not. His. Problem. As I headed for the back door, I called over my shoulder, "You ordered a load of mulch for me? Really?"

"Yeah." His boots creaked over the kitchen linoleum. "Ashleigh, about your job—"

"Like I said, I should have handled it a different way. Now I've learned something—something I can't put into practice today." I grabbed my gardening gloves from the table beside the door. "Let's go play in the dirt. My dad always says if we greet disappointment with productivity, we can solve any problem."

The look on Blu's face told me my charade didn't fool him in the least, but he had the good manners not to press me. Praise the Lord. If he kept looking at me with that mix of sympathy and guilt, I'd probably give in to impulse and a healthy dose of lust disguised as fear for my future and climb into his lap. Knowing what happened the last time I did that, I had no doubt he could quite easily make me forget the last two days. Which would only make my situation worse.

♪

We spent the rest of the day planting flowers in my yard. I still couldn't wrap my head around Blu's interest in helping me. The questions he asked as we worked together showed he had a genuine interest in my little hobby—and not for the first time, I found myself forgetting his day job and reputation. When it was only the two of us, Blu became a regular guy—an extremely attractive regular guy—and what was I doing with him?

As the shadows lengthened and my back and knees began their ritual protest against my heart's desire to create a showplace on a shoestring budget, my inner censor took a nap. Imagine my surprise when I heard myself inviting Blu to join me for dinner.

"Sounds great, Ash. I gotta admit, all this manual labor has had my stomach growling for the last hour."

Sitting back on my heels, I eyed him. "Why didn't you say something?"

A smile bloomed over his face. "'Cause I've been enjoying watching you having such a good time playing in the dirt."

That smile, so open and relaxed rather than his usual smirk, reassured me I hadn't bored him completely to death with my horticultural enthusiasm. It was another aberration for me to ponder—later.

"Well then, let's go see what I have in the fridge. No promises you'll get anything gourmet like you do at home."

"I'm not complaining about your cooking, babe."

Something in the way he said the word jerked my attention to him, but he studiously kept his eyes on tidying up the area where we'd been working.

After we finished a meal of grilled burgers and salad, to my ever-lasting shock, I heard myself again inviting him to stay to watch a movie. Honestly, the consequences arising from my morning email must have turned off my brain completely.

"What do you want to watch?" I asked as I scrolled through the menu on Netflix.

"Whatever you want."

"Seriously? What if I want to watch politics or something? Maybe a show about gardening?"

"I'll learn something."

That was unexpected. But the accompanying smirk wasn't.

"How 'bout this?" I asked as I settled on an old Bruce Willis action movie, one of my favorites.

"I love this one. Good call." He settled comfortably in the middle of my couch, preempting my plans to stay away from him. As if he read my mind, he patted the cushion next to him. "Have a seat."

"I-I'll grab us some dessert while the movie queues up."

Tossing him the remote on my way past the couch, I nearly tripped over my feet as I hustled into the kitchen. When I opened the freezer door, I let the cold air waft over me, cooling off my embarrassment at the way my libido leaped at his one small gesture. After grabbing two ice cream sandwiches, I returned to the living room in a way I hoped looked more sophisticated and nonchalant than the clumsy way I'd raced out of it.

"I hope you like coffee-flavored ice cream sandwiches since that's the only kind I buy."

"Your guilty little pleasure?" he asked, his eyes sparkling as he reached for the treat I offered him.

"They're my favorite. No guilt whatsoever."

I sat on the couch in the only space I could, being careful not to touch him, which was a feat considering how little room he left on either side of him. His long lean muscular frame took up much more than his fair share of space, a feat I suspected he'd perfected.

After a while, I became engrossed in the movie. When the action slowed for a minute, I discovered myself tucked up against Blu's side, his arm across my shoulders, his fingers absently tracing a pattern over the bare skin of my upper arm. He smelled of outside and grilled burgers and manly sweat. His solid body fit perfectly to mine, his touch on my skin natural and right. With a sigh, I turned a deaf ear to the warning bells clanging in the back of my mind and enjoyed spending an evening with an incredibly sexy man who, against all my preconceived notions about him, was also incredibly decent. As that thought crossed my mind, I smiled a little to myself, doubting his rock 'n' roll persona would appreciate that assessment.

When the closing credits started rolling, Blu slid a calloused finger along my jaw, tipping my face up to his. "I can't remember a day I was more relaxed. Thanks, Ashleigh," he said, his baritone voice rumbling through me, mesmerizing me.

I didn't move. I'm not sure I even breathed as he lowered his head and brushed his lips over mine. I hadn't forgotten the way his mouth felt, the exquisite pleasure of his kisses from the last time we'd ended up on my couch. Like that time, I couldn't stop myself from savoring the sensation, lifting my chin higher in a silent request for more.

I didn't have to ask twice. My response flashed Blu's kiss into a conflagration of desire, and before I knew it, he'd tangled his hands in my hair as I wound my fingers into the front of his T-shirt. Our tongues danced together, our lips and teeth playing the rhythm. The whimpers I heard coming from the back of my throat harmonized with the groans coming from him. When he deepened the kiss, my whole body started singing his praises.

From some distant place, his phone chimed, the sound escalating until I panted, "You'd probably better get that," against his lips.

He groaned as he reached into his back pocket to retrieve his phone.

"Dakota. Gotta tell ya, buddy, your timing sucks."

He listened for a minute before, "Fuck you too."

I could hear Dakota laughing before he said something else. "Yeah, yeah. I'll put it on my calendar."

The timing of the call probably saved me from making an irrevocable decision, and I moved to stand. Blu exerted just enough pressure with his palm on the top of my shoulder to let me know what he thought of that plan, so I stayed put. But my acquiescence to his silent command wouldn't change anything.

"Listen, man, I'm kind of in the middle of something here. I'll call you in the morning."

He ended the call and tossed his phone onto the coffee table in front of my couch. "Now, where were we?" he asked with a smile.

"We were remembering the movie is over and so is our night."

I stood then, and he let me.

"Damn it. When you were kissing me a few minutes ago, I thought you'd finally admitted my interest in you is real."

"Yeah, I figured that out. I've also figured out that you're going back out on tour in the next month or so, which means I might not be a one-night stand, but I'll be the next closest thing. Like I told you before, I'm not good at casual sex or relationships on a deadline."

He stood and faced me. "Nothing that's happened between us so far has been casual, and you damn well know it."

"Please, Blu. Like you said, we had a nice day together. Let's not ruin it."

A smile ghosted over his features. "Did your dad ever teach you anything about battle tactics?"

"What?"

"'Cause I'm letting you win this little skirmish, but I'm also putting you on notice that I'm going to win the war."

"We're at war?" I asked, confused.

"Only until I win you. Kind of like in that Shakespeare play my English teacher made us read junior year. When the Greek guy went to war with the Amazon lady and not only won the battle but also won the lady." He stepped into my space. "Good night, Ashleigh. See you tomorrow."

He butterflied another kiss over my lips then brushed his body against me and headed out the door.

♪

After he left, I spent another restless night. Between trying to determine my next course of action since I no longer wrote for the blog and trying to keep images of Blu and his hot sexy kisses out of my head, I tossed and turned until dawn made its way beneath my curtains. Dragging myself out of bed at the butt crack of nine o'clock in the morning only darkened the cloud I woke up under. When my phone rang, it was tempting to ignore it, but one look at the caller ID had me fumbling to answer.

"Today? How soon would I have to be there? Well, I could make it by ten. Will that still work? Great! See you then."

I leaped out of bed and raced into the bathroom for a quick rinse in the shower. Yesterday, I would have turned down a substitute teaching job on such short notice, but with my financial situation taking a potential nosedive into the great red unknown, I thought better of turning down a chance to make enough money to eat for the next two weeks if I was careful.

The job opportunity took my mind completely off a certain hot lead singer for two minutes until I nearly ran him over as I barreled down the sidewalk to my garage. He grabbed me by the shoulders, his touch searing through the thin cotton of my summer dress.

"Hey gorgeous. Where are you off to in such a hurry? Aren't there still some flowers to plant?"

"They called me in to sub at the school this morning. Very short notice. I'll finish planting them tomorrow."

For several seconds, he held me as he processed what I said. I tried to slow down my heartbeat, which tripped into double time because I was in a hurry and not because he stood in front of me with his wonderful hands on me. Yeah, I was going with that.

"When will you be home?"

"Sometime after four." I glanced down at his hands where they still rested on my shoulders. "Not to be rude, but I have to go."

Before he released me, he leaned in and stole a kiss. "Have a good day, Ash. I'll be here when you come home." With a brilliant smile that started in his eyes, he stepped aside and let me by.

Him kissing me goodbye checked my speed, but I still fumbled with my key in the lock on the door to my garage. My laser focus retreated to scattered thoughts all colliding with an image of Blu. Damn the man. He insisted on starting something we both knew he had no intention of finishing. What was I supposed to do with that?

♪

Since it was summer school, the class periods were longer to accommodate students working on independent or small-group projects. Today, my students were doing something with physics, figuring out the math to build cardboard boats they were going to paddle and race in the pool at a nearby college. On the one hand, I would have liked to have substituted on the day of the race. On the other, I would have been highly overdressed had the race occurred today. At any rate, the teacher's preparation meant I didn't have much to do beyond keeping the students on task. Since the project engaged them so well, I didn't have to work at that either.

Which left me way too much time to think about Blu Connolly. Memories of his hands on my body, the erotic way he kissed me, the sounds he made as he pressed himself against me kept finding their way into my consciousness, causing me to lose focus on my class. The way he greeted me and sent me on my way this morning warned me he hadn't been kidding when he told me last night he was embarking on a campaign to win me. I had to guard my heart, but my traitorous body seemed to have the intention of joining forces against me, heating up at the mere thought of his lips on mine, at the image of the sizzling looks he gave me with his molten gold-green eyes.

On top of that, there was his voice. Truly, I had no defense against it, especially when he sang to me. Even the radio conspired against me, playing a Balefire song as I pulled my tiny car into my garage at the end of the day.

Sighing, I locked up the garage and walked around the corner of the house to my backyard, hauling up short as I heard the soft sounds of a guitar coming from the direction of my patio.

Chapter Eleven

Ashleigh

"**H**AVE YOU BEEN here all day?"

"Nah. Had some work to do for Mom. How did your day go?"

"Easiest day ever, I think," I said as I lowered myself into the empty chair on my patio, stretching my legs out in front of me. "The kids were working on a physics project, something they're super excited about, so I mainly hung out and watched them work."

"You like physics?"

"Their project looked fun, but it's good I didn't have to help them with it. Much to my father's despair, I never did like math. From what I saw, their project requires quite a bit of it," I said with a chuckle. "Considering how handy you are with mechanical things and carpentry and whatnot, you must have enjoyed physics in school."

"I liked all of school, math, physics, English. Music especially." Blu grinned at me. "But I learned how to fix stuff out of necessity. Without a dad around and Mom's job not paying all that much, I needed to learn how to do some things to keep us going. Dakota's dad helped me too."

"Yeah?" I couldn't help it. I was curious, and he seemed to want to talk.

"Before Dakota's mom walked out, I went to his place after school to wait for my mom to come home from work. Rich, Dakota's dad, would usually be in his garage working on an old car he was fixing up, and he'd let Dakota and me help." He strummed a note, fiddled with the tuning pegs, and strummed the strings again. "After Dakota's mom spooled up on them, his dad spent a lot of time at the bar, so the two of us tried to work on the car ourselves."

Blu stopped talking, and his face took on a faraway look. After a bit, I prompted, "How did you do?"

"Trial and error is a good teacher. When we fucked up the carburetor, Rich screamed at us for half an hour at least, but he started coming home a little earlier and helping us." He strummed a note. "About that time, we cooked up this plan to get our parents together so his dad would stop spending so much time at the bar and my mom would stop spending so much time crying."

My heart broke for two little boys and their parents who were left behind by the people who'd promised to stay forever, for two little boys who needed the parents they did have to pay attention to them, for two adults so lost in their own pain they couldn't see how much their children needed them. Taking the risk of stirring up bad memories with my curiosity about him, I asked, "How long had your parents been gone?"

The events in question happened years ago, I knew, but the feelings were obviously still raw. Blu's matter-of-fact tone sounded at odds with the way his hands tightened on his guitar. "By then my dad had been AWOL about four years, Dakota's mom for about a year."

"I'm sorry." Clearing my throat over the lump that suddenly

formed in the back of it, I asked the question I'd wanted to ask Diane for months. "Have you ever heard from them?"

"No." He replied with so much hostile finality I knew to stop pressing. On a dime, his demeanor flipped again. Smiling, he continued, "We schemed all sorts of ways to throw Mom and Rich together. Even skipped school so they'd have to come to the principal's office at the same time." He chuckled at the memory. "But it never worked out. Nine-year-olds don't know much about matchmaking, especially when the adults involved are so heartbroken." He sobered, his features hardening, and I knew he'd headed into a dark place in his memories.

"Is that why the two of you are best friends?" I asked, hoping to keep him out of that dark place.

It worked.

"Nah. We're best friends because we know too much about each other." He smirked. "That and the music. In the end, music is what kept us together. When we both took an interest in guitar, Mom convinced Rich to pay for Dakota's lessons. I have no idea how she afforded mine." He strummed another note and tuned again. "I figure she thought if we were playing music, we couldn't get into trouble." He chuckled. "Funny thing about boys, though. No matter how much parents try, we're always going to get into trouble."

His eyes sparkled with mischief, daring me to ask.

"Poor Mr. Smith."

"Grumpy old bastard had every prank coming and a few we didn't get around to."

"Yeah? What stopped you?"

"Girls. Parties. Starting a band. Although practicing till all hours in Mom's garage did the trick a time or two." He smirked. "Until Old Man Smith started calling the cops. That's when we moved all our gear to Tron's place."

My brow shot up in question.

"His dad had a big shop where we could play as loud as we wanted without bothering too many people."

"Ah." I nodded. "Are you working on something new?" I asked, indicating his guitar.

"Just messing around with some ideas I've had."

"May I hear?"

"Sure."

He warmed up with a series of wild arpeggios and some furiously strummed chords before he flexed his hands and fingers and settled into a soft melody. The music immediately pulled me in, and he'd already sung a few words before my focus shifted from the sound of his voice to the words he was singing.

". . .so beautiful. Reaching out to me
"You're scared, I know, and maybe you have reason to be
"My beauty.
"I can't promise you forever 'cause forever is a mystery,
"But I can give you now, and I can give you all of me
"If you'll take a chance
"My beauty."

Blu played a bridge before trailing the song away on a few harmonious chords. "It's something I started working on this afternoon. What do you think so far?"

The breath I'd been holding whooshed out of me. "You started working on that this afternoon? Wow."

"You like it?"

"It seems a little tame to be a Balefire song, but it's pretty."

He leaned his hands over the body of the guitar. "Hey, Jack's not the only member of the band who can write a love song."

I think he was trying to sound offended, but I didn't believe it, not with the way his eyes sparkled.

"Playboys writing love songs. No wonder the stage is covered in women's underwear during your concerts," I scoffed, waving my hand in a teasing gesture.

"Ashleigh." Blu's tone sounded a warning, which didn't make sense with the way he'd been messing with me.

Standing to stretch, I sighed. "Well, watching teenagers do physics all day wore me out. I need to shuck these clothes—and these shoes. I forgot what wearing them all day was like."

I headed into my house, only to discover Blu right behind me.

"Hey, what are you—?"

"Making sure you don't mess around, woman." He made a shooing motion with his free hand. "Change your clothes so I can take you out to dinner. I'm starving."

"W-We're going out to dinner?" I stammered. "Since when?"

"Since I've been waiting for you on your patio for at least an hour. Hurry up." He nodded toward my bedroom, his look severe except for that ever-present sparkle in his eyes that I was coming to know meant he was enjoying himself.

"Casual?"

"Whatever you want, Ash. Just move it."

Hustling off to my bedroom, I changed into a low-slung pair of skinny jeans and a halter, which I pulled together with a light jacket. After forcing my feet to endure four-inch wedges for eight hours, I gave them a break with a pair of strappy flat sandals and hoped we weren't taking the bike.

"Quick enough for you?" I asked when I reentered my kitchen.

"Impressive. You do the quick-change like a pro." He ran his eyes up and down my body, his slow perusal jacking up the temperature in the room by ten degrees. Or maybe that was my own body heat.

"The shoes aren't going to work on the bike, Ash," he said at last.

Blowing out a breath, I returned to my bedroom where I rummaged around in my closet until I found an old pair of short-heeled ankle boots I'd worn back in college. They didn't do much for my outfit, but I couldn't face any other pair I owned since they all sported sky-high heels.

"Better?" I demanded when I returned to the kitchen.

"Yeah."

He walked over to the door and held it open for me. When I turned back to lock it, I bumped squarely into the broad expanse of his chest with an "Oomph!"

"Easy there, Ace." He laughed as he wrapped his free hand around me.

"I need to lock the door." I spoke into his chest.

"Got it."

Neither of us made an effort to move. Maybe I was supposed to angle back so Blu could step away from my door, but he smelled so delectable, like soap and something citrusy and musky. Snuggled up tight against his hard body, it was like I belonged there.

That thought sent me backpedaling like a madwoman. *This is Blu Connolly, playboy lead singer for Balefire and way out of your league.* I struggled free of his embrace.

"Something I said?"

"N-no. I thought you wanted to eat. You said you were starving," I tossed over my shoulder as I led the way to the gate separating my yard from his mom's.

♪

Blu throttled the bike down in front of an out-of-the-way bar and grill, a place tucked into a niche between the edge of a strip mall and the repair shop for a car dealership. Its location, coupled with its low-key exterior, made me wonder how he even knew the place existed.

Finding no parking out front, he wove through the show lot of the car dealership to an alley behind it, which opened out into a parking area directly behind the eatery. After locking the helmets to the bike, he grabbed me by the hand and led me to the back door, which looked more like the main entrance to the place anyway. Inside, we found a lively mix of people from the mechanics next door, to businessmen with their suit jackets thrown carelessly over the backs of their chairs, to a crowd of bikers sipping beers at the bar, to a group of cowboys taking up air space with their ten-gallon hats. Of course, after my surprise at Vaughn Hamilton's occupation, I conceded that my assessment of the last group could be completely wrong.

The hostess looked to be sixteen, but maybe her perky enthusiasm for her job made her seem young. Either way, she slanted Blu a look like she recognized him before shrugging and leading us to a booth toward the back—or was it the front?—of the restaurant. She handed us menus, informed us Jared would be our server, and wished us a pleasant meal.

The menu tended to barbecue, not my all-time favorite, so I decided on the grilled chicken salad. When I gave my choice to Jared, Blu shot me a look and proceeded to order a full rack of ribs and a beer.

"You not in the mood for barbecue?" he asked when Jared moved off to put in our order.

"Not a big barbecue fan. But you clearly are, or you wouldn't even know about this place. How did you find it, anyway?"

"Dakota's dad used to work at the dealership next door. This bar and grill has been around forever because they make the best barbecue anywhere outside of Texas. You're missing out by having that pansy-ass salad." He challenged me with a grin.

"No worries. You ordered a full rack, so I bet I can steal a taste off your plate."

Sighing dramatically, he said, "Ash, we haven't been dating long enough for you to be stealing food off my plate already."

"We haven't been dating at all."

Arching a brow, he gave me a once-over that nearly lit my panties on fire. "Could have fooled me."

Ignoring how his hot look made me want to squirm in my seat, I asked, "What are you talking about?"

"Let's see. We played pool to determine who paid for dinner for our first date. We went to a bluegrass show for our second date.

We stayed in to watch movies for our next four dates. Now we're out to dinner again. And that's not including all the nights we've had dinner with my mom, which can't count as dates since we had a chaperone." He leaned his forearms on the table, daring me to argue.

"You consider us dating?" I sputtered, dumbfounded by the sincerity in his eyes.

"You didn't?"

"But—"

"Ashleigh, you're gorgeous, fun—"

"Convenient."

"Don't do that," he growled. "The fact you happen to live next door to my mom has fuck-all to do with my interest in you. I'd have made a run at you no matter where or how we met."

"But you have your pick of any woman you want," I said, hating how small my voice sounded.

He leaned across the table, capturing my hand in his. The stroke of his thumb over my skin sent shivers up my arm. "Yeah. And I want you."

Wow. Oh wow, wow, wow.

Mercifully, Jared interrupted our conversation by delivering our drinks. I hid behind my beer and took an exaggerated look around the room as I tried to process what Blu had said. He thought we were dating? He *wanted* to date me? How the hell had that happened? More importantly, *what was I going to do about it?*

"Ash, whatever's going on in that gorgeous head of yours, knock it off. I'm not playing games with you." He reached across the table and took my hand in both of his again, sending sparks of electricity up my arm to gather in my solar plexus, jump-starting my heart into overdrive. "I'm dating you, and you're dating me. People who are interested in each other do that, you know," he added with a wink.

"What makes you think I'm interested in you?" I sassed him before I nearly choked on my audacity.

His gentle smile did all kinds of wild things to my belly. "Oh,

I don't know. The way you patiently answer even my most stupid questions in your garden. The way you always give in when I suggest you cook me dinner. The way you choose a movie rather than kick me out whenever I make myself at home on your couch afterward." He gave my hand a tiny squeeze. "The way you melt a little every time I sing to you."

"All the girls melt every time you sing. Do you even pay attention at your concerts?" I countered, trying to put some distance between his words and the way they made my heart trip into hyperspeed.

Calling my bluff, Blu ran a calloused finger over the top of my hand, his leonine eyes heating up to sizzling as he stared into mine. "None of those women melt the same way you do Ash. You're right there with me through every single note and you know it."

The touch of his skin against mine, his words spoken in his velvety baritone, the heat in his eyes burning me all the way to my core sent a riot of emotion through me I couldn't disguise and couldn't control.

He smiled at me in triumph. "Dating you keeps getting more and more interesting. More and more fun."

Jared arrived with our meal, a welcome distraction from our current conversation.

"Thanks, man." Blu glanced down at his dinner with undisguised delight. "Could you come back with more napkins and another finger bowl, please? My *date*"—he stared hard at me— "thinks she might like to share a few of these."

"Sure thing. Anything else you need, Mr. Connolly?"

"That'll do it for now, thanks."

I gaped after Jared as he bustled off to take care of Blu's request. Snapping my jaw shut and turning back to Blu, I said, "You're a regular here. That's why they leave you alone. That's why you have this booth."

"You're quick, Ash. Must be the journalist in you or something," he teased as he started pulling apart the monstrous rack of ribs on the platter in front of him.

He gnawed some meat from the bone he held delicately between his fingers and swallowed a bite, closing his eyes in culinary ecstasy. Watching him eat such messy food should have turned me off. Instead I stared at his lips, his eyes, his fingers, fascinated at his obvious pleasure in his meal and his equally obvious lack of self-consciousness about it. He grinned at me as he conspicuously licked sauce from his fingers, and I had to look away to keep from squirming in my seat.

When the waiter returned with the extra napkins and the finger bowl of warm, lemon-scented water, Blu thanked him again and gestured at his plate. "Give these a try, Ash. I promise, they'll change your mind about barbecue."

I reached for the piece of meat Blu offered and took a dubious taste. Smokey sweet flavor burst over my tongue as I bit down on melt-in-your-mouth pork. Never before had I tasted anything quite so succulent. Without thinking, I stuck my fingers into my mouth to lick off the sauce and glanced up to catch him watching me with a hungry expression that had nothing to do with dinner.

Clearing his throat, he slanted me a cocky grin. "Good, huh? Bet you wish you'd ordered this instead of that lame salad."

Helping myself to more of his dinner, I primly replied, "The salad has meat in it. And I'll share. After all, it's not good for you to eat nothing but meat for dinner." I grinned back at him before taking a big bite of his barbecue.

The look of fascination on Blu's face as he watched me eat should have warned me.

"Ash, for such a proper lady, you're messy with barbecue."

"What?"

He answered by reaching across the table to slide his thumb against the side of my mouth, using the perfect amount of pressure to make me open my lips. He glided the rough pad of his thumb over my bottom lip before plunging his thumb into my mouth. Reflexively, I closed down on him and sucked off the tiny taste of sauce before releasing him. His eyes darkened and his nostrils flared as he slowly lifted his thumb to his own mouth to lick and suck off the nonexistent sauce left there. Now I watched him, my lady parts revving up quicker than his bike at the sight of him licking a taste of me from his skin. This time I couldn't help it. Suddenly, my jeans were a bit too constricting, and I had to adjust my seating a little.

For several seconds, we stared at each other. If someone had paid attention to us at that moment, they could have seen the electricity sparking between us, pulling us closer to each other. Jared fortunately wasn't paying attention when he broke the spell.

"Everything all right here? Food good?"

"Yeah," Blu said absently, not taking his eyes from me.

"Anything else I can get you? Some extra dressing for your salad?"

At the mention of my meal, I realized I hadn't even touched it yet.

"No, no. I'm fine. Thanks."

As the waiter walked away, I busied myself with my fork and knife, cutting the grilled chicken resting on the salad greens into bite-size pieces. The activity allowed me to look away from Blu and try to regain control of my responses to the man.

"You can't hide, Ashleigh," he said quietly.

Forking a bite of chicken into my mouth precluded me from having to respond.

It didn't stop him from talking though. "There's something happening between us. I know you feel it too, so don't even try to deny it."

Studiously, I kept my attention on my dinner. *I'm going to deny everything.*

CHAPTER TWELVE

Ashleigh

ONSIDERING HOW MUCH I'd come to know him over the past month, I should have anticipated Blu wouldn't let the little scene the waiter interrupted drop without comment. When we arrived back on our street, he parked in his mom's driveway, cut the engine on his bike, and slid his helmet over the handlebars as I tried to drag myself away from the magnetic heat of his body. On the ride home, I'm sure he intentionally made several sharp turns so I'd wrap my arms around him tighter. He sang to me throughout the ride, the intimacy of his voice through the speakers in my helmet causing my body to spark and heat even in places not directly contacting his.

At last, I unglued myself from him enough to swing my leg over the seat and stand beside his Harley. While I removed my helmet, he kicked the stand down and swung his leg over the gas tank, leaning against the seat to face me. The smoldering expression in his eyes had my stomach doing backflips before he reached out, grabbed me by the hips, and pulled me into the space between his legs.

"Hey!" I breathed.

"Hey yourself. You have a nice time tonight?"

"Yes. Thank you." My response came out even more breathy, much to my disgust.

Not knowing what else to do with them, I placed my hands lightly on his shoulders and willed my heart to slow down.

"Me too. Especially the part where you discovered you *do* like barbecue."

He smirked at me, and I replied with an eye roll.

Blu laughed out loud. "You're not going to give in easily, are you, Ash?"

"I have no idea what you're talking about," I said with feigned exasperation.

"Hmm. Maybe I should remind you."

The way he stared at my mouth mesmerized me, and I couldn't move as he leaned in and brushed his lips over mine. The feather light touch of his mouth tantalized me to lean in closer to him. I expected him to intensify the contact, but instead he butterflied kisses over my lips, my cheeks, my closed eyelids, and back to my lips before he pulled back.

"Thanks for going out with me tonight, Ash."

He still held my hips lightly as he pushed himself up to stand, the movement brushing his hard chest against my hyperaroused nipples. He held me against him for several seconds, and the look on his face told me he was having some sort of inner debate. Then he gently moved me to the side before he let me go.

"I'll see you to your door."

My confusion at his change of mood must have shown on my face because he smiled at me and gestured with his outstretched hand that I should precede him to my house. After I unlocked the front door, I turned back to him. "Thanks again for dinner."

He traced the calloused pad of his index finger over the contours of my cheek. "My pleasure, Ash. See you tomorrow."

He turned and walked back over to his mom's, the picture of

nonchalance with his hands in his pockets and a tune on his lips. From right inside my open door, I watched him in stunned disbelief as he strolled away after he'd revved me up and left me hanging. Especially after all that talk about us dating.

♪

After spending yet another restless night thinking about Blu Connolly, I finally fell asleep in the wee hours of the morning. Since I didn't have work, I'd turned off my alarm somewhere during the endless hours of tossing in bed. When the insistent banging started at my back door, I didn't want to deal with it.

"Come on, Ash. Open up. I know you're home. Wake up, Ashleigh!" Blu yelled from my patio as he continued to pound on my door.

Groggily, I rolled out of bed, shrugged on my bathrobe, slid my feet into my favorite fuzzy slippers, and dragged myself out to my kitchen to shut up the racket that was Blu Connolly.

"Seriously? The sun's barely up," I groused as I opened the door.

He gaped at me for several seconds before he audibly shut his mouth. I watched his Adam's apple in fascination as he swallowed several times before he spoke.

"Sun's been up for a while, babe. I thought we could finish planting that pallet of daisies and whatnot I picked up yesterday." The scrape of his deep voice over the playful words said planting flowers was not really on his mind.

"Um, sure."

He cleared his throat and continued. "I bought a few things for Mom's yard. After we finish at your place, maybe you could come over and help me decide where to put them, yeah?"

In a badass sort of way, he looked kinda cute with his hands buried in the back pockets of his jeans while he desperately tried to keep his eyes on my face. I discovered I liked the Blu who came to my house this morning and found me attractive with bed hair and fuzzy slippers.

I smiled. "I'd like that. But can it wait until after I have a shower and maybe some breakfast?"

Blu

I hoped like hell the reason Ashleigh had so much trouble rolling out of bed before nine in the morning had something to do with the way I'd left her hanging last night. Especially considering how I almost blue-balled myself in the process.

Trying not to think about her naked in the shower when she disappeared into the bathroom nearly did me in, though. After seeing her in daylight in that sexy baby doll robe, her tousled hair falling in disarray around her shoulders, her voice all sleep roughened, it was all I could do not to scoop her into my arms and carry her back to her bed where I'd wake her up properly. I'd already jacked off once in the shower today to images of Ashleigh from our date last night. But one look at the woman in the flesh left me rock hard again. *Damn.*

She'd said something about breakfast. Breakfast I could do, and maybe the thought and smell of food would quiet down my needy dick. While I scrambled eggs and cut up cantaloupe and strawberries I found in her fridge, my mind wandered through a gallery of pictures of Ashleigh. It took me a little while to realize that as badly as I wanted her, the pictures I kept focusing on were of her laughing or sharing her enthusiasm for her hobby or talking to me like a professional about music. As gorgeous and sexy as she looked standing in front me in that tiny robe, it was the conversational Ashleigh Baker who truly turned me on.

The thought stopped me cold. Watching the eggs turn golden in the pan, I had to admit that I had it bad for her. Dakota was going to laugh his ass off at this new turn of events, which was a thought that should have had me high-tailing it out of Ashleigh's kitchen. Instead, I set the table with her goofy collection of dishes and called out to her, "Breakfast is ready. Come and get it while it's hot."

"You cooked me breakfast?" She was busy twisting her damp hair up into a messy bun as she came around the corner into the kitchen.

When I looked up from transferring scrambled eggs into a bowl, she stole my breath—again. *Da-amn.* The woman made a plain T-shirt and cutoffs look like something off a New York runway. Even her bun had my fingers itching to comb it out, preferably over her pillow.

Clearing my throat, I replied, "You said you needed breakfast before we could finish planting all that stuff I picked up from the greenhouse. So I whipped up a gourmet feast of eggs and fruit. Allow me."

I pulled out her chair and made a big show of placing her napkin on her lap before I helped her slide her seat up to the table. With a flourish, I picked up my own napkin and seated myself across from her, her laughter singing in my ears.

"I take it you've dined in some pretty fancy restaurants, sir."

"The finest being Chez Diane. It's local, you know. With the best cuisine on the planet." I waggled my brows.

"Which begs the question of why you've been eating over here so much."

Her skeptical expression told me I wasn't done convincing her of the sincerity of my interest.

"Because I've gone all Zen with this gardening thing. Plus, I'm dating my gardening teacher, so it goes without saying that I'd spend as much time as possible with her."

"Blu—"

"How's it going with shopping the interview to other media outlets?"

Ashleigh sighed, but as I hoped, she didn't pursue her ridiculous denial of us having a relationship.

"It's not. I don't have the contacts or the reputation to have anyone believe the interview is real. The rejections have been steady and some of them even professional. Several editors, though, have reminded me they don't do business with people who live in fantasyland."

Shit. All I'd wanted to do that day was show off for her. How was I to know my stunt would cost her that job and jeopardize her career?

"I have contacts."

"What?"

After I swallowed a bite of scrambled eggs and wiped my mouth with my napkin, I repeated, "I have contacts. If you'll let me help you, I'm pretty sure you could see that interview in print."

"Blu, I don't want to use you." The way she dragged her fork through her eggs told me more than her words.

"It's not using me if I'm the one making the offer. Besides, I owe you one for getting you fired from your blog in the first place." It wasn't an argument.

"I don't know . . ."

Or maybe it was.

"Will you at least give me a chance?"

Stubborn girl. The look on her face told me she planned to turn me down flat, so I gave her my best puppy dog eyes and said, "Please?"

She blew out a breath. "I'll think about it."

♪

We spent the morning planting flowers first in Ashleigh's yard then in Mom's. Honestly, I couldn't see where Ashleigh had another square inch of space for another flower in her yard, but somehow, she found room. The place could be a showpiece for *Better Homes and Gardens* or some shit. I hoped Old Man Smith's daughter appreciated what Ashleigh had done with the yard. Maybe give her another break on her rent.

Finished with her morning shift at the diner, Mom showed up right as we finished edging her patio with daisies.

"Oh my! You two have been busy. These beds look marvelous, like I have a professional gardener or something," Mom gushed.

"Nah, just a hobbyist and her minion," Ashleigh said with a sly grin in my direction.

"Minion," I scoffed. "I thought we established at breakfast this morning that I'm your *student*."

"So when you swore at the second pallet of daisies, that was you being all *studious*, right?"

She gave me no choice but to wipe that cocky grin right off her face. Since I held the still-running hose in my hand, I covered the stream with my thumb, creating the perfect power wash. She squealed and tried to run, but made the mistake of running toward the fence where I trapped her with the water, the spray soaking her T-shirt, making it cling deliciously to her delectable curves. Once I got a look at her puckered nipples poking through the layers of her bra and T-shirt, I forgot all about teasing her with cold water. I also forgot all about my mom standing on the patio.

Dropping the hose, I walked over to where Ashleigh stood, watching me now with wary eyes.

"What are you doing, Blu?"

I didn't say a word until I stepped into her space. "Minion, huh? Do your minions do this?"

Crushing her beautiful body against the hard planes of my own, I lowered my head and kissed the shit out of her. At least that was my intention. But when she wrapped her arms around my waist and melted her soft curves over me, I forgot everything except how incredible she felt in my arms. Her sweet body molded perfectly to mine like she'd been created for me alone.

Sliding one hand up to cradle the back of her head, I held her where I wanted her as I glided my tongue between her plump lips, insisting on a dance with hers. Ashleigh's response slayed me. She tightened her arms around me while she deepened the kiss until I didn't know where I ended and she began. As I pulled back from her mouth enough to grab a breath before plunging back in, I heard a cough from somewhere to my right.

"Do I need to use the hose on you two?"

Resting my forehead against Ashleigh's, I tried to drag my breathing under control. "Don't think so, Mom."

Ashleigh pushed away from me, touching the back of her hand to her mouth and mumbling, "Sorry, Diane."

Experience taught me how fast she could pull away from me, so I preempted her. "Geez, Ashleigh. Look what you did to the front of my clothes. How could you go and soak me like that after all I did for you this morning?" I teased.

"I soaked *you?*" she sputtered.

"Now, now, kids," Mom began.

"That's probably enough for one day anyway." Ashleigh let out a sigh. "I need to go change into something dry."

She slipped through the gate between the yards and disappeared into her house while Mom and I watched.

"You really like her, don't you, son?"

"Yeah."

"I knew it!" Her glee carried across the yard. "I knew the moment I met her the two of you would hit it off."

"Don't get carried away." I walked over to the house to shut off the hose and coil it up.

Without my knowledge or permission, Ashleigh had sneaked under my skin. By the time I realized it, she'd embedded herself so deeply, I didn't think I'd ever stop feeling her, thinking about her, needing her.

Oh hell. I'd jumped off the deep end without a life jacket. Worse, I caught myself smiling. I didn't care. I knew Ashleigh didn't believe me about my very real feelings for her, but her response to that kiss made me think I was making progress.

Chapter Thirteen

Blu

ONE NIGHT THE following week, I was absently tracing patterns on Ashleigh's shoulder as we watched another action movie on her TV. Touching her like that soothed me, grounded me somehow, and I found myself feathering my fingers over her skin whenever I had her close to me. She liked it too and showed me as much by pushing back into my hand if I stilled my movement for some reason.

Tonight, she'd started tracing her own patterns across my stomach where her hand rested. The sensation aroused me of course, and I discovered I'd missed an important bit of the action on the screen when an explosion blasted out of context.

Taking her hand, I pulled it up to my neck. When she looked up at me in question, I leaned down and kissed her. And I didn't start slow. Our make-out sessions on her couch had been increasing in intensity over the last several nights, and I knew I was wearing down her resolve to keep me out of her bed. Not that I hadn't been enjoying taking it slow. Building a relationship with her had felt right. But my cock not seeing any pussy action since the last night of Balefire's

Asian tour, combined with how much I'd wanted Ashleigh since the first night I saw her, meant far too many cold showers when I wasn't stuck jacking off to yet another fantasy about her.

As her sexy tongue tangled with mine, I smoothed my hand down her body until I found her ass. Cupping her, I urged her to climb onto my lap. She rolled into me a little without breaking the kiss and pulled her knee over my thighs, sliding it down on the other side of my hip to straddle me. The hot kiss I started didn't stop as she settled herself on top of me.

She felt so good I couldn't keep my hands still. Skimming them up the sides of her body, I palmed the outsides of her full tits while my thumbs gave her puckered nipples all kinds of attention. The whimpering sound she made in the back of her throat drove me wild, and I deepened the kiss. She responded by grinding her center into the front of my jeans. Even through the layers of our clothes, her heat drove me wild. Before I could stop myself, I surged up against her, answering the siren call of her pussy. With a groan, I remembered my promise to myself to let her lead and only go as far as she wanted to go.

I put on the brakes.

Dropping my hands to her waist, I attempted to push her away from me a little, but she tightened her arms around my neck and her knees along my thighs. Tearing my mouth from hers, I panted, "Baby, we have to slow down. There's only so much of all your sweetness I can take before I turn into some greedy bastard who tries for more, and I'm working hard here not to do that. Cut me some slack, would ya?"

I smiled at her to soften my words.

A look of confusion flashed across her beautiful face before she smiled back at me, a smile that revved my motor right back up to Mach 7 in a heartbeat. Never taking her gorgeous sapphire eyes off mine, she reached between us and undid the top button of the tight cutoffs she'd been wearing me out with all damn day. Then she crossed her hands over her taut belly, slid them inside her shorts, and pulled them out along with the hem of her camisole. She didn't stop until her top came up over her head, and she dropped it into a pool of silk on the cushion beside us.

I stared at her lacy white bra and thought about how much I wanted to take advantage of the friction I could cause with my tongue and that lace on the hard peaks of her breasts. Ashleigh apparently had other plans as she reached behind her and unclasped her bra with one hand while she used the other to tug it off her gorgeous tits, the bra joining her abandoned top on the couch.

I couldn't take my eyes off the absolute fucking perfection that was Ashleigh's body. Her heavy round breasts peaked with dusky pink nipples were so ripe and inviting, like having my own private feast of sweet strawberries and cream. With a smile, I palmed and played with the bounty she offered before I lowered my head and took one puckered nipple into my mouth. She sighed and arched into my touch, silently giving me permission to do what I was already busy doing.

Sucking her deep into my mouth, I flicked my tongue over her tight skin before pulling at her with my teeth. She gasped, and I laved the tiny sting with the flat of my tongue. My ministrations to her beautiful breasts had her grinding her pussy on me again, but this time, I didn't back off. Instead, I surged against her, my cock straining the confines of my jeans as I dry humped her, my hands and my mouth busy with her luscious naked breasts, my ears drinking in the sounds of her moans and whimpers and sighs. Whether or not she knew it, her fuck-me song drove me nearly as wild as her body.

Thoroughly involved with pleasuring her breasts, I didn't at first catch on that her breathing had changed to panting, almost like she was close to orgasm. That is until she put her hands on my face and lifted my mouth away from all that sugar that was her body.

"Blu," she whispered, "let's turn off the TV and go to bed."

The way she said it sounded like we were in the middle of

something we did all the time. Like starting things on the couch before heading for the bedroom was normal foreplay for us. The thought of finally getting naked with Ashleigh Baker nearly had me coming in my jeans on the spot.

Instead, I smiled at her. "Whatever you want, Ashleigh baby."

It seemed to me she slipped reluctantly off my lap, like she didn't want to break contact. I understood the feeling, so she only managed one step before I scooped her high in my arms and carried her the short distance to her bedroom.

After gently laying her on the bed, I reached over and flipped on her bedside lamp. I wanted to watch her as I took her for the first time. Skimming my hands up her long, smooth legs, I concentrated on the feel of soft skin covering resilient muscle, my fingers memorizing the beautiful contours until I reached her shorts.

As I grabbed the waistband, I stopped. "Are you sure about this Ashleigh?" If she suddenly decided to stop the train, I'd respect that. But I sure as hell hoped we were going to finish the ride.

She answered my question by covering my hands with her own and pushing her clothes down off her hips.

"Thank God," I mumbled, smiling at her before I finished undressing her. For a second, I felt a little cheated at not being able to check out her panties, especially after seeing the sexy bra she had on beneath her camisole, but the sight of her naked pussy more than made up for it.

I had to take a minute to stare at her. Never in my life had I seen a more stunning woman, and tonight, I was going to make her all mine.

"I'm glad you're enjoying the view, cowboy, but maybe it would be better if you were naked too?" she asked with a teasing grin.

Laughing, I made short work of stripping off my T-shirt, jeans, and boxers, leaving the whole works in a heap on the floor beside her bed. When my hard cock sprang up from my boxers as I dropped them, I have to admit I liked the way Ashleigh's beautiful blues popped at the sight of me before they turned to smoke. Good to know looking at me turned her on as much as looking at her turned me on.

Reaching into the pocket of my jeans, I extracted the condoms I'd been packing around for when she finally decided I wasn't going anywhere and put a couple on the nightstand, reserving one. Catching and holding her eyes, I tore open the packet with my teeth and smoothed the latex over myself.

"Bend your knees, Ash," I commanded.

When she did as I told her, I knelt on the bed and pushed her legs wider apart, making room for me. "Fuck, baby. You are so beautiful," I said as I stared at her pretty pussy. In the lamplight, I could see she was already wet for me.

She lifted her hips, inviting me to join myself to her, but I needed something more. Staring into her eyes, I licked my finger before rubbing it over the tight nub of her clit. She rewarded me with a gasp and an upward surge of her body, seeking more of my touch.

"You want this."

"Please, Blu."

"And you'll beg for it." I grinned. "This keeps getting better and better."

Smiling at her, I leaned forward enough to push the head of my cock an inch inside her slick lips. She tried to lift herself to pull more of me in, but I wanted to tease her a little, hear her beg me for more, so I pulled back, only enough to play with her.

She fisted the covers on either side of her hips and demanded, "I want you inside me. Now."

Oh yeah. The best six words in the English language.

"That's what you want, Ashleigh? Right now?" I grinned and barely kissed her pussy again with the head of my cock.

"Yes!"

And there it was, my all-time favorite word.

Smoothing my palms from her ass to her knees, I lifted her legs.

She took the hint and rested her delicate ankles on my shoulders, my fantasy come to life. Wrapping my arms around her thighs, I held on to her as I plunged my cock into her slick, wet heat, nearly losing my breath at how tight she was, how perfect she felt.

Her inner muscles pulsed around me. Gritting my teeth, I grasped the base of my cock to slow down my response to the absolute heaven of being inside Ashleigh Baker. This being our first time together, I wanted to make it special, make it last, but the sensation of being inside her was too incredible. I couldn't remember a woman ever feeling as amazing as Ashleigh did.

Positioning my hands on either side of her shoulders, my own shoulders rubbing against the backs of her thighs, I changed the angle and pumped into her. She was right there with me, her nails scoring the tops of my thighs, her head rolling back and forth on the pillow, her breathy moans driving me wild. Her eyes flew to mine as she arched her back, and a scream tore from her throat as she came hard, her pussy a velvet vise locking down on my cock. The gathering sensations of my own orgasm concentrated at the base of my spine, and I thrust hard into her a couple more times before I let go with her name on a shout and joined her in blissful oblivion.

At last, I let her feet drop from my shoulders to rest on the mattress on either side of my thighs. My eyes followed the pad of my finger as I traced a path from the hollow at the base of her throat, along her collarbone, and down the swell of her breast, pausing to pucker her nipple a little more before continuing down her taut stomach to the sensitive spot where her thigh met her torso.

"So fucking beautiful," I whispered as I looked up into her eyes.

She smiled a sad half smile, her eyes clouded in an emotion I couldn't understand before she blinked and gave me a smirk. "That's what you get for teasing me, rock star."

Click.

She thought I was leaving her. After she'd given me what I

wanted, she thought now I'd move on. Except there would be no moving on after she'd given me the best sex I'd ever had.

"Remind me to keep teasing you," I said before I leaned down and smashed my mouth on hers, demanding she open for me and give me everything.

I fucked her mouth with my own, leaving her no doubt that was exactly what I was doing Before I let either of us up for air, she was clawing my back, and I was hard again inside her.

Eventually, I tore my mouth away from hers, and panting, I said, "Got something to take care of. Don't go anywhere."

I pulled out of her and crossed the hall into the bathroom to dispose of the condom. When I returned to the bedroom, I grabbed a second off the nightstand and sheathed myself before returning to the bed. This time I wanted to take her from behind, go even further with her, plunge myself even deeper into her, claim her completely, but I sensed she wouldn't understand that to be my intention just yet.

Instead, I pushed her pretty knees apart and stared long and hard at her glistening pussy, letting her know exactly what I was about to do to her. Then I buried my face in all that glorious flesh, licking and kissing and sucking and biting, thoroughly eating every delicious part of her. She writhed and bucked against me, so I grabbed her hips and held her still while I kept at her, relishing the salty-sweet taste of her. She tasted like sex, my favorite flavor, and I didn't quit eating her until she arched her back into a bow, lifting her hips and giving me even more of herself as she came all over my face.

Not giving her a chance to recover, I crawled up her body, positioning myself to plunge into her pussy.

"Blu, I—"

"We're not done yet, Ashleigh. I'm not sure we'll ever be done."

I shut her up with a kiss, letting her taste herself on my lips and tongue as I thrust deep inside her. Her moans combined with my own as I started a rhythm she met. Wrapping her arms and legs around me, she moved with me, her inner muscles pulsing in time with the rhythm I set. Never in my life had I been so in sync with a woman, and I couldn't get enough.

Rocking and rocking and rocking into her, my body crescendoed, readying for the huge encore. When Ashleigh screamed her orgasm, an explosion of sensation, light, and color went off inside my head.

Best. Fucking. Sex. Ever.

When I finally came back to myself, I discovered I was lying full length on her, pinning her beneath my weight. Groaning in sated exhaustion, I rolled off her. I didn't have the energy to climb out of bed and put away the condom this time, so I knotted it and wrapped it in a tissue from the box on the nightstand and dropped it somewhere on the floor.

"That was off the charts, Ash," I mumbled into the pillow as I rolled back over, throwing my arm across her waist. I'd meant to cuddle her close, hold her all night, but she, with her exquisite, responsive body, had demanded I give her everything I had. In the end, I passed out before I could do the afterplay thing I intuitively knew she needed and that I'd wanted to give her.

The next thing I knew, the warm sun shone full morning across the bed, and Ashleigh's side of it was stone cold.

CHAPTER FOURTEEN

Blu

WEARING NOTHING BUT my boxers, I stood in the eerie silence of an empty house. Before I called out her name, I knew she wasn't there. I called anyway.

"Ashleigh! You home? Hey baby, where are you?"

That, of course, was the hundred-thousand-dollar question.

Padding barefoot out to the kitchen, I found a note she left on the table:

Thanks for last night. I forgot I had some errands to run today. Make yourself some breakfast.

-Ashleigh

Bullshit. When we were couched up watching the movie, she said she didn't have any plans for today. I thought I'd take her to the botanical gardens, let her educate me some more about flowers and shit, have a picnic lunch. In other words, we'd go on another date.

Errands my ass.

I jerked on my jeans, threw my T-shirt over my shoulder, and stomped out of her house, slamming the door behind me. When I stalked through Mom's back door, I found her at the stove flipping a pancake in a skillet.

"Blu!" She covered her heart with her hand. "What are you doing here? I thought you'd be sharing breakfast with Ashleigh this morning."

"That's what I thought too. Seems I thought wrong." Sniffing the heavenly smells of pancakes over her shoulder, I asked hopefully, "You make enough batter for two of those?"

"Yes, and don't change the subject."

Smelling Mom's food put the brakes on my anger and hurt for a minute. So did the idea of talking about my current dilemma with my girlfriend not believing herself to be my girlfriend. "Let me grab a quick shower, and we can talk over breakfast."

♪

"I think this is good for you, Blu." Mom propped her elbows on the table and blew over her second steaming cup of coffee. "It's been a long time since you've wanted something bad enough to work hard for it."

Standing from the table, I walked my dishes over to the sink. "What do you mean? I work my ass off for my music, for the band, for our shows." Still, I knew full well what she meant.

"Blu, I'm your mother. I see right through you, so stop trying to pretend with me."

"All right, all-seeing one. What's your suggestion for helping me convince Ashleigh this is for real? That I'm for real?" I asked as I gathered up Mom's dishes from the table.

"Be there for her. When she comes home today or tonight or tomorrow morning or whenever, be waiting for her. Tell her what you've told me. Show her you're not going anywhere." She gave me a mom look over her coffee cup. "And be patient with her. She walked away first because she has her pride, and she doesn't want you to know you have the power to hurt her."

"Yeah, well, her lack of faith stings a bit too."

"I know, son. I'm sorry." She patted my hand when I topped off her coffee. "But think about it from Ashleigh's point of view. You're a celebrity rock star. Women throw themselves at you all the time. Why, I can't imagine." She rolled her eyes playfully at me. "If they knew how you always leave your dirty socks lying on the floor, they might have a different opinion," she said with a smirk.

I shot her a look from beneath my brows and finished cleaning up the kitchen before grabbing another cup of coffee and rejoining her at the table.

"So, what? I hang out at Ashleigh's all day till she decides to come home?"

"Yeah, baby. Sometimes you have to be patient and wait for people to come back home to you."

The wistful look on her face nearly killed me. Reaching across the table, I covered her hand with mine. "Uh, Mom? You know he's never coming back, right? It's been twenty-three *years*."

She sighed. "It's not the same for you and Ashleigh. You're starting a relationship as adults, not kids. Neither of you needs time to grow up. Which doesn't mean that one or the other of you can't run scared," she added. "If you're there waiting for her when she comes home, she'll know you're not going anywhere. When she sees you there, she'll know you mean it when you tell her how much you care about her."

I blew out a breath. "Yeah, all right. I'll wait for her."

♪

Ashleigh finally returned home a little after dark. I hadn't bothered to turn on any lights since I didn't want to alarm her and make her think someone was waiting in her house. Besides, I could read my phone just fine. My phone on which Ashleigh hadn't returned a single damned one of my texts all day.

"Blu! You scared the hell out of me! What are you doing here?" she screeched when she stepped through her back door and flipped on the lights in the kitchen.

"Lots of errands, huh? I could have helped you with 'em, you know." I tried to keep my tone even, I truly did, but it was hard considering how worried she'd made me all day long.

"Look, I know I'm just another notch on the bedpost for you—"

In one quick movement, I stood and faced her. "There was never going to be a one-night stand with us, Ash. The next time we spend the night together, like tonight, you damn well better still be in bed with me when I wake up in the morning."

I stalked toward her, and though her gorgeous blue eyes rounded into saucers, she stood her ground. I stopped a hairbreadth away from her and continued. "We have been *dating* for a month. Exclusively. Not because you're convenient. Not because my mom likes you. Not because I only wanted to get into your panties." I let that sink in for a second. "We've been dating because we like each other, because we have a good time with each other." Taking a step, I crowded her against the counter behind her. "We both knew we were headed to the bedroom eventually. But the mind-blowing sex isn't the reason for our relationship."

Ashleigh blinked up at me. "Exclusively? Are you saying you haven't had sex since you returned to Denver?"

"Not until last night."

Her questions annoyed me and I turned away. Running a hand over my head, I turned back around.

"I admit this is new territory for me, Ash. Dating, spending time with one woman, sleeping with only one woman. But with you, it feels right. So I want to give it a try, see where it leads."

She blinked up at me. "Y-you do?"

"Yeah, baby. I do. And don't go getting your panties in a wad because I called you 'baby,'" I said when she started to bristle at the endearment. "I know exactly who you are and who I'm with. You're my girl, Ash." Because I couldn't help it, I finally touched her, gently tucking a lock of chocolate-colored hair behind her ear and lingering my fingers on the silk of her skin. "You're going to have to get used to being called all sorts of pet names. Have you ever *listened* to my mom? It comes with the territory, *darlin',*" I tacked on for emphasis.

Taking her beautiful face between my hands, I stroked my thumbs over her cheeks and stared deeply into those sapphire eyes I'd been drowning in from the first time I ever looked into them. "I'm nuts about you, Ash. And I have a pretty good idea you feel the same way about me. 'Cause if you didn't, you wouldn't have given me the best sex of my life last night—twice—then walked away this morning to give me space 'cause you think that's what I want."

"You waited here all day for me?" she whispered.

"All the damn day," I emphasized. "When I woke up to an empty house, I was thoroughly pissed. So I picked up my guitar and spent the day on your patio writing songs"—I jacked a brow—"and texting you."

She dropped her eyes, and in the glare of the overhead light in her kitchen, I could see the blush spread over her cheeks.

"When suppertime rolled around, I came inside and cooked myself some dinner and spent the rest of the evening on the couch with my phone. So yeah, I spent the day here waiting for you. What were *you* doing?"

She blew out a breath and seemed to relax a fraction. "Driving mostly. Hanging out at a bookstore with a coffee shop inside. Trying not to give in to my feelings."

"Give in, Ashleigh," I dared before I lowered my lips to hers.

She hesitated a second before meeting me halfway. Then she wrecked me—again—with her incredible response to me. Wrapping her arms around my waist, she dragged me as close as she could hold me and parting her lips, invited my tongue to party with hers. The whimpers and moans coming from the back of her throat sang a beautiful descant to the deep sounds resonating from the back of my own throat. We kissed each other to the brink of consciousness before I pulled away from her exquisite mouth at last.

"I'm going to spend the rest of the night proving to you that you're my girl, Ash. I hope you're up for that."

Not giving her a chance to respond, I bent and picked her up at the waist. She shrieked in my ear when I tossed her over my shoulder and carried her to the bedroom where I dropped her across the bed.

"I meant what I said earlier, babe. We're going to make love until we completely exhaust each other. And when I wake up in the morning, you're still going to be in this bed with me. Are we clear?"

"Anyone ever tell you you're kind of a caveman?" she sassed.

"Oh, darlin', you have no idea how much of a caveman," I said with no apology whatsoever.

Ashleigh squealed when I crawled over the bed onto her, but the dare in her eyes and the way she rolled her body into mine told me she was with me all the way. I made short work of removing the pretty sundress she wore before sitting back on the bed to enjoy the picture of my woman in lacy panties with a matching light pink bra. With a smile, I appreciated her good taste in underwear. Leaning forward, I ran the tip of my tongue over the tight bud of her nipple pushing at the lace of her bra and reveled in the way she writhed beneath my touch. Her breathy moans told me I wasn't the only one who couldn't stop thinking about the two of us together.

Kissing my way over the exposed mounds of skin above her bra, I paid equal attention to her other nipple before I trailed my lips down the center of her belly. She arched and gasped as I stopped to swirl my tongue in her belly button on my way to the prize hiding behind the fabric of her panties.

Not bothering to remove them, I pulled her underwear aside and went to work kissing her pretty pussy, paying special attention to the tight nub that swelled and hardened as I licked and sucked and nibbled at it.

"Blu!" she gasped, her fingers pulling at my hair. "Please."

Taking her plea to mean "please, more," I slipped one finger inside her as I continued to plunder her clit with my mouth. She rewarded me with a scream, her fingers pulling hard on my hair, and I added a second finger, curling inside her until she shouted herself hoarse.

I gave her half a minute to gather herself while I shucked my clothes and sheathed myself with a condom from the stack I'd left on her nightstand.

"On your hands and knees, Ash."

She blinked up at me. "What?"

"And if you like this pair of panties, I suggest you take them off."

I sat back on my knees, telegraphing my intent as I stroked myself, my eyes lasered in on the sapphires of hers.

A tiny smile played over her lips as she took her sweet-ass time following my demands. When she rolled up onto her hands and knees, my mouth went dry. The sight of the smooth skin of her bare ass, the long lush curve of her spine, and all that silky hair sliding over her shoulders left me harder than I could ever remember.

"Widen your knees, Ashleigh. Let me in."

She wiggled her pretty ass as she did as I said, and I couldn't help but run my hands over her soft skin. Her sharp intake of air told me all her teasing was a front. My woman was every bit as turned on as I was. To prove it, I trailed a finger over her pussy from front to back, and she cried out as her juices covered my skin. I lubed the condom with her wetness before I positioned myself and thrust inside her as deep as I could go.

"Blu!"

If anything, hearing my name on her lips made me harder, and I leaned over her back, changing the angle as I pulled out and thrust into her again.

"Yes!" she screamed, and I couldn't help but shout in triumph.

Ashleigh was mine, and before the night was over, she was going to know that beyond any doubt. But when I clamped my hands on her hips and started moving, I lost all ability to think beyond the present moment and the way her body responded to mine. The world and all its expectations fell away as she pushed back into me while I pumped inside her, the slap of our bodies in perfect rhythm as we chased our climax together.

In the morning, she still lay with me, her head heavy on my chest, her silky chestnut hair tickling my skin, her soft exhales soothing me. I smoothed my fingertips over her shoulder, down her arm, and lower to the pretty curve of her waist. She sighed and snuggled closer to my body, throwing her leg over my thigh. Like I hadn't woken up with morning wood already.

Yet I wanted to spend a few minutes enjoying the contentment that stole over me almost from the second I opened my eyes and knew she'd stayed with me. Somewhere in the back of my head, a kid with dreams of chasing wild women and music and a good time asked me what the fuck I thought I was doing. I ignored him while I concentrated on Ashleigh's fingers tracing patterns over my belly.

"Mornin', my gorgeous woman. Sleep well?"

She tucked in even tighter to my side and mumbled, "Did we sleep? 'Cause I think I missed that part."

Chuckling at her morning grumpiness, I lifted my head off the pillow enough to stare down at her, catching a ghost of a smile playing over her lips.

"Sleep is overrated, Ash. Didn't anyone ever tell you that?"

"I dunno. I think I'd like to give it a try anyway."

"Nah. You wouldn't, not with the sun up high and everything else in the world awake," I said as I rolled her onto her back and crawled on top of her.

"*Something* is definitely awake," she all but growled before she smiled up at me.

"I can't think of a better way to start the day."

Leaning down, I kissed her full on the mouth then trailed my lips over her jaw to nibble her ear before licking and sucking my way down the column of her throat. Ashleigh moaned and arched into me, and just like that, we picked up right where we left off sometime in the wee hours of the morning.

Chapter Fifteen

Ashleigh

WITH A STEAMING mug of coffee in my hands, I stared out my kitchen window at my mini-masterpiece of a yard. As much as I adored the view, this morning all the individual flowers and plants blurred into a kaleidoscope of color and texture, a backdrop for the swirling images of Blu and me together that jumbled my thoughts into incoherence. I couldn't decide if the mind-blowing sex or the lack of sleep prevented me from being able to focus.

Or maybe ending up in the middle of a full-blown fantasy was to blame. *Having out-of-this-world sex with your favorite singer? Come on, Ash,* I chided myself. *Who in her right mind believes daydreams like that have a snowball's chance in hell of becoming real?* The bigger question, of course, was what would I to do when I woke up, when the fantasy ended as it surely must? Though I'd tried, over the last month, I couldn't stop looking forward to Blu's appearances at my house to help me garden or to invite himself for a meal or to entertain me with his guitar as he worked on writing new songs. I had to force myself to face the truth: I'd been falling for him slowly from the moment I met him. Even though he'd said we were dating, even though he'd called me his girlfriend, even though he'd waited for me all day yesterday, in the end he would leave. At some point in the not-so-distant future, I could expect my beautiful little bubble to burst, so I owed it to myself not to let my heart burst with it.

He'd been telling me about the new album Balefire would be cutting later in the summer and the tour to support it that would start in the fall. His contagious excitement about the band's next endeavors infected me too, and I often daydreamed about tagging along, being his actual girlfriend. Always, I hauled myself up short with a reminder that I was only an Air Force brat who truly did want those roots Blu said my gardening hobby revealed about me. I was nothing special, certainly not rock star girlfriend special.

Then I'd given in to my desire for Blu, the man I was coming to know, rather than for Blu Connolly, the fantasy lead singer of Balefire, which landed me in bed with him. I'd spent all of yesterday driving around trying to forget how in one night he'd imprinted himself on me inside and out . . . only to return home to find him waiting for me in my living room. Only to spend another night with him, one that completely wrecked me. More than anything, I had to wrap my hands around my feelings and hold on to them tight. I had to protect myself from falling in love with Blu.

As though I'd conjured him with my thoughts, he sauntered into the kitchen, a towel wrapped low on his waist, water droplets gathered in the light dusting of hair on his chest, and thought, coherent or otherwise, left my mind completely.

With laughter dancing in the golden-green light of his eyes, Blu took my mug from my hand and swallowed a drink of my coffee. "Usually, I take mine black, but I kind of like the way you make yours with a shot of cream in it." He took another taste and added, "Or maybe it's the sugar."

Scowling at him, I retrieved my mug. "I don't put sugar in my coffee."

"Must be you I taste then. 'Cause I definitely noticed something sweet."

He leaned in and stole a kiss. When he pulled away from me, he'd stolen my coffee too and tipped the mug up and drained it.

"Hey! Get your own!"

"Ashleigh, didn't your mama ever teach you it's nice to share? Besides, it tastes better after you've already had half of it."

"Ugh! You're impossible," I grumbled.

"And you adore me." Grinning, he wrapped his arms around me and hauled me against him as I tried to walk away.

Tried being the operative word. Once I felt the hard planes of his chest and his taut belly against my back and his arms around my waist, I couldn't go anywhere. With a touch, he'd tethered me to him. He felt so good as he held me to him, and he damn well knew it too. Not that he'd ever take advantage—like now.

When he nudged my hair from the side of my neck, I angled my head to give him better access and sucked in air in anticipation. I couldn't help myself. After only two nights with him, he'd become even more addicting than coffee.

He feathered a breath across my skin. "You'd probably better get dressed, Ash. I don't want Dakota to see you in this robe 'cause that could very easily lead to having a physical disagreement with him about how much attention he's allowed to give you."

"What?" I asked, confused. "What does Dakota have to do with anything?"

"Well, darlin', Dakota and I have a standing tradition of having breakfast together at the diner where Mom works on our first morning back to rehearsals for a tour or an album. Since we're starting rehearsals for both today, I expect him to show up any time to pick us up for breakfast."

"Us? But I'm not part of the band."

"You're my girl, Ash. So I want you to come with me to rehearsal, meet the guys, see what I do for fun." He cleared his throat. "I mean, what I do for a living." The grin I detected on my skin still didn't convince me.

"Won't I be in the way?"

Though the thought of attending a Balefire rehearsal thrilled me to my bones, it also scared the ever-living hell out of me.

"Did you think I was in the way when I helped you in your yard?" he asked in a deceptively quiet tone.

"No, of course not. But that's different."

"Really? How?" He cocked his head.

"Gardening is my hobby. It doesn't matter to anyone else. Balefire is a monster band. Your rehearsals affect your whole team, not only you." Needing some space, I stepped away from him. "Music is your life, not something you do to entertain yourself during your down time."

"You're right. Music is my life, and now you're a big part of my life." He stepped into me, his fingers digging into my hips. "So I'd like you to see what I do. Come on." He stared hard into my eyes. "Don't walk away from me again."

The words so at odds with the whispered plea in his voice nearly undid me.

"All right," I pretended to huff. "If I'm going to change, you're going to have to let go of me."

He trailed kisses from my ear to my collarbone and back up. His hands weren't idle either. His fingers traced patterns over my belly, puckering my nipples and moistening the apex of my thighs. I sighed and melted a little into him.

Abruptly, he pulled his mouth from my skin with an audible pop and said, "Seriously, Ash. You have to go put something else on. This bathrobe wears me out, and that fuck boy I call my best friend will have no willpower if he sees you in it."

Stepping away from me, he left me off-balance, which he righted with a well-placed smack on my ass.

I spun around and glared at him. "You did *not* just go there."

Blu barked out a laugh. "Get dressed, Ash. Dakota's going to be here any minute."

He whistled a little tune as he headed out the back door wearing nothing but one of my bath towels while I stared disbelievingly after him.

Only one of us could win here. Only one would walk away eventually while the other would be hurt. Though I had no doubt which of us fit which category, I couldn't stop myself from giving in to Blu's demands. I was in so far over my head that even if there was someone out there who would throw me a lifeline, I'd never see it, let alone grab onto it and save myself. It was too late, but I wasn't ready to admit it.

♪

True to Blu's prediction, I'd no sooner dressed in a floral tiered blouse with spaghetti straps over cropped skinny jeans and wedge sandals when I heard the god-awful racket of a loud pickup roar up Diane's driveway. Since Blu had nonchalantly walked out of my house wearing nothing but one of my bath towels, the jeans and T-shirt he'd worn last night were still tossed over the chair beside my bed while his boxers and socks lay scattered across my bedroom floor.

As I stared at the mess Blu had left behind, I heard my back door slam. "Ashleigh! You ready?"

Fluffing my hair and taking one last quick look at my makeup in the mirror behind my bedroom door, I determined I looked as good as I could for meeting the other members of my favorite band.

Inhaling one long breath, I opened the door and stepped into my living room, where I discovered Dakota Perri and Blu Connolly standing together. Seeing all that rock god male perfection in one place left me light-headed. I don't know if Blu noticed or if he just wanted to touch me, but before I could do something dumb, like pass out, he stood beside me with an arm wrapped tightly around my waist.

"Dakota, I want you to meet my girl. This is Ashleigh Baker. Ash, this is my best friend, Dakota Perri."

Extending his hand to me, Dakota said, "Definitely a pleasure to meet you, Ashleigh. Blu didn't say a word about how hot you are."

Tentatively extending my hand to him, I replied, "Nice to meet you too." In my ears, my voice did its best Minnie Mouse impression, which I guess Blu noticed since his fingers flexed against my waist. Clearing my throat, I tried again. "Blu tells me the two of you used to prank my landlady's dad like it was your job. Guess it must be weird being invited into his house."

Dakota laughed, delight dancing in his eyes. "Blu told you about those days, did he? We had some fun times back then."

"You can let Ashleigh go any time, buddy," Blu said with a pointed look at where Dakota still gripped my hand, his thumb gliding lazily across my skin.

"You say that like we're not sharing or something, Blu. What the fuck?" Dakota asked. Confusion played across his handsome features as he let me go.

The look on my face must have mirrored Dakota's along with a dose of disbelief judging from how fast Blu corrected him. "Ashleigh is my *girlfriend*, Dakota. She's not a groupie or a casual fan looking to get lucky with the band."

"So?"

"So, she's off-limits to you and to everyone else in Balefire."

Dakota's brows went up. "Uh-huh."

Blu took a step toward him. "I mean it, Dakota. Don't even think about making a run at her. She's *mine*. And I'm not sharing." The feral tone of his voice shocked me.

"Blu? Are you six? You're talking about me, right? Not some Matchbox car or plastic guitar you played with when you were kids." *Seriously? Do these guys share women? Are they talking about sharing me?*

"Sorry, Ashleigh. But remember what I said about Dakota this morning when I was holding you in your kitchen? He makes a run at you, and somebody's million-dollar hands and somebody else's million-dollar face are going to collide. That's all I'm sayin'."

The smile that spread across Dakota's face should have had Blu backing up. I know I wanted to hide from the mischief dancing in his sea blue eyes.

"Fuck, Blu. We take a short break from each other, and you went and got yourself all mothered up." The "aw shucks" tone of his voice was at odds with the unholy lust in his eyes. "Though I gotta say, if this little hottie lived next door to my place, I might be the one mothered up instead."

Dakota made a slow perusal of my body, and Blu wrapped his other arm around me.

"I mean it, Dakota. Ashleigh is not on your radar. At. All. You got me?" he growled.

"Hey buddy. I won't be able to help it if she decides she likes lead guitarists with magic fingers better than diva lead singers who spent their hiatus from touring with their mom," Dakota teased. He had the audacity to wink at me like I was somehow in on the joke. "Did you spend any time at your place at all while you've been off the road?"

"Diva lead singers? We're starting with that, dude? Not only are you driving, you're buying. Let's go."

While I tried to make sense of what Dakota had said, Blu turned me toward my back door.

The new information I learned about Blu in the first few minutes of meeting Dakota made me feel like I'd met two new guys rather than one. He shared women with the other guys in the band? He had his own place? A place he apparently didn't want me to know about since this was the first I'd heard of it?

I pulled against him, effectively stopping our progress out of the house. "I don't know, Blu. Maybe inviting me along when you and the rest of the band reconvene isn't such a good idea. I don't want to be a distraction."

"Reconvene—ooh, you hooked up with a smart hottie, Blu. I like her even more now."

"Knock it off, Dakota," Blu grumbled before turning his attention to me. "You're the best kind of distraction, babe. I want you with me. Aside from dumbass here"—he jerked a thumb toward Dakota— "the other guys in the band will be cool with you hanging out with us too. What they won't be cool with is us being late to practice, so how 'bout we go grab some breakfast, huh?"

He pressed a kiss to my mouth and held me tight to his hard body. The caresses felt natural, like we headed out together to Balefire rehearsals all the time. Still, there was so much I didn't know about him, so much maybe he didn't want me to know. So much of not knowing that likely would lead to a whopper of a heartbreak if I wasn't careful.

The whole morning so far had seemed surreal, exactly like Dakota's pickup, a white and lime green behemoth jacked up on four monster tires. Like the man himself, everything about his ride screamed, "Look at me!" It would have taken me some effort to hoist myself up into the cab, but Blu helped me by placing his hands on my ass and nearly launching me up and into the truck. As I maneuvered to sit between the two men, relief flashed through me when I saw the size of the custom guitar-shaped gearshift centered on the middle of the floor of the front bench seat. At least I could keep some distance between Dakota and me since he seemed determined to use me to have fun at Blu's expense. Or maybe he actually was interested in me too—an even more unsettling idea.

Blu's reticence to share me with Dakota mollified me, but I'd be lying if I said the thought of the two of them sharing women didn't bother me. Then there was the knowledge of Blu's private residence, a place so private he hadn't even told me about it. Silly me. I assumed he lived with Diane whenever he was off the road since he'd stayed at her place for the past month. Of course, when I thought about it, it made sense that a twenty-eight-year-old rock star with Blu's wealth and fame would have his own place. Which begged the question—what had he been doing staying at Diane's all this time?

"You're quiet, Ash. What's going on in that gorgeous head of yours?" Blu whispered into my ear before he feathered a kiss along my cheek. He'd slid his arm behind me on the seat, pulling me closer to him when he'd climbed into Dakota's truck.

"Trying to wrap my head around the fact that I'm going to see a Balefire rehearsal. Too bad Camille fired me."

"Someone fired you? What was your job?" Dakota interrupted as he peeled the truck out of Diane's driveway.

Though I tried to be cool about it, I still grabbed the dash as I answered his question. "I used to write for a music blog. Now I don't. Which is a bummer since I'm about to experience every Balefire fan's wet dream."

"Babe, I have a plan to make that up to you." Blu nuzzled the side of my head. "So, if you feel like putting that little stylus of yours to work during our rehearsals today, knock yourself out."

"That's okay, Blu. Like with the exclusive interview you gave me, no one would ever believe any article I wrote about attending a Balefire rehearsal. I'll just stay out of the way and hang out, enjoy the experience."

Deliberately changing the subject, I turned to Dakota. "Do you write songs on your hiatus too? It seems like Blu spent almost every afternoon working up something on his guitar."

"I put my axe down for two straight weeks while I worked on this truck. What do you think of the sound of it, Blu? Pretty bitchin', yeah?"

"Noticed it right away. What all did you do?"

The two of them launched into a conversation about carburetors and exhaust systems or something, and I went back to my worries about how I'd survive the aftermath of living out my fantasy and watching it end. When we rolled up in front of the diner, I still had no clue.

Chapter Sixteen

Ashleigh

THE BUILDING WE parked in front of looked like a Quonset hut on steroids and did not fit my idea of a state-of-the-art recording studio. Instead, after we finished breakfast, it appeared Dakota had made some sort of pit stop for something for his truck. But when Blu opened his door and stepped out, turning to help me to the ground, I knew my already surreal morning had tripped into space.

He smiled and said, "Remember when I told you we moved the band out of my garage and into a shop at Tron's parents' place?"

"Yes." I dragged out the word.

He swept a hand in the direction of the Quonset. "We still use the shop. Only now, it's not only our practice space—it's also our recording studio. Leaving the exterior intact means we can work in peace, which maybe wasn't our initial goal when we were first starting out, but it comes in handy these days."

He twined his fingers with mine, and we followed Dakota through a side door, which opened into a reception area surrounded by offices. Beyond the plate glass windows of the offices, several people were hard at work behind computers or on phones. I turned to question Blu, who preempted me.

"Our team is headquartered here. The people you see in these offices are setting up our next tour, working on publicity, marketing, that sort of thing."

My eyes widened as I took in the relatively small office spaces encircling the large reception area. "Does anyone have an opportunity to see the sun in here?"

He laughed. "Everyone focuses when they're working. Even the band, as you'll see. But this is a big ole place with lots of amenities. Upstairs, we have a gym and a rec room with a hundred-inch projection screen and theater seats, pool tables, game consoles, the works." He grinned wide, obviously happy to show off the band's success. Knowing where he came from, I couldn't fault him. "We have a state-of-the-art kitchen with a full-time chef catering meals, and the conference room has spectacular views. People who work here can use anything in the place, so these little offices aren't a big deal."

I looked around the reception area, in the middle of which sat a young woman behind a massive black and chrome desk. Couches and groupings of end tables and plush chairs lined the rest of the room. The prevailing colors were silver and black from the silver swirl designs in the black area rugs covering the polished wood floor to the black seating and chrome tables, to the dove gray walls bordered at the top with a wide black band of paint. All of which drew attention to the red flames licking along the ceiling and the edges of the walls. On closer inspection, I could even see flames painted along the edges of the floor where it met the walls. Red threads subtly woven through the fabric of the furniture echoed the flame theme. The room reminded me of all the Balefire cover art I'd ever seen.

"Obviously, you guys have learned some things about branding yourselves," I said with admiration.

"Glad you approve. But we're only getting started, babe," Blu said as he guided me to the receptionist's desk. Seated there was a beautiful Asian woman with perfect skin and straight black hair falling to the middle of her back. With a smile, he said, "Hello, Emory. How's your summer going?"

"Decent. I've been chauffeuring my son to baseball games for most of it. You?"

"Decent." He looked at me and winked. "I've been learning all about gardening."

I admired Emory's professionalism when her deep brown eyes didn't even twitch at that description of Blu's summer.

"Em, this is Ashleigh Baker. I need a pass made up for her."

"You got it, Blu. Nice to meet you, Ashleigh," Emory said as she stood and offered her hand.

"Same."

"If you'll step over here, I can take your photo real quick and have that pass ready in a few minutes."

I followed her to an office space dedicated to equipment like printers and copiers and such where she lined me up against a wall and snapped my photo. No doubt, the photo looked as bad as the one on my driver's license.

"Why do I need a pass, Blu?" I asked as I rejoined him in the main reception area.

"So you have access to the place whenever you need it," he said like I'd asked a silly question. Turning his attention back to Emory, he added, "Benson Strauss from *Rolling Stone* is going to show up sometime this afternoon. Let me know when he gets here. Thanks."

I stared hard at Blu when he dropped that little bombshell, but he didn't say another word. Instead, he ushered me through a door cleverly concealed by the room's paint job. Someone who wasn't allowed in the band's inner sanctum would have a difficult time even noticing it if they could bypass the security of the front office team. We walked down a hallway lined with framed gold and platinum records of Balefire's hits before we stepped out into the main studio area. The soundproofing in the studio was so excellent that until Blu opened the door to let me through, I didn't even hear all the noise of Dakota and Adam Tron, Balefire's bassist, tuning their guitars or of Jack Whitehorse banging furiously over his massive drum kit.

Blu leaned in to speak into my ear. "This is our rehearsal space. The recording studio is through there." He pointed toward an area directly behind Jack's one-story drum kit. "There are couches around the room if you want to get comfortable while we practice. I have to warn you, Ash. Sometimes we drop into the zone, and rehearsals and recording can go on literally for days." He brushed a kiss over my cheek. "Bathrooms are through there." Again he pointed toward a doorway behind and to the right of Jack's drums. "If you have any questions, ask. If you need anything, Emory will get it for you."

By now, the tuning and banging had faded away as Tron and Jack seemed to realize someone other than a Balefire member stood in the room. Tron broke the sudden silence. "Blu, this one is gorgeous, but at the risk of pissing you off—what the fuck is she doing at our rehearsal? We have rules for a reason."

"Nice to see you too, Tron. You have a good summer?" Blu asked deliberately and gestured to me. "This is Ashleigh Baker, my *girlfriend*. She also happens to be a kick-ass music reviewer. So I invited her to our rehearsal to see how a Balefire album and tour begin. There's an editor from *Rolling Stone* who's been on my ass for an interview. Ashleigh has an exclusive to sell to him, so I brought her along to see how we work, maybe add some material to her article."

As we listened to Blu speak, I could see my shock mirrored on the faces of the members of the band.

Tron recovered first. "You invited the press to our rehearsal and didn't think to run it by any of the rest of us first? Excuse us, Ashleigh is it? We have some family business to discuss."

At Tron's pronouncement, Emory materialized at my side. "If you'll come with me, we'll finish some paperwork for your pass."

Though her smile and tone said friendly, her eyes said wary. I couldn't blame her.

"Blu, it's obvious I shouldn't have come along today. I'll call an Uber and head back home."

I turned to follow Emory out of the room when he grabbed my arm, hauling me up short.

"Ashleigh, wait. We'll sort this out in a minute." He shot a meaningful look at his band. "Go with Emory to take care of your pass, but please don't leave." He leaned in to whisper for my ears only, "Sometimes we do go for days in a rehearsal. But I don't want to go for days without seeing you. Please stay."

Shit, I am in so deep, I thought desperately as I nodded my assent. "Okay."

Blu

Emory barely closed the door behind Ashleigh and her when Tron started in for real. "What the fuck are you thinking, Blu? We don't bring women to the studio, ever. They're a distraction we can't have if we're going to do this thing the right way. We agreed to that, you as much as any of us." He turned to Dakota. "Did you know about her and his plan to bring her here?"

"Before this morning? Nope. Not a clue. But he says he's not sharing."

It was all I could do to stop myself from punching the smirk off Dakota's face.

"For the last time, Dakota, Ashleigh's my *girlfriend*, not a groupie or some random woman I picked up. She's mine," I growled.

"That's not the issue right now." Tron shook his head. "We agreed to vote on whether or not anyone outside the band and our management attends our rehearsals and recording sessions. You had no right to bring her along," he gritted out. "Not without a discussion and a vote ahead of bringing her here."

I ran my hand through my hair as I paced a circle in front of the guys. Yeah, I knew the rules. Hell, I'd come up with most of them.

But this thing with Ashleigh was so new, so intense. Fragile. With the way I knew we could drop into the zone during a rehearsal, I couldn't risk her thinking I'd truly walked away from her after sleeping with her or that sex was all I wanted with her. I couldn't risk appearing to be exactly what she'd accused me of being from the start—a player in every sense of the word.

Because with her, everything was different.

Sighing, I said, "You're right, Tron. I should have run it by you guys first. It's just that—she's special. Really special."

Tron rolled his eyes while the huge smile Dakota had sported till now dropped off his face. I think he finally figured out that I hadn't been kidding about how much Ashleigh meant to me. As usual, Jack remained quiet, but I noticed the way he gripped his drumsticks in his hand and wondered at what thoughts pounded through his head.

"Up until she met me, she freelanced music reviews for the local press and for Colorado Music Works blog. She even reviewed our show at Red Rocks last summer. Check this out."

I pulled up her review on my phone and handed it to Tron.

"Impressive. You're right. She's good." He returned my phone. "Still doesn't give you the right to bring her here without letting the rest of us have a say about it."

"Let me see that." Dakota snatched the phone from my hand. "What did she say about my incredible axe-playing skills?"

"That they're incredible." I laughed. "And you call *me* a diva," I couldn't resist adding.

"What do we do now? She's here though she did offer to grab a cab and leave," Tron said pointedly.

"Listen. We've got a ton of material to sort through: what we wrote on the last tour and what any of us wrote during our hiatus. I wrote four or five songs—"

"About Ashleigh," Dakota teased in a singsong voice as he returned my phone to me.

"If we let a journalist see how we decide what to include in an album, we could give the fans something new that can only help make us even more interesting, make our music more special to them."

"Since you're dating her, you would control the spin on her review?" Tron challenged.

"Hadn't thought about it," I said truthfully.

"Think about it. She gonna want you looking over her shoulder, telling her what she can and can't include in her work? Tell me something, Blu. Did she hook up with you for the chance you're giving her? Whose idea was this anyway?"

Tron's hostility frayed my last nerve, but Jack interrupted. "I saw the look on her face when Blu said someone from *Rolling Stone* would be talking to her about an exclusive interview she's already done. If anything, I'd say she was even more surprised than we were."

"Thanks, Jack," I said as I shot a filthy look at Tron. "Ashleigh didn't want one damn thing to do with me from the moment we met. I pursued the hell out of her until she finally gave in. Because she tried to protect the band from her boss at the blog, her boss fired her." Again, I directed my explanation at Tron. "I gave her the interview her boss wanted, but her boss blackballed her with any reputable outfit in this region. I kind of owe it to Ashleigh to let her have this chance." Crossing my arms over my chest, I dared my brothers, my only family outside of my mom. "You read what she wrote about us before she met any of us. Why would she change her view now? Especially since she's dating me."

"I kind of like Blu's idea of letting the fans see how we work. It could give us another way to connect with them, Tron," Dakota said.

"So we're going to let her stay?" Jack asked.

"Not without a vote," Tron insisted.

"Fine. I vote Ashleigh stays," I said.

"Me too," Dakota seconded.

"Fine," Tron huffed. "But she better not say one damn word. Stay in the background and take notes or whatever."

"Thanks, Tron," I said, relieved and turned to Jack. "You haven't voted."

"Majority rules," was all he said.

"If you have something to say against Ashleigh being here, now would be the time to say it, Jack."

"I don't have anything against her being here. I wish I'd known that all it would take to change the rules would be to bring your girl to rehearsal."

"What are you talking about, Jackie-boy? Since when do you care about any girls?" Dakota asked, a sly smirk on his face.

"Since my girl gifted me with a daughter while we were on our last tour."

In the silence that greeted Jack's pronouncement, his expression didn't change at all.

The room exploded with questions.

"You have a woman?"

"What the fuck, Whitehorse?"

"When in the hell did you have time to make a baby with someone?"

"A kid? You have a kid?"

"Didn't see this one coming at all."

"It appears you guys were even busier than usual on your hiatus," Garrett Phillips, our manager, drawled as he materialized out of nowhere to join us in the rehearsal studio.

"Appears so," Tron said, eyeing Jack like he'd never seen him before.

I could see my own astonishment reflected on the faces of my two oldest friends.

A small smile spread across Jack's face at last. "Guess you'll have to stop calling me the monk now, huh?"

"And today of all days, you invited the press, Blu," Tron said as he ran a hand through his hair. "Peachy. Fuckin' peachy."

CHAPTER SEVENTEEN

Blu

S EVERAL HOURS INTO our rehearsal, we were tired, sweaty, and generally jacked. Two of the songs we'd written on tour showed real potential, and playing together gave each of us a high no other experience could replicate. Yet, in spite of our rock god reputation, we needed to take a break. With the sound of our latest effort still reverberating around the room, I noticed Emory standing patiently near the door to the offices.

"A Mr. Strauss has been waiting for the last half hour to see you, Blu," she said.

"Perfect timing. You ready, Ash?" I asked as I extended my hand to her. "Let's go sell an interview."

"What? Now?" Ashleigh stammered as she stood up from one of the couches where she'd been watching us.

She'd spent the morning and early afternoon in our rehearsal studio. Though she stayed on the edges of the room, I knew where she was the whole time. Even as she wandered to the back of the space to peer into the recording studio behind us, I could sense her precisely. The knowledge that she was here with me centered me, relaxed me somehow, and I performed at a higher level than usual, something Tron noticed.

"I hope I'm wrong about her," I heard Tron say behind me as I escorted Ashleigh toward the door. "'Cause Blu is singing in the best form I've ever heard."

She glanced over her shoulder at me when he said that, and I answered her with a grin. As we walked down the hallway back to the reception area, she spoke to me for the first time since we'd started rehearsing.

"*Rolling Stone*, Blu? I'm a nobody. This guy is going to laugh his ass off when he hears your proposal. You know that, right? Then he's going to demand your time for a real interview, and the rest of the band is going to have a fit." The way she lagged behind me told me she believed every word she said.

I stopped and cupped her face in my hands. Staring deep into the sapphire pools of her eyes, I said, "You gotta sell it, Ash. While I make nice with him, you grab a copy of your interview from Emory. I emailed it to her yesterday."

She blinked. "What? You planned this all out? Why?"

"I owe you for taking it in the shorts to protect my mom and me. Strauss wants an interview, I gave you an interview, you need a chance, and it all comes together here." Taking her hand again, I led her up the hallway.

In front of the door to reception, I stopped and pulled her into my arms. "You're going to be great. When he's done reading your work, I bet you have more than a sale. I bet you have a job." I punctuated my confidence in my girl with a quick kiss. Anything more would have put my whole plan in jeopardy, but that didn't mean I didn't think about it with her sweet body pressed so perfectly into mine. Pulling away enough to open the door, I ushered her through before she had a chance to react—to any of it.

"Blu! Nice to see you again. Thanks for seeing me. How much

time do we have?" Benson Strauss asked in the rapid-fire way he had as he stood and offered me his hand.

"Benson. It's been a while. This is Ashleigh Baker."

"Nice to meet you," Ashleigh said, extending her hand.

I didn't like the way Benson looked her over as he said, "Likewise."

So I interrupted. "She's a local music reviewer, earned her degree in English from the University of Denver. I'd like you to take a look at a piece she did a couple of weeks ago. Camille Watson at Colorado Music Works blog turned her down, said she'd made this up. Watson's loss is your gain," I said. "You want to grab that, Ashleigh?"

Emory stood at Ash's elbow with the interview in her hand. Yeah, there's a reason we pay Emory like the queen of executive assistants that she is.

Recovering herself, Ashleigh said, "Blu did me a favor and let me have the interview after Camille blew the opportunity I set up for her with him. Then she turned down the piece when I submitted it."

"How do you two know each other again?" Benson asked as he scanned Ashleigh's article.

"We're neighbors," we said in unison and looked at each other in surprise.

Fortunately, Benson didn't look up from his reading.

"This is good. You wrote this?" Before Ashleigh could reply, he added, "Really good. You didn't shy away from the hard stuff, and you write well." He glanced up from the page. "This for sale?"

"Yes."

"Have you offered it to anyone else?"

Ashleigh gave me a look, and I nodded.

"Yes. I've offered it to about every regional outlet."

"And they've all turned you down?" Benson asked, incredulousness written large across his features.

"Well, Camille put it out that I made up a story about a cameo appearance a certain lead singer from a certain rock band made with a local bluegrass group. Blu did sing with Lightning Strikes one Sunday afternoon, making their lead singer look like the backup he should be. My review didn't go over so well with some of the bluegrass fan base, it seems." She fidgeted for a second before she squared her shoulders and stared Benson in the eye. "Camille's way of apologizing for me was to discredit me."

"Some photos accompanying the interview would go far toward giving your words credibility," he commented. "May we send a photographer over?"

"I don't know if the rest of the band will go for a photographer here at the studio," I hedged. "Of course, I might be able to talk them into it if Ashleigh interviewed each of them too, maybe even went out on tour with us. Write an exclusive about our next tour for your little rag."

"'My 'little rag' he calls it." Ben chuckled and turned to Ashleigh. "Do you know how long I've been trying to get this guy to sit down with one of my reporters and give them something? I don't know how you did this, but I'm interested in hiring you on a probationary basis to follow Balefire on tour."

"Really?" Ashleigh's voice nearly jumped into the stratosphere for the second time today. I had to work to keep from laughing out loud at the comical way her eyes rounded at Benson's proposal.

"There's one thing you need to know up front, Benson. Since I gave her the interview, Ashleigh has become my girlfriend. If that's going to be a problem, now is the time to let us know."

His good humor morphed into deadly seriousness in an instant. "You weren't his girlfriend when you interviewed him for this? You swear?"

"No. I've been trying hard not to be attracted to him even after we started dating," Ashleigh said.

He stared at her for a beat before busting out a laugh. "If you're interested in pursuing this gig, we're interested in your work. Do you have a few minutes? Can we work out some logistics right now?

Since I thought I was getting this interview, my flight back to New York isn't until early this evening, so I have some time."

"Sure. I have time now," Ashleigh said before she shot me a look of equal parts fear and excitement.

I knew the feeling. Stage fright, adrenaline rush, call it what you want. It's the essence of every performer's ability to be *on* when the moment calls for it. Now was Ashleigh's moment in the spotlight.

Smiling back at her, I said, "Great! I need to go back to work. Your pass will let you back into the studio when you're finished here, Ash. Nice to see you, Benson." I shook his hand and walked over to have a word with Emory.

Keeping my voice down, I said, "Pay attention to them for me, would you? Make sure Ashleigh doesn't sign anything yet."

"You got it, Blu. Also, the chef wants to know if you all would like to break for lunch now," she said.

"I'll ask."

With one last surreptitious glance over my shoulder to see Ashleigh listening attentively to whatever Benson was saying, I let myself back into the studio.

♪

"Got *your girl* all set up, buddy?" Dakota greeted me when I reentered the rehearsal space.

Rolling my eyes, I replied, "Ashleigh sold the interview. *Rolling Stone* would like additional interviews with each of you to add to her article."

"Girl works fast," Tron said.

"Maybe too fast," Garrett added.

"Already had this conversation with Tron, Garrett. Ashleigh is not with me because she saw an opportunity. I'm pretty sure the next time we're alone, I'm going to hear all about how she can take care of herself and set up her own gigs."

"Sure," Garrett drawled.

"But she's not stupid enough to turn down this chance right now either. When you read the article she wrote from my interview, I bet each of you—even you, Garrett—will want her to talk to you."

"Yeah, we'll see." Garrett crossed his arms over his chest. "You ready to get back to work?"

"Actually, Emory sent me back with a message that the chef has some eats ready if we want 'em."

"I'm all over that," Jack said from somewhere behind his massive drum kit.

"Me too," Dakota added as he headed toward the hallway that led to the kitchen at the back of the rehearsal space.

The rest of us followed, and I smiled to myself that my little gambit to have my girl join us on tour might even work out.

Ashleigh

After a week of watching Balefire rehearsals, I needed a break from "the zone." Yet, it didn't seem like being in the zone affected the band at all. Instead of being at each other's throats like I'd anticipated, if anything, they were more in sync, more fired up about the work they were doing. And boy howdy were they ever working. Sometimes they replayed a single measure ten or twelve times in ten or twelve different ways until they found something they all agreed on. Other times, it seemed a melody or a lyric clicked immediately—they played it through once, liked it, and determined to practice it that way. Their patience, musicianship, and genuine camaraderie astounded me.

Though I heard the occasional frustrated snipe, not once did I hear real hostility or anger between any of them. If anything, the more upset one or the other might become, the funnier his jibes at the rest of the band.

"Oh yeah, Tron you're steady all right. Rock steady like standing on shale in an earthquake."

"Hey Blu, I think my cat could sing that line that way too."

"Jack, know what they say about drummers? They can't dance to a beat."

"Dakota, if you played an actual lick, you might even get into a pair of those panties some girl tosses at you onstage."

And so it went. There were times when the entire band couldn't continue to play because they were laughing too much, a situation I came to associate either with a meal or a nap since one or the other usually followed such an outburst.

I'd had no idea the day Blu loaded me into Dakota's truck that not only was I not likely to return home that night, but I might not return home for a week. At some point during the week, Emory took pity on me and brought me a fresh pair of jeans, a band T-shirt, and some clean underwear. I'd been showering in the band's locker room, and consequently smelled like the boys, but at least I was clean.

Over the course of their rehearsals, I'd found time to talk to each of the guys individually. Since I'd met him first, I started with Dakota, who I discovered was the true diva of the band. Jack spent most of any downtime he had texting or talking on his phone, and he didn't want to share any details about the special lady with whom he kept in contact. Tron remained standoffish even after he read my article about Blu. One afternoon, though, he walked in on Blu trying to get me to join him in the shower. He witnessed my determination not to go there in the band's special space, and somehow after that, Tron started to warm up to me.

Like Blu had already told me, Dakota learned to play guitar as a way for his dad and Diane to keep their boys out of trouble. Jack was the second son of a large family of six boys, born to a contractor and a nurse who gave him his first set of drums and knew about every type of earplug and its properties before Jack turned thirteen. Tron's dad ran an industrial mechanics business that outgrew the shop at about the same time the band decided they needed their own studio. His mom ran her own accounting firm, and she sometimes consulted on finances for the band.

The retired short school bus they'd scraped the money together to buy at an auction, which had served as the band's tour bus in their early days, was parked behind the shop. The original three members said they held on to it as a reminder of where they'd started. Tron's dad kept it tuned up, and sometimes they even took it out on short road trips for a lark. When Jack joined the band, they'd rolled up to his parents' place to pick up his drum kit and told him the old ride was still the band bus. He'd laughed and asked which one of them would be riding on the bumper after they loaded all his gear into it. They'd ended up playing rock-paper-scissors for who had to stand on the steps for the ride back to the studio. Dakota lost, so of course he climbed to the top of the bus and played Superman from the luggage rack all the way back to the studio.

From my observations, Balefire's success lay in the members' true friendship and affection for each other. Sure, they were each virtuoso musicians and consummate professionals, but in the end, their relationships with each other were what made the band tight musically and personally. Having never lived anywhere long enough to build such strong connections with other people, I envied their closeness.

The couches lining the walls of the studio were all oversized to accommodate anyone who needed someplace to sleep. On more than one occasion, I woke up to find Blu spooning me, snoring softly in my ear. At first, I was embarrassed about the other guys seeing us that way, even though we were both fully clothed. Turned out, their reactions ranged from disinterested to indifferent except for Dakota who asked several times when it would be his turn.

One evening, he made a pass at me. Before I could even react, Blu backed him up against a wall faster than the speed of sound.

"Dammit, Dakota, Ashleigh is off-limits. I warned you the morning I introduced her to you, and I've been reminding you ever since. She's not a groupie or a casual fuck. She's my *woman*. And you need to keep your fucking hands to yourself. Got it?"

"Blu!" I gasped.

Tron, standing nearby, made a casual statement that stabbed my conscience even as Blu's words warmed my heart. "That's why we made a rule about bringing women into the studio."

"All right, already. Jesus, man. I was having some fun. Relax, Blu," Dakota said as he pushed back at him. "Ashleigh's yours, and you're not sharing. Understood."

When I glanced at Jack, he merely raised a brow and meandered over to his drum kit, climbed up onto his stool, and started banging out the rhythm I'd noticed him tapping against his thigh earlier. His actions deflated the volatility of the situation as Tron joined him on his bass. Slowly, Dakota and Blu made their way back to their guitars and took up the melody Jack's and Tron's rhythms created. Like flipping a switch, the band came back together and wrote a song. It was the most astounding thing I'd ever seen. Still, I didn't want to create friction inside my favorite band even with—or maybe because of—my intense attraction to its lead singer.

At last, I convinced Blu that I needed to go back to my place, check on my yard, and gather up some of my own clothes. The guys, knowing what to expect, kept a closet with changes of clothes in it, so they didn't share my problem. Besides, I thought it would be in the band's best interests to rehearse for a while without an audience. Even though I'd done my best to remain unobtrusive, I often caught one of the guys, usually Blu, watching me. After their little scuffle, however, Dakota studiously avoided me in every way. Another reason for me to disappear for a bit was to help the two of them repair any damage my presence caused to their relationship.

After spending a couple of days dealing with the damage of a week's neglect in my garden and working on my article for *Rolling Stone*, I finally received a text from Blu. Now knowing how the band worked, I wasn't surprised at not hearing from him sooner, but I'd be lying if I didn't admit that his radio silence bothered me a little. Still, I had to laugh when I read: *Hey babe, send me a pic of your posies.*

Having been up to my elbows in flowers the moment Blu texted, I snapped a quick photo of a row of roses and forwarded it to him.

He shot back almost immediately: *Those are nice, but I was thinking about some other even prettier buds.*

With a smile, I texted back: *You'll have to reach into your imagination for those, rock god.*

I miss you, Ash. When are you coming back to the studio?

I have a sub job tomorrow. The day after?

Jack's girl sends him pics. Send me a photo, Ash. I need something to snuggle when I take a nap.

=).

I took a selfie in my floppy gardening hat and sent it to him.

You truly are the most beautiful girl in the world.

I had no idea how to respond to that, so I didn't.

CHAPTER EIGHTEEN

Ashleigh

WHEN I ARRIVED at the studio a couple of days later, the front office throbbed with activity. Emory barely acknowledged me with a quick hello before she returned to the phone call that held her attention. With everyone else in the office equally focused, I wondered what was up.

Using my pass, I keyed into the rehearsal studio to find it empty. Before I could panic and wonder if I'd waited too long to return, I looked past Jack's giant drum kit and noticed the band working behind the thick glass of the recording studio. A red light above the window warned me they were recording, and once again, I marveled at their prolific creativity. They'd been rehearsing and even writing new material for a little more than two weeks and already they were recording? I mean, I knew they wrote music all the time. I'd seen it with Blu most afternoons on my patio, but still. To put it all together and record it so fast? Wow.

Not knowing how long they'd be working, I made myself at home on one of the sofas where I could unobtrusively watch the action inside the studio. Each of the guys wore oversized headphones and sang into giant mics hanging from the ceiling in front of them. The stripped-down drum kit Jack sat behind didn't seem like enough after watching him on the behemoth he used for rehearsals and shows, yet the way he moved over the surfaces of the skins told my eyes everything my ears couldn't hear through the soundproofing of the space. The same could be said for the way Dakota and Tron wielded their guitars. The band's musicianship truly transcended the skill of mere mortals.

And Blu? Even with the barriers of equipment between us, the man simply mesmerized me with the way he moved. I could almost hear his voice, the notes raw and unrefined or soft and caressing, his range and vocal timbre calling to me even through the walls and glass of the studio. Since he didn't know I'd arrived, I could watch him surreptitiously, enjoy his love for his muse without disturbing him. It was a heady experience and one I didn't want to end, especially not the way it did.

"So you're back," Garrett whispered in my ear from somewhere too close to me.

"Garrett!" I jumped away from his voice. "You startled me. I thought you were somewhere inside the studio too."

"I was. Then I saw you arrive and thought I'd come out and hang with you. They're going to be a while in there."

"If you're supposed to be a part of that, please don't let me interrupt. I can entertain myself," I said as I put more distance between us on the couch.

"Actually, I was wondering why you didn't interview me for your article. I've been Balefire's manager for ten years." The pride in his tone was for him, not the band.

"You've been with the band since the beginning?"

"Almost. I took over managing them right before they cut their first record, guided them through the process, helped them with their finances and touring." He slid his arm across the back of the cushions behind me, a self-satisfied expression marring his handsome features.

If Blu hadn't told me otherwise, I might have considered Garrett the unsung hero of Balefire, judging from the way he puffed himself up. Since I didn't truly know how much the guys relied on him and in what ways, I thought it prudent to play along with him even though a latent smarminess about him made me uncomfortable. The way he crowded my space had me attempting to make myself smaller, a circumstance I loathed but couldn't seem to stop.

Yeah, he came across as "dressed down" chic in designer jeans, an expensive T-shirt, and Johnston & Murphy slides, but clearly, he was trying too hard. The band dressed in off-the-rack jeans and lace-up boots or Converse, and each of them usually sported some rock band T-shirt. Whenever Blu and I went out, he wore an expensive long-sleeved dress shirt with the sleeves rolled up, but the jeans and boots remained the same. Also, there was Garrett's trendy haircut and the expensive cologne he must have bathed in. I was certain I would smell of it too merely from being in his vicinity for a few minutes.

Not wanting to cause problems after the band had given me the chance to launch my career, I pulled out my phone and stylus and asked Garrett a few questions. It took me a minute to notice he'd been inching back into my space as we talked, his knee nearly touching mine.

Standing abruptly, I said, "If you'll excuse me for a minute, I need to use the facilities."

Garrett coming onto me worried me more than interrupting the band, so I deliberately walked along the outside of the studio where Blu could see me if he looked away from his mic. When I came out of the bathroom, I saw that someone had turned the recording light to green, and Blu awaited me outside the studio door.

"About time you got here, babe," he said as he reached for me.

Before I could comment, he had me in his arms, a smile spread wide across his face, and then his mouth was on mine. He'd made a game out of stealing kisses and the occasional grope during the week I'd spent with the band in rehearsals. After the two nights he'd spent in my bed, I'd known what I was missing, so those encounters hadn't been enough. But over a week without his kisses had been even worse.

At the moment, I didn't care that my response to him left me vulnerable, that he would know how much he'd come to mean to me. All I cared about was his incredible mouth on mine, his tongue tangling with mine, his body promising pleasure as he held me close, his hands roaming freely over my back and down to cup my ass, holding me tight against his hardening cock. Wrapping my arms around his neck, I pushed my breasts into the solid wall of his pecs, relishing the feel of our bodies together as I returned his kiss and lost all sense of where we were.

From some distance, I heard a throat clearing followed by Dakota's raucous laughter. "Hey you two. Get a room why don'tcha?"

My face burst into flame as I pulled away from Blu who smiled again before leaning in to whisper in my ear, "Glad you missed me as much as I missed you."

"The guys were saying Blu had found himself a girl, but no one mentioned how beautiful you are," a man said from somewhere behind me.

Blu turned me, sliding an arm around my waist and holding me close to his side. "Nick, this is my girlfriend, Ashleigh Baker. Ash, this is Nick Parker, our producer. He flew in last night and put us in the studio at dark-thirty this morning."

Extending my hand, I said, "Nice to meet you, Nick."

"Likewise." His grip said we were equals, and I liked him immediately. "But I don't want you to get the wrong idea. These guys were on the phone with me already last week, pushing me to come in. So the taskmasters here are the boys in Balefire."

With his long dark hair pulled back in a neat ponytail and his tall lean frame, Nick looked to be somewhere in his forties, but I was aware of him by reputation and knew he clocked in somewhere north of fifty. The twinkle in his light blue eyes, the deep dimples in his cheeks when he smiled at me as he shook my hand, and the enthusiasm in his voice contributed to his youthful appeal. Either that or the fact that he produced one of the biggest rock 'n' roll bands in the world, and every one of their discs was excellent. The man was a genius.

"Ashleigh is a music reviewer. She's doing a piece on us for *Rolling Stone*. Maybe you'd have time to let her to ask you a few questions later," Blu said, giving me a tiny squeeze.

"Yeah? You don't seem pushy or in-your-face obnoxious. Are you sure you're a reporter?" Nick deadpanned.

"Not a reporter. A music reviewer. But I'd love to chat with you about music and your current projects when you have a minute."

I admit it had kind of pissed me off at first that Blu set me up with Benson Strauss at *Rolling Stone* without my knowledge or even a warning. Yet I wasn't stupid enough to turn down such an amazing opportunity. I understood I'd have to be scrupulously objective in everything I wrote and I'd made that clear to the guys as I'd interviewed them. In the end, though, the game was what it was. In this business, it was as much who you knew as what you knew that put you ahead. Interviewing one of the biggest producers of rock music for the past twenty years certainly wouldn't hurt my résumé.

"Beautiful and diplomatic. Is that how you landed my man Blu here?"

"She blew me off when we met. One of my buddies and I had to cheat at pool to even score a first date with her and her friend," Blu said as he smiled down at me, affection in his eyes. "Of course, the girls might have been ringers themselves. I'm not sure."

I rolled my eyes and tried to suppress a grin.

Nick barked out a laugh, and about that time, Dakota stepped up to us and said, "Hey Ash. Want to come into the studio and see how we cut a record?"

"We've been at it for hours, Dakota. Maybe we could take a break," Blu said.

"Yeah, but it's my song we're working on. And we're at a critical point. Maybe we could finish it before you sneak your girl off to a dark corner, yeah?" Dakota pouted.

Blu laughed and kissed my cheek though I swear he had one eye on Dakota, taunting him with the caress. "Sure, D. We'll finish your song." The affection in his eyes warmed me to my toes, telling me my sacrifice the past week had been the right thing to do. "How 'bout if you watch from the sound booth with Nick?" he suggested to me.

"Is that okay?" I asked. Though I tried with all my might, I couldn't keep the eagerness out of my voice.

"Guess you have an apprentice, Nick." Blu gave me a tiny squeeze, and I might have melted a little.

I spent the rest of the afternoon in heaven, or as close as I'd ever been outside of my bed with Blu in it. Through my headphones, the man's voice alternately caressed me and teased me, enticed me and soothed me. Each member of the band contributed his own unique sound, but Balefire wouldn't be the same band without Blu's voice fronting it, something I already knew as a fan but now reverberated through me as I listened to the band build a record.

"Pretty sweet, huh?" Nick said several hours later when the team decided they'd finished the track.

"Amazing," I breathed.

The guys were fist-bumping each other and laughing when they entered the sound booth a few minutes later.

"You like that one, Ashleigh?" Dakota asked. Though laughter colored his tone, there was something serious going on in his eyes.

"I loved it. That one will top *Billboard's* charts within a week after you release it," I said with all sincerity.

Dakota's grin could have lit up all of Denver. "You hear that, Blu? Your music connoisseur girlfriend thinks I write number ones. Fuck, yeah."

He fist-bumped me, and it felt like I'd somehow become a part of the Balefire family. Especially when Blu slipped in behind me and wrapped his arms around me like we'd been together since the inception of the band.

Before I could dwell on the surrealness of the whole experience, Emory appeared at the sound booth door to announce the chef had something prepared for us, and would the band please take some time over dinner to peruse the tour schedule?

♪

Two weeks later, I was flying over the Atlantic in Balefire's private jet, accompanying the band on their European tour. We were going to be out of the country for six weeks before returning stateside for a series of concerts leading up to Christmas. From heated exchanges I'd overheard, I gathered Garrett had wanted the band to play shows over Christmas as well, but Jack had flatly refused and Blu backed him. Somewhere in there, something was said about women in the picture messing up the dynamics of the band, and I wondered for the thousandth time since meeting him if Blu was only going to break my heart or tear it completely to shreds.

Which had me attempting to remain as unobtrusive as possible. Being the only woman traveling with the band made me stand out anyway. The plush captain's chairs spaced at intervals around the expansive cabin allowed me to sit away from the guys who were enjoying the bar and each other at the front of the cabin. Inside jokes about groupies and wake-up calls, which I decided I didn't want to know about, flew faster than the jet we were flying in.

Balefire would start their tour in London playing Wembley Stadium, something I couldn't wait to experience. Growing up an Air Force brat, I'd spent quite a bit of time on a base outside of London. I remembered Christmas in the UK capital as being modern and Dickensian all at once, and I'd loved it. Seeing Blu and Balefire perform there was a fantasy I hadn't even dreamed.

The downside of the experience, of course, was missing the fall in my garden, something I'd looked forward to all summer. Diane assured me she'd take care of it and send me photos every week, so that would have to be enough. To make up for missing it, I had plans for touring some European gardens on days off if I could talk Blu into it.

The man in question found his way to me, turning the chair beside me to face me. "Ashleigh Baker, what do you think of the tour so far?" The wicked gleam in his eyes put me on alert.

"This jet is amazing, and you boys take your beer seriously."

"I take you seriously too. Know what's behind that door at the back of the cabin?" He gestured to the door in question.

"The head?"

"The one for the cabin is through the door to the right. Through the big door in the middle is a comfy king-size bed. I have it on good authority that the sheets are fresh and one thousand-thread-count Egyptian cotton. Wanna go check it out?"

"Blu! Everyone here will know where we are and what we're doing if we go behind that door," I hissed.

"And the problem with that is what again?" He tapped his chin in phony contemplation. "Oh, yeah. They'll be jealous." He waggled his eyebrows, and I had to smile.

Placing his hand on my knee then sliding it slowly up my thigh, he lowered his voice. "You know you want to, Ashleigh."

"My mama always told me good things come to those who wait." I placed my hand over his to stop his progress up my thigh. His touch sent tingles dancing all the way to my center, but an outburst of laughter from the area around the bar reminded me where we were. I looked away from Blu to catch Tron giving us a speculative look. As wild as I was for Blu, something I'd grudgingly admitted to myself and to my friend Jamie weeks ago, I couldn't have sex with him with the rest of the band on the other side of a small door on a jet.

Blu looked over his shoulder to see what had grabbed my attention, and Tron smirked at him before saluting him with his beer. Blu nodded and turned back to me.

"You're right, darlin'. Good things come to those who wait. We're going to join the mile-high club together one day, but not today." He leaned back in his chair and shot me a lopsided grin before tipping back his bottle of beer and draining it. "Tell me, Ash, what are you looking forward to on this tour?"

"Everything," I said. "Especially the chance to see a dozen Balefire shows. After all, you guys already were my all-time favorite band before we met."

"Yet I haven't heard you sing a single lyric of any of our songs," he challenged.

"I'll say some lyrics, if you need proof."

"Okay. But how do I know you know the tune?"

"Honestly, Blu, you don't want to hear me sing. I'll scar your ears for life," I said with a laugh.

"Your laugh sounds like a melody. Did you know that? I love to hear you laugh, so I'm pretty sure I'd like to hear you sing." He put his hands on my knees and turned up the wattage of his smile.

"Not on a plane flying over the ocean. I'd rather you be on solid ground when you take a flying leap to escape my caterwauling."

"As stubborn as you are, babe, I'm even more. Keep that in mind," he warned as he slid his hand up my thigh and squeezed.

I gasped and tried to move away, but he prevented me with his other hand on the arm of my seat, caging me in with his body. "In the end, I always get what I want," he said with a gleam in his eye that I didn't trust.

He leaned in and kissed me, a soft brush of his lips at first before he tasted my bottom lip with his tongue, a move he knew I couldn't resist. Without hesitation, I opened for him, and the gentle heat of soft lips whipped into a flame of desire that left me weak. Of their own volition, my hands slipped up the nape of Blu's neck and over his head to tangle fingers in his hair and hold his mouth to mine. We kissed each other into a conflagration that threatened to burn us to cinders even as we flew over half the world's water.

A not-so-discreet throat clearing from somewhere nearby cooled me off enough to resume normal hearing rather than the roar of desire in my ears.

"There's a perfectly serviceable bed at the back of the plane. Unless you want an audience, in which case, don't stop on our account." The sneer in Garrett's voice washed over me like a bucket of ice water, and I tried to melt back into the cushions of my seat away from Blu who'd moved barely a fraction of an inch from me.

"Fuck off, Garrett." He rested his forehead on mine and said for my ears only, "First thing when we reach our hotel, we are taking care of each other. I promise."

Chapter Nineteen

Blu

I FORGOT THE ONLY way to stave off jet lag is to stay up all day after an overnight flight. Which meant I couldn't keep my promise to Ashleigh. Garrett had us running from the time we touched down until well after midnight, giving interviews to the press and catching dinner with some local celebrities. By the time we checked into our hotel, we'd been awake for nearly two days, and neither of us had the energy for bedroom shenanigans.

We spent the next day on sound checks and last-minute rehearsals. Before I could catch my breath, it was showtime. My boys and I were so amped to try out our new material in front of a live audience. With the Brits being some of our biggest fans, we were especially excited to hear their reaction to some cuts from our new album.

Of course, there was the additional attraction of knowing Ashleigh would watch the entire show from a VIP seat in front of the stage. I wanted her to have the full experience, especially after she told me she sat so far back the only other time she'd seen one of our shows. Rehearsals for the last month didn't count since she hadn't seen the pyrotechnics and lights when we were in the studio.

We opened the concert with a flash of green light followed by the blistering guitar solo Dakota incorporated into the song Ashleigh had liked so much when we recorded it. The crowd roared its approval then nearly broke the sound barrier when Jack and Tron layered in the beat behind Dakota accompanied by more flashes of light in shades of orange, yellow, and red. At last, I joined the show with a primal scream—I'd had to warm up for thirty minutes to pull it off as an introduction, but we wanted to set the tone of the performance immediately.

When I settled into the melody, the lights came up, and I instinctively searched for Ashleigh. Finding her in the VIP section stage left, I smiled and sang directly to her. Her eyes rounded before she smiled back at me, and I literally felt my heart expand in my chest. Nothing in the world could compare to playing music in front of ninety thousand screaming fans except playing for the one person in the world who truly mattered.

That thought flying through my mind nearly knocked me off my game before I looked away from its source and concentrated on my job. As I sang to the crowd, the usual assortment of sexy and skimpy lingerie rained down on the front of the stage and occasionally landed on one of us. Between songs, Dakota did his regular bit of admiring some piece or another, draping a bra over his mic stand, attaching a thong to the pegs of his guitar, shooting a pair of bikini panties up at Jack on his massive traps so he could enjoy the fun too. Of course, I encouraged this behavior by commenting on how hot English roses were, and Tron even theatrically pocketed a pair of zebra-striped panties after admiring them for everyone's enjoyment.

Throughout the show, though, I couldn't keep my gaze from straying stage left, and always, Ashleigh's smile shone up at me, rivaling the light show our tech crew created for this tour. A couple of times I even caught her singing along to our songs, and I winked at her, causing a rosy glow to spread across her face. But she didn't stop singing along with the rest of the crowd and me. After the finale and the three encores the audience demanded, we finally left the stage for the night, our clothes soaked with sweat, our spirits flying. The sold-out show came together even better than we'd rehearsed. Some of that had to do with the adrenaline rush of playing live, which always resulted in a heightened performance. But most of it was the audience's reaction to our new material. Judging from their applause, Ashleigh had been right—we had a number one song on our new album and maybe three or four more. The kicker? We hadn't played them all yet.

We were euphoric when we entered the suite for our private after-party. We had a ritual of just the band and crew partying together after the first show on a tour. Tonight was no exception. Except I wanted Ashleigh to be there. Even though I'd had my way with having her at rehearsals and now on tour didn't mean I would always get my way, as Tron so pointedly made clear.

"I like her, Blu. I really do. She's good for you. Tonight you sang better than any time I've heard you, and that's sayin' something. But this party is a band thing, a man thing, and she doesn't have any place here."

I pulled a face, and I'm sure Tron could see the wheels turning in my head, so he preempted me. "Think of it from her point of view. Flying alone with the four of us and Garrett makes her uncomfortable. Imagine how she's going to feel with all the roadies and techies we bring along. We do this party for them. Think about it, Blu."

Dammit. Tron was right. But I didn't have to like it.

"Fine. I'll send her back to the hotel. Save me a beer," I said as I walked over to the green room where Ashleigh awaited me.

"Hey babe. You like the show?" I asked nonchalantly as I entered to find her chatting with some staff who were preparing to move the refreshments left over from the preshow to the giant space they'd set up for the post-show party.

"Blu, I've never witnessed anything more incredible in my life. You blew me away."

The sincerity in her voice, in her smile, in her eyes made me feel ten feet tall and bulletproof. All by herself, the woman did more for my ego than ninety thousand screaming fans.

"Come here," I demanded.

She didn't argue or give me one of her flip comments about my rock star entitlement. She walked into my arms and kissed me like I was the only man on the planet.

Which is when Garrett interrupted us. "Thought I'd find you here, Blu. Maybe you want to speed this up? The guys are waiting."

"I know where the party is, and I don't need an escort. Be there in a few."

Garrett stood there for several seconds like he didn't believe me before he shrugged and walked back out the door behind one of the caterers who was struggling with an unwieldy platter. Garrett didn't even offer to hold the door for the woman, which pissed me off, so with a hasty, "Excuse me, babe," I let Ashleigh go to hold the door long enough for one person to walk through. A satisfied smile might have crossed my face when Garrett yelled, "What the fuck?" as the door started to close in his face when I let it go behind the caterer.

As I took my woman back into my arms, I tried to explain. "Ash, the band has a tradition of a private after-party on the first night on tour. It's only this one, I promise." I cringed inwardly with the knowledge I'd already made one promise on this tour so far, and I hadn't kept it. "I'll be back at the hotel in a couple of hours, okay?"

Ashleigh looked nonplussed, and I couldn't blame her. Yet she didn't whine or make a fuss. Instead, she nodded and tried to step around me. Oh no. I was having none of that.

She stood stiffly when I stopped her progress by pulling her back into my arms. "It's not what you think," I said quietly into her ear. "It's only the band, the roadies, and the tech crew. No groupies, no fans, no women. That's why you can't be there. I'll be alone when I come to you at our suite later."

I kissed her, and even though she tried to pretend she didn't feel anything, eventually, she gave in and softened against me, her mouth molding to mine in the sweetest way only Ashleigh could do. After a while, I pulled away enough to say, "The town car is waiting right outside the back doors. Bailey Saunders, our head road engineer, will walk you out to it. I'll see you in a bit, okay?"

She nodded again, and I followed her out into the corridor where Bailey waited.

♪

When I awoke at the crack of nearly noon, I found myself wrapped around Ashleigh's soft, warm body, my morning wood happily pillowed along the cleft of her ass. While she slept peacefully, I spent some quiet time looking at her, running my fingers over the satin perfection of the curves of her shoulder, the side of her breast, the sweet indentation of her waist, the pretty swell of her hip, my libido in the back seat for once as I admired the incredibly beautiful woman in my bed.

Weird.

On the other occasions on tour when I woke up with a woman in my bed, my first thoughts had nothing to do with touching her purely for the sake of memorizing every inch of her. With Ashleigh, all I wanted was to touch her inside and out.

Where the fuck did that come from?

My fingers stilled on the top of her hip as her body tensed with wakefulness. I slid my hand over her taut belly and held her to me the second before she tried to bolt out of bed.

"Hey gorgeous girl, where do you think you're going?"

"Blu! H-how did I end up in your bed?"

"I put you here."

"When? How?"

"I came back to the hotel from the concert to find my bed empty, so I took a little tour of the suite and discovered you next door. You were out cold, so I gathered you up and carried you in here. You were in the wrong bed, but at least you were in the right state of dress."

I pushed up on my elbow to gauge her expression and caught a smile curving her cheek. As much as I wanted to pursue where this particular conversation led, another took precedence.

"You wanna tell me why you were in the wrong bed?"

Her smile slipped away as she turned her face into her pillow, her words muffled. "I didn't want to presume on your space."

"What the fuck does that mean?"

She must have heard the irritation in my tone because she turned slightly to look at me at last. "You're a rock star on tour. You suggested I leave the venue after the show because the boys needed a band night out. I thought that meant I should sleep somewhere else."

"Ash, you're my girl. My girl sleeps in my bed, even when the only thing she's doing is sleeping. Are we clear?"

"Um—"

"Listen, I know I'm new to this whole exclusivity thing, but what I'm figuring out is that having you all to myself is the best time I've ever had. I don't intend to fuck it up. You pickin' up what I'm puttin' down?"

Mercifully, she laughed, and my dick perked right back up. She'd had him worried there for a minute that she didn't understand she was the only one who turned me on these days. Fact was, from the first time I laid eyes on her, Ashleigh Baker had been the only woman to hold my attention. Right now, I didn't want to think too hard about why. Right now, I wanted to remind her why she should always share my bed.

Ashleigh

The tour took us to several of the major cities in Europe. After London, we traveled to Paris, Vienna, and Prague, a place Balefire had never visited before, so we spent a couple of days there. Then it was on to Hamburg and Munich where the band encountered another audience that loved Balefire as much as the Brits. They performed in Barcelona and Madrid before moving on to Lisbon. Next came Athens with the guys wishing they could perform in the Parthenon but settling for entertaining eighty thousand screaming fans in the Olympic Stadium. The tour ended in Scandinavia where Balefire rocked venues in Copenhagen and Stockholm.

In every city, I insisted on finding and touring a garden, something that became a standing joke with both the roadies and the band. I used the fancy camera the magazine loaned me to take photos of flowers and plants almost as much as I used it to take photos of the tour. All the guys teased me without mercy, but instead of taking it personally, I cajoled and teased and even bribed them to come along and see what all the fuss was about. By the last stops on the tour, several of them were finding gardens for me to explore.

My favorite one was at Schonbrunn Palace in Vienna. I could have spent days in the Orangery alone with the lingering heady fragrance of its hothouse citrus trees. Dakota nearly had us kicked out, though, when he picked an apple from one of the special apple trees growing inside the greenhouse and ate it as we wandered through the greenery. The perfect geometric patterns of the massive gardens leading to the main entrance of the palace were intended to impress dignitaries, adversaries, and regular people visiting the palace back in the day. As I studied the gardens, I tried to figure out how I could train my petunias at home to grow to such uniform heights as those edging the gravel paths of the garden. The exotic animals—camels, elephants, even a leviathan—sculpted out of living shrubs fascinated me, and I took so many photos Blu threatened to steal my camera. The gardens looked like a painting done by a French master, and I couldn't gaze at them enough. The wine tasting at the end of our tour certainly helped my cause with the guys too.

Blu went with me to every single garden I wanted to see. Of course, whenever we toured one, just the two of us, he sneaked me into some secluded bower or found a bench hidden in a hedge. Dragging me there, he kissed me senseless. When we made it to the inside of a particularly tricky maze in the middle of a park in Paris, he "rewarded" us by taking a tour of my panties with his fingers. When we emerged to find a long line awaiting a trip through the maze, I'm sure my face rivaled the blood red roses along the exterior hedges. After each of our private tours, Blu would pick a flower or find some pretty leaf and tuck it into my hair—or my cleavage— and smile.

Though I tried desperately to keep my heart distant and enjoy the ride that was touring with Balefire, Blu insisted I was his girlfriend. By the end of the European leg of the tour, I'd started to believe he meant it.

When we entered our hotel suite after the Copenhagen show, he hauled me up against him, my back to his front, and whispered against my ear, "Ash, this tour has the been the best one I've ever done, and it's all because you've been with me."

He nuzzled my hair away from my neck and nibbled his way from my shoulder to the sensitive spot he'd discovered behind my ear.

"Yeah?" I asked. "Checking out all of those gardens really did it for you, huh?" I teased—or tried to. With his mouth moving over my skin as he tasted me, and his hands exploring the sensitive skin of my belly beneath my shirt, I sounded breathy even to my own ears.

"The garden tours certainly added some culture to it, especially that maze you insisted on exploring."

I could hear the smile in his voice as I tried hard not to react to his words evoking the memory of that day. But I'm sure he detected my belly muscles tightening because his explorations took a decidedly southern direction.

"You up for recreating the moment, Ash?"

Already he had the fly of my jeans undone enough to slide a hand inside them. He played his fingers over the top of my clit, and when I squirmed at his touch, he held me closer with his other hand. While he touched me with his body, he also touched me with his words.

"You're the best thing that's ever happened to me, Ashleigh. You've made me happy in ways I didn't even know I was missing until you came into my life and showed me. You're beautiful, intelligent, sexy, and easy to be around. I'm damn glad you have a thing for gardens. If you didn't, you might not have moved next door to my mom, and we might never have met. I would hate that." I could feel his smile on my skin. "So I like your little garden obsession. And you like this."

While he mesmerized me with his pretty words, he'd pushed my jeans and panties down enough to access my pussy, dipping his long musician's fingers inside me. Now I was moaning as well as squirming against him.

"That's it, babe. Let me take you for a little ride."

He stopped talking to lick and kiss and nip the side of my throat while his other hand moved from my belly to my breast where he toyed with my nipple through the lace of my bra. All the time, he never stopped playing with my pussy. I lifted my hands to hold his head to me, anchoring myself to him while I ground my ass against the front of his jeans. He was deliciously hard, and I wanted to feel that hardness elsewhere.

"More. Please! I need *more*," I pleaded.

"I do love it when you beg, Ash." He added another finger to the party, his thumb expertly pleasuring my clit.

In seconds, I was flying off into outer space, screaming his name as I came apart in his hands.

Before I could catch my breath, he'd spun me to face the wall, and I braced my hands on it as I listened to him tear open a condom packet.

"This what you wanted?" he asked as he guided himself into me from behind.

"Blu!" I screamed when he filled me full.

He thrust into me again. "I asked you a question, babe."

The sound of his words coming through gritted teeth thrilled me, knowing I wasn't the only one lost to sensation.

"Yes," I panted. "Yes. This is what I wanted."

"You could have had this in the gardens if you could control your volume."

The grin in his voice might have ticked me off if he hadn't chosen that moment to rub his finger over my clit while he plucked at my nipple with his other hand. I pushed back into him, silently demanding more as a loud moan escaped my throat.

"There's my girl. Come on, Ash. Take it. Take it all."

The smell of sex, the loud slaps of skin on skin, his clever fingers working me as he pumped into me drove me to the edge. Sliding his hand up to my collarbone, he pulled me back toward him and bit down where my neck met my shoulder. Waves of sensation overcame me, and I screamed my climax so loud Blu covered my mouth with his hand. A couple more thrusts, a grunt, and his groan echoed mine as he joined me on our freefall over the edge into bliss.

As I came down from the ether into which he'd blasted me, he whispered in my ear, "Oh yeah, Ash, I've especially enjoyed the garden excursions you've insisted on taking during this tour."

Afterward, we headed to bed where he spent most of what was left of the night showing me, in so many ways I lost count, how happy he was that I'd spent the last several weeks on tour with him. I didn't want to give in to my feelings for him, but it turns out that was never going to be an option. Blu Connolly's expertise as a musician came from a deep place of determination inside him, and when he turned that determination onto having me and making me fall for him, I didn't stand a chance.

CHAPTER TWENTY

Blu

I LEANED BACK IN my seat and thought about what would happen now. We were flying home to start the US leg of our tour with a half-time show at the Dallas-Washington Thanksgiving Day football game. Our tour would be over in a couple of weeks. Thanks to Jack for demanding time with his new family, we'd have a month hiatus over Christmas. The way I saw it, I'd been with Ashleigh since July, my longest relationship outside of with my mom and the band and certainly the longest I'd ever experienced with a woman. That thought probably should have set alarm bells clanging through my brain, but as she slept in the seat next to me, I found myself trying to figure out a new plan for keeping her near me.

One thing I'd learned about her was she didn't want anyone giving her a free ride. The whole garden thing aside, she'd spent our entire tour so far working as hard as we did. She'd submitted at least ten articles to *Rolling Stone,* becoming a traveling correspondent for the magazine. Ashleigh's work spoke for itself, which was good since Camille Watson, her former boss, wrote a scathing letter to the editor after Ash published her first piece, the article from the interview with me that Watson fucked up. Instead of sabotaging Ashleigh's career—again—Watson's letter seemed to fuel a demand for more articles. In the end, Ashleigh profiled each of the band members and wrote about the grueling work of the roadies and the tech crew. All of which did fantastic things for our PR leading up to our shows stateside.

Her current article would be about the music videos Garrett decided we needed to make from our live shows. In October, Nick, our producer, had finished and released the new album we were supporting with the tour. Garrett thought the time was right to add some videos. He'd lined up a director, some big fan of the band who made videos for bands like Godsmack and Shinedown, and had a secret plan for the one we'd make in Dallas. Something about the way Garrett worked on this new project bugged me. It also irritated me the way he always checked Ashleigh out and tried to chat her up, sometimes even when I had my arms around her.

Like this one night after our show in Lisbon.

"So, Ashleigh, would you like to have a drink with me?" Garrett had asked as I stood with my arm around her near the bar.

"I'm with Blu, Garrett," she responded.

"Yeah, so, about that drink, Ashleigh," he said like he hadn't even heard her response. "I wanted to talk to you about the profiles you've written so far."

"I've published them, already, Garrett. The time to talk about them was weeks ago."

I could hear the exasperation in her voice, but Garrett seemed oblivious.

"Yeah. I read them. They were great, but there were some things I think you missed and maybe want to consider in your next article."

"I'm writing about the roadies in the next one, so I'm not sure what could be relevant from the band profiles."

I'd stood there watching the conversation like a spectator at a tennis match. Garrett would lob a ball, and Ashleigh would overhead smash it back at him. Yet he didn't seem to catch on how much he wasn't even in the game.

It didn't take long before I had enough. "In case you didn't notice, I'm standing right here, Garrett. Move on. This lady is spoken for. Has been since the day you met her."

"You used to share." Garrett pouted.

"Not with you," I said, and I didn't even try to keep the surliness out of my tone.

"I don't know why you bother with her. She's a writer, nothing special," he complained like Ashleigh wasn't standing right beside me.

She stiffened beneath my arm, and I pulled her even tighter against me. "Which begs the question of why you won't back the fuck off, Garrett. I tried to keep this civilized, tried to spare you the embarrassment, man, but you won't quit. Ashleigh. Is. My. Girlfriend," I snarled at him. "She's not a casual fan or a groupie or whatever. She's my woman. She also happens to be a kick-ass writer whose articles are jacking up all kinds of interest in this tour. So stop insulting her and embarrassing yourself by panting after her."

I pulled Ashleigh away from the bar then because I could tell she was upset.

"What is wrong with that guy, Blu? I've done my best to be professional and courteous to him, but honestly, he makes my skin crawl."

"I'll take care of him, babe."

It was the only time I heard her say something negative about Garrett, but it was enough for me to watch him around her and to have the rest of the band make sure to interrupt if they ever saw the two of them together. Ashleigh never encouraged him. If anything, she went out of her way to avoid him. Whatever the problem was, it was Garrett's.

Beneath my arm, Ashleigh shifted in her seat. Lightly, I stroked my hand over her hair before settling her head on my shoulder.

With a tiny sigh, she snuggled in closer to me, her breathing light and even. As I watched her sleep, another thought occurred to me. Though we'd been together so much, we hadn't had much downtime to talk to each other. Something else I needed to work on—extended time alone with Ashleigh. I wondered what she might think about a ski vacation over Christmas for the two of us. A sound from the front of the cabin pulled my eyes away from her to land on Garrett. The expression on his face as he stared at Ashleigh defied description. Anger? Lust? Perplexity? When I moved to catch his eye, he glanced away.

Tightening my arm around my lady, I held her to me as we flew through the night.

Ashleigh

The half-time show in Dallas put everyone in the band and on the crew in high spirits. Balefire had played a half-time show the previous Thanksgiving to rave reviews, which meant they were invited back for an encore performance. This one, they all assured me, would be even bigger and better than the last one. They'd be playing the chart topper from their new album for the first time for the American public on national television. They'd also be debuting a new song Jack had written, something special to him that the band had kept quiet from everyone, even from Garrett I think.

Once we arrived in the States, Garrett was so busy setting up the music video that he didn't have time to follow me around, make up reasons to be near me, or alternately insult me or come on to me even in Blu's presence, all of which was a huge relief. I could concentrate on how the band and crew prepared for the show and the video simultaneously and how hard they all worked to entertain the fans.

When we arrived at AT&T Stadium in Dallas, I couldn't believe the size of the venue. The state's residents weren't kidding—everything is bigger in the Lone Star State. The thought of playing before a hundred thousand fans would have terrified me, but it energized the guys. They laughed and joked and generally appeared more relaxed than I'd ever seen them as they rehearsed for their show. The tech crew shipped in even more pyrotechnics than anything they'd had in Europe. The pyrotechnics required a professional specialty crew from some tiny Montana town that produced fireworks for events like the Superbowl. Even though I'd grown up in a military family, I'd never understand the boyish enthusiasm for blowing things up, which seemed to possess otherwise grown men. Fascinated, I watched as both crews prepared for the event, their laughter and excitement showing how much they anticipated the fireworks part of the show.

As the football teams played the first half of the game, I focused on the live preparations for the half-time show. Like a well-oiled machine, the roadies assembled at their designated stations. While I could see their lips moving as they spoke into their headsets, I couldn't hear anything over the roar of the fans watching the last seconds of the first half of the game. Somewhere along the line, I'd moved from writing notes on my phone to speaking them into it and transcribing them later. The choice gave my writing more immediacy, my articles more of the flavor of the semicontrolled chaos that passed for Balefire's concert preparation. This time, I added a few hasty words with my stylus—I wasn't sure my voice would record clearly over the noise of the crowd, which echoed down the tunnel leading out onto the field.

When I hustled out with the crew to station myself in my designated space near the stage, Garrett caught me. "It's vitally important I speak to you after the show. Meet me in the green room afterward, please."

His demeanor was so professional and uptight, especially for him, that I wondered what could be up. Still, I nodded my assent and returned to trying to add some notes into my phone over the din of the crowd.

The second the portable stage rolled to a stop in the middle of the field, the lights in the stadium dimmed. A minute later, they flashed back on after an explosion of fireworks rippled around the field to accompany Dakota's opening guitar solo. The crowd lost its collective mind as Balefire launched into their new hit. When they finished it, the fans barely quieted down enough to hear the opening strains of a tune I'd never heard before, and I realized we were listening to Jack's newest song. "Far Away" softened the mood from Dakota's raucous opening, but when the song concluded, if anything the audience's approval of it thundered through the stadium, and I knew Balefire had delivered its biggest hit to date.

The band followed that up with a couple of fan favorites from previous years accompanied by a light and fireworks show to rival any New Year's Eve or Fourth of July extravaganza. To say they blew me away would have been the understatement of all time. I was so caught up in the show that I forgot about the music video crew filming the event until a cameraman near me panned the crowd around the stage and stopped on me. When I realized what he did, I melted back into the people around me and comforted myself with the idea that the footage would likely end up in the editor's trash folder.

Back in the green room, I tried to find Blu, but instead, Garrett met me. "The boys have another part of the video to film, so Blu asked me to escort you to the town car. They'll be a couple hours, and he didn't want you to be stuck here."

"I don't mind. I could watch the second half of the game while I wait."

"I didn't think you liked football. All those intimidating men bashing each other around out there." Garrett sniffed, and I couldn't decide if he sounded surprised or disdainful. Either way, I think I was insulted—or meant to be. Before I could respond, he added, "At any rate, you need to return to the hotel since we'll need the town car back here to pick up the band, and traffic after the game will be brutal."

I hadn't thought about that. "Fine. Great. I'll wait for him at the hotel then." Though I would have rather shared my excitement with the band themselves, Blu especially, Garrett was the only one around. "They put on a great show tonight, didn't they?"

"One of the best I've ever seen. Having so many cameras on them probably did that," he said, and I swear I could see him visibly puffing himself up for his contribution.

"Jack's new song is incredible. Did you hear it before tonight?"

His face clouded for a split second. "They kept that one from me. I take it that was your first time hearing it too?"

"Yeah. What a wonderful surprise," I gushed. I couldn't help it. The song was that good.

"It's a surprise all right," he said under his breath, but I heard him all the same and wondered why the song upset him. Turning his attention back to me, he pointed to the exit. "I have to get back to the band and the video, so I need you to hustle on out to the car."

He reached for my elbow, but I deftly stepped around him and headed up the ramp to the VIP parking area where we'd arrived before the game. When I saw the car idling there, a bad feeling stole over me.

♪

After I returned to the two-bedroom suite Blu and I shared, I ordered room service—turkey, dressing, mashed potatoes, the works—and slipped into the baby doll robe Blu liked so much. As I awaited my dinner, I called my parents to wish them a happy holiday. I called Diane to wish her well too. We talked for nearly an hour about the show, which she'd watched with some friends from the diner. It felt weird to be eating Thanksgiving dinner alone in a luxury hotel suite, and more than once my thoughts strayed to Blu and the video the band was shooting.

At last, I turned down the covers on the bed and pulled out my laptop. Popping my earbuds in, I started transcribing my notes. Somewhere in the midst of my transcription, it occurred to me I should have stayed at the game to see how the rest of the video was filmed since that was part of my article. That's when a truly awful thought intruded. Did Garrett want to sabotage me now after I'd turned down his advances? Was that why he wanted me to leave so much? But he said Blu had asked that I leave. Which didn't make sense at all, now that I thought about it.

Loud feminine laughter and someone bumping against the walls in the hall outside our suite interrupted my thoughts. I pulled out my earbuds and looked up in time to hear someone keying into our room. Before I could react, the door flew open, and Blu stumbled in with his arms around two busty women who between them maybe wore a scrap of clothing. He kissed one on the mouth and turned to kiss the other one when he caught sight of me on the bed. A puzzled look flitted over his face before the woman who hadn't been kissed put her hand on his chin and tugged him to her.

I didn't wait to see what happened next. With my laptop in one hand and my phone in the other, I launched off the bed and dashed into the adjoining bedroom where, mercifully, my still mostly packed suitcase lay open on the bed. On my way into the room, I elbowed the door closed behind me, dropped my things into my suitcase, and tore off my robe, flinging it in on top of my computer. Trying not to think about what was going on in the other room, I threw on the clothes I'd worn earlier and slammed my suitcase shut. I gathered up my purse and raced out of the room into the hall.

Out in the hallway, people were laughing and drinking—so many people. The video shoot must have been a success, and the after-party was taking place in the hall right outside the band's hotel rooms. It took me several minutes to maneuver my suitcase through the throng to reach the elevators. Someone called out to me—I think it was Garrett—but I didn't stop moving. Once the doors on the elevator closed, I leaned back and took a breath, the first one since Blu stole it when he walked into our room with two women in his arms.

Then I was gulping in air as I desperately tried to hold back the sobs threatening to erupt from my chest. How could he? He said he cared about me. He said he'd never felt so connected to another woman before. He said I was special. And I believed him. How many other women had heard those same lines over the years? Dozens? Hundreds?

That day in my tiny house when I'd met Dakota, he wanted to share me with Blu. Apparently, Blu had finally become bored with having one woman. Had he wanted to try three? Was that why he sent me ahead? Because he knew I'd be waiting for him in bed? Or was this his not-so-subtle way of telling me we were over?

The doors to the elevator opened to a bustling lobby, effectively cutting off my jumbled thoughts. So many more people. Were they all there for the band? For the party? The one going on upstairs in our suite? I pushed my way into a nearby restroom and barely made it to a toilet before I threw up. I'm not sure how long I sat on the floor of the stall before I finally decided I'd retched up all my Thanksgiving dinner as images of Blu and those women swirled in my head. Rousing myself at last, I splashed cold water on my face and rinsed out my mouth. I grabbed my suitcase and wove my way through a mass of people to reach the concierge desk.

After handing the clerk my key card, I stumbled out of the hotel.

"Please drive me to the airport," I implored the taxi driver as he loaded my suitcase into the trunk of his car.

It being Thanksgiving Day following a big game, the airport seemed deserted when we arrived. Everyone must have been out celebrating the holiday and the win. I creamed my credit card buying a standby ticket for the first open seat to Denver and tried to keep my shit together long enough to pass through security. Mercifully, I only had to wait for about an hour before an airline attendant announced an open seat, and I was in the air headed for home.

CHAPTER TWENTY-ONE

Blu

TWO MONTHS. IT had been two fucking long months since that awful night when I'd walked into our suite with the two actresses from the video and surprised Ashleigh in bed. The camera crew behind us had caught only a flash of Ashleigh as she raced out of the room ahead of us. Why the hell she was there in the first place, I had no idea. When I asked why she wasn't with us to finish the video shoot, Garrett told me she'd scored an interview with one of the football players, something she thought she could use for another publication. The way he wouldn't quite meet my eyes as he said it should have warned me something wasn't right.

We were on the road until Christmas, so there was nothing I could do about her not responding to any of my texts or returning the messages I left on her phone. After a couple of days, she blocked me, and I knew I had to do something special to convince her to even talk to me. Which was impossible until Christmas. That old Theory of a Deadman song "What Was I Thinking?" kept playing on a loop in my head. Though I knew I'd fucked up by agreeing to let the video crew follow me into our suite, which should have been off-limits no matter what, I needed Ashleigh to know none of that shit was real.

At the end of our European tour, she'd started believing in me, believing in us. And I got cocky. She was mine. Hadn't I been telling her and anyone else who would listen that she was my girl? She had to believe it. Yet on a night when I walked on air following one of the best performances of my life, I forgot the one thing about me that Ashleigh had believed from the start. I was a player—in every sense of the word. The night after the Dallas show, all that cockiness came back and punched me square in the mouth.

Still, I thought I could make it right, but when I arrived home, Mom met me in Ashleigh's front yard after the town car dropped me off. I was pounding on her door, but Ashleigh wasn't home. I freaked the fuck out when Mom blew my world to hell when she told me Ash had moved out and left no forwarding address. She told Mom the two of them could remain in contact as long as Mom didn't bring me up in conversation, which killed her. Especially after she saw the way I reacted to Ashleigh's disappearance from my life. At no time had Ash revealed to Mom where she'd moved or what she was doing now. All I knew was that she was out there somewhere.

A couple of weeks earlier, I'd discovered through Benson Strauss that she continued to write for him. So I arranged for her to be assigned to cover an up-and-coming band while she followed the tour that Strauss had already assigned her. Conveniently, the band she followed would be coming through Charleston, South Carolina right behind our performance there, so we stayed an extra day to play the set that would bring her to me.

I instructed the crew to watch for her, and when she arrived at the venue, a local brewery that featured live acts, a couple of roadies would escort her to an office behind the bar to wait for me. They had my permission to lock her in if that's what it took.

I'd talked the guys into doing an acoustic set at the brewery on a night off after we resumed the American leg of our tour, and they agreed. Because of where I positioned myself on the small stage, I noticed Ashleigh the instant she walked into the bar. It took her several seconds to realize the sound she heard belonged to us and not to a cover band. She stood in the shadows near the back of the venue and listened, and I sang directly to her.

Tonight, we'd toned it down, playing mostly ballads, which is what I'd been writing for her. The timing couldn't have been more perfect as she heard me sing one of the many songs I'd written for her—something we had yet to record. It cheered me that she seemed rooted to the spot, unable to look away from me any more than I could look away from her. After the applause died down at the conclusion of our song, I noticed her turning to leave and two of the guys intercepting her. Giving a tiny sigh of relief that so far my plan was working, I spoke into the microphone.

"Thanks for indulging us with this little experiment, folks. We have a couple more songs to share before we return the stage to the band you came out to see tonight."

Even without the amplifiers and the fireworks and the lights, the audience responded to us with a roar of approval. Judging from the grins on my band mates' faces, they'd enjoyed our little experiment too. We played our final two songs and exited the stage at the back while our crew gathered up our equipment.

"She here?" Dakota asked when he followed me out the stage door.

"Yeah. Arrived as we finished 'My Beauty.' She's waiting for me in the office."

"You hope," Dakota said with a smirk.

"We all hope," Tron added from somewhere behind me. "Jack was bad enough on the last part of the tour when he and Clio were separated. These last months with you doing without Ashleigh have *not* been a joyride. She better be waiting in that room. That's all I gotta say."

I left the rest of the band and walked back to the office where

Bailey Saunders and one of his road crew stood guard outside the door.

"She's spitting mad, just so you know, Blu," was all Bailey said as he stepped away from the door.

Nodding to him, I said, "Thanks for helping me out, man."

I faced the door, took a deep breath, and turned the handle.

Ashleigh stood on the other side of the massive walnut and chrome desk in the middle of the office and glared at me as I entered the room, closing the door behind me.

"What little game are you playing here, Blu?" she demanded, arms crossed tightly over her gorgeous chest.

"You blocked me, Ash. You wouldn't respond to me. You moved away from your house and left no forwarding address. You left me nothing else to do but this." I tried my damnedest to keep the hurt out of my voice.

"You're surprised why again? You sent me ahead to the hotel so you could show up with your kind of party, knowing full well that I'm not into sharing. At. All. And I certainly didn't want to watch," she snapped.

I could tell she had to work at sounding harsh and nasty—the quiver of her lower lip gave her away. Slowly, I circled the desk toward her.

"Those women were *actresses*. They were part of the video. Didn't you see the cameras coming in the door behind us?"

"Which explains why you were so into kissing them that you didn't notice me on the bed at first when you slammed through the door? Jesus, Blu. Give me a little credit."

"The director gave me the cue about how to enter the room."

"Uh-huh. So that explains why you were enjoying yourself so much. Because you all were *acting*."

"Ash, it was like the two of them were having a contest for which one could shove her tongue far enough down my throat to make it to my dick."

"Now there's a visual." Her sardonic tone couldn't hide the visible shudder that went through her as I described the actresses' lack of skill or finesse.

"No one kisses me the way you do, Ashleigh. All sugar and fire. There is absolutely no other woman in the world who turns me on the way you can with a single kiss."

I'd been slowly making my way around the desk toward her, angling my pursuit to back her into a corner. When she bumped up against the wall, she looked up at me with equal parts hurt and anger in her beautiful sapphire eyes.

"You don't believe me," I said quietly, caging her in with my hands resting on the wall on either side of her. "After every woman I turned down during the whole tour, you don't believe me? You were there. You knew we were shooting the video—"

That's when it dawned on me. "Did you have an interview with one of the football players that night?"

The puzzled look she gave me told me the answer to my question before she responded. "No. I'm a music reviewer. Why would I interview a professional football player?"

"Son of a bitch!" I hissed. "Now it's starting to make sense."

"What are you talking about? You're not making any sense," she said.

"What did Garrett tell you that night after the show?"

"He said you wanted me to return to the hotel. Which I didn't understand, but he said you needed the car returned, that with the crew and everyone, there wouldn't be enough room, so I needed to go ahead."

"He told me you were interviewing a football player and would be joining back up with us when you finished. Then we were involved in filming, which for some reason included way too much tequila—the good stuff, not something watered down in bottles to imitate the good stuff. By the time we arrived at the hotel, I wasn't thinking too clearly."

From the look on her face, that was the wrong thing to say. Before she could duck under my arm and run from me, I rushed on.

"I saw you in our bed, which made no sense at all, and when that actress finally let me up for air, you were gone. I thought I'd made you up. We finished my part of the shoot, and I went next door looking for you. That's when I discovered your suitcase was missing, and I sobered up on the spot."

She hugged her arms tighter over her chest and, if anything, seemed to try to melt into the wall behind her.

"You were in that bed when we arrived, and you had no idea what was going on." I ducked my head down to catch her eyes. "That explains two long fucking months of radio silence."

Lowering my voice, I touched her then, my chest pressed to her crossed arms. "There was never anyone else, Ashleigh."

She remained rigid, telling me I had no choice but to pull out the big guns. Leaning in close, I sang softly into her ear.

"Every time you look at me
"I drown in your eyes.
"Every time you smile
"My spirit flies.

"Because nothing in the world compares
"To my beauty.

"Every time you laugh
"So precious and rare,
"My spirit flies
"Every time you take me with you there.

"Because nothing in the world compares
"To my beauty.

"You let me in, you let me see
"Your world.
"You shared your love, you came to be
"My girl.
"You gave me more, you made my life
"So real.
"And I'll love you every single day.

"Because nothing in the world compares
"To my beauty. My beauty,
"Nothing in the world compares—to you."

When I finished singing Ashleigh's song, she was in my arms, and I noticed the front of my T-shirt was soaked. I pulled away enough to slip a finger beneath her chin and tilt her face up so I could look into the endless blue of her eyes. Tears shimmered there, but I also saw something else. "You do believe me, don't you, Ash?" It wasn't really a question.

She nodded and gave me a watery, lopsided smile.

"From the moment I first saw you, it's only been you." She blinked up at me, and I knew this was the moment of truth. "Ashleigh Baker, I'm in love with you."

A loud knock on the door made both of us jump.

"You about done in there? I need to get the keys to the back room," someone said from the other side of the door.

I looked at Ashleigh and grinned.

"How 'bout we go somewhere more private and finish this conversation?"

"Okay."

"Since I don't want to be anywhere near that son of a bitch Garrett right now, let's go to your hotel," I suggested as I led her by the hand around the desk.

"It's not what you're used to, I'm afraid. The magazine only springs for two, maybe three-star hotels unless the reporter is popular."

"Does your room have a clean bed and a shower?"

"Yes."

"That covers it," I said as I held the door for her and ushered her through it ahead of me.

CHAPTER TWENTY-TWO

Blu

ASHLEIGH KEYED US into her hotel room and flipped on the lights. Stopping, she glanced back at me. "It's not what you're used to," she apologized again as I closed and dead-bolted the door behind us.

The room was spartan, a bed, a nightstand, a TV mounted on the wall.

"It has the only thing I need in it."

She gave a nervous laugh, her smile not reaching her eyes. "The bed?"

"You."

Seconds that felt like hours ticked by before she took two steps back to me and wrapped her arms around my waist. Resting her cheek on my chest, she whispered, "I've missed you so much."

I wrapped my arms around her, pulling her even closer, trying to absorb her into me. We stood quietly holding each other for long minutes, our hearts syncing in rhythm to each other before I finally said what I needed her to hear.

"When I came home at Christmas, I barely closed the door

on the town car before I tore over to your place. It took me a long time to realize you weren't coming to the door no matter how hard I pounded on it." I tightened my hold on her as if she might disappear like smoke before she heard everything I needed to say. "Mom walked over, told me you'd moved out and left no forwarding address." She stiffened against me, but I had to finish. "When I looked out into the yard, I saw the 'For Rent' sign and lost my mind. I ripped it out and flung it into the street before I dropped to my knees and cried."

Ashleigh tightened her arms around me and said nothing.

"Ash, it was as if I was five years old again. I couldn't understand how I could love you so much and you could walk away from me."

I pulled away from her enough to see her face, and the tears shimmering in the sapphire depths of her eyes cheered me. My story wouldn't make her cry if she didn't love me too. Still, I had no choice but take the biggest risk of my life—bare my fears and lay my heart at her feet. "Please, baby. Promise me you'll never leave me like that again. Promise me we'll talk it out when you're upset or worried. Please, Ashleigh."

She nodded, closing her eyes tightly, but a couple of tears spilled over to slide down her cheeks anyway. I kissed them away and pulled back to look at her again.

"Ashleigh."

"I promise, Blu. I'm so sorry." She sighed. "You're right. We're a pair, you and I. We both need to learn how to talk to each other," she said into my chest before she looked up into my eyes. "I want to try."

"Me too."

Framing her face with my hands, at last I kissed her beautiful mouth. I meant it to be a seal of our promise, but I could never control myself where Ashleigh was concerned. The kiss we shared burned so hot it could have launched a rocket. That strip of bare skin peeking from beneath the hem of her shirt begged for my touch, a temptation I couldn't resist as my hands slipped from her face to her waist.

Arching into me, she moaned and seemed to try to meld our bodies together. In a nanosecond, I'd backed her against the wall beside the bed, my thigh wedged between her legs. The silk of her skin beneath my fingertips drove me wild as I smoothed my hands over her, touching her everywhere I could reach beneath her shirt.

As I played my fingers over her, together we deepened our kiss, our mouths fused in a conflagration, the temperature rising with every stroke of our tongues.

She dug her nails into my biceps as I skimmed my fingertips over her belly. I palmed her full breasts through the lace of her bra as tiny whimpers escaped her throat and she rubbed her pussy along the top of my thigh.

Tearing my mouth from hers, I pulled away to push her shirt all the way up and off her body. But it wasn't enough.

"I do love your taste in lingerie, Ash, but this has got to go," I ground out as I slipped my fingers beneath the band of the sexy pink lace bra she wore and pushed it off her body to join her shirt on the floor.

For a heartbeat—maybe two—I feasted my eyes on the beauty of her full tits with their dusky pink nipples all puckered up and begging for my mouth. Then I swooped down and kissed her nipple before opening my lips and taking her in a deep hard suck.

Ashleigh gasped and arched into me, giving me all the encouragement I needed. I sucked and licked and kissed her tits as she begged me for more.

"Blu, please," she whimpered, gyrating her hips against me.

Her skirt had rucked up around her waist, and when I dropped to my knees in front of her, I welcomed the sight of skimpy lace panties the same color as her bra. Skimming my palms up the outsides of her thighs, I reached the top of her panties and jerked them down to her ankles in one motion, paying no attention to the ripping sound of lace giving way to desire.

"Please what, Ash?"

"Please, more."

"Your command is my wish, princess-girl. Open for me."

Anchoring herself with her palms flat against the wall behind her, Ashleigh obeyed, offering me her pretty pussy. Testing her, I ran my index finger from her clit along her folds, discovering to my everlasting happiness that she was soaking wet. Never taking my eyes from her face, I pumped my finger inside her before withdrawing it and sucking her sweet juices from it.

"Blu!" she gasped as her knees buckled.

"Oh yeah, baby," I groaned as I caught her and kept her standing right where I wanted her

Focusing my attention on her perfect pussy, I ate her exactly the way I knew she needed. When I added two fingers to my lips and tongue, she plunged her hands into my hair, alternately tugging my hair and holding my mouth on her while she pulsed hard on my fingers, her sighs filling my ears with satisfaction before she filled the room with my name on a scream.

Once again, her knees threatened to buckle with her orgasm. Her response made me feel like Superman, and I couldn't help the smile that spread across my face as I held myself against the heaven of her body.

With my hands on her hips, I steadied her as I stood in front of her. "Oh yeah, Ash, we're just getting started," I said as I stared into the deep oceans of her eyes.

Lifting her high into my arms, I turned and dropped her onto the bed where she watched me from beneath her lashes, those gorgeous eyes now nearly black with desire. I toed off my boots and dragged my T-shirt over my head and shucked my jeans and boxers into a pile beside the bed.

Noticing her skirt still bunched around her waist, I said, "For this next part, I want you completely naked."

She took the hint and lifted her hips to unzip her skirt so I could tug it down her endlessly long legs.

"These can stay on though," I said, indicating her heels as I flung her skirt to the floor.

"So, not *completely* naked," she teased.

"Bend your knees, Ash," I commanded.

I grabbed her ankles and arranged her legs with her bent knees spread wide, her feet flat on the mattress. Diving in, I gave her clit another kiss before I pulled myself up to lie between her legs.

"You taste so sweet. Let me show you."

The kiss we shared fired me up even more than I already was. Rubbing myself over the top of her G-spot only inflamed both of us more.

Eventually, I couldn't take it anymore. The months apart, the response of our reunion, the love I felt for her all came together in a blazing need to be inside her *right now*. Tearing my mouth from hers, I panted, "Hold that thought, babe."

Leaning over the side of the bed, I retrieved my jeans and started going through my pockets. *What the fuck?* I found nothing but my hotel key card and my wallet in my pants. My alarm built as I dug through my wallet and discovered it devoid of the one necessity for the night.

"Fuck!"

"What is it?" Alarm sounded in her voice as she leaned up on her elbows.

"I can't fucking believe this! All the careful planning I did to find a way to see you again, to talk to you, to work things out between us, and I didn't come prepared for *us*."

"No condoms?"

"No condoms," I confirmed as I threw myself onto my back against the pillows, so many levels of frustration overwhelming me.

Not the least of which was the specter of blue-balling myself with my gorgeous and very willing lady lying right beside me.

Turning my head to her, I asked hopefully, "You wouldn't happen to have any with you, would you?"

Ashleigh laughed. "Haven't needed any since Thanksgiving, Blu."

I flung my arm across my eyes. "Great. That's fucking peachy." I couldn't very well beg her for a blow job. Then again . . .

Ashleigh had other plans.

"Ash, what are you doing?" The pitch of my voice leaped three octaves I think as she straddled me. "We already established we don't have any protection."

She smiled sphinxlike at me as she stroked the length of my cock with her hot wet pussy lips. "You told me you weren't with those two women the night of the film shoot on Thanksgiving, and I believe you." She slid along the length of me, and I fisted the sheets beside my hips, willing myself not to surge up into her.

"You told me you haven't been with anyone since I left that night, and I believe you." Another long slide along the length of my cock had me grinding my teeth hard enough to crack the enamel. "You told me you'd only been with me since the end of your Asian tour almost a year ago, and I believe you." She added her hand to the party, stroking me, and I nearly tore the sheets to hold myself back. "You told me you were clean, and I believe you," she said as she jacked me, and I did my damnedest to hold on and let her have her way.

"You told me tonight that you love me. And I believe you." She slid down my body enough to take me into her mouth, licking and kissing me before she pulled me completely inside the sweet heaven of her mouth and sucked.

Again, I tried not to surge up into her, but all our foreplay—most of which I admit I initiated—had driven me right to the edge of my control. Ashleigh took me, hollowing her cheeks on the upstroke and driving me out of my mind. Pulling off of me with a pop, she slid back up my body, her pussy hovering a breath above my rock-hard cock.

"I'm on the pill, Blu. So I guess we can be completely naked when we make love. I've never been completely naked with a man before." She smiled softly. "I'm glad you're my first."

"And your last, Ashleigh. Just like you're my first . . . and my last."

She slipped her hand between us, grabbed my cock, and pumped me, dragging a groan from me I couldn't suppress. Positioning herself above me, she kissed the head of my cock with her slick pussy lips, then pulled herself up and sat down on me, sheathing me fully inside her.

"Ashleigh!"

She closed her eyes and dropped her head back while her walls pulsed around me.

I grabbed her hips, my fingers digging deep into her flesh as I lifted her nearly off me before slamming her back down my length.

"Oh, baby, you feel—" I couldn't form the words, my mind a jumble of incoherent thoughts and emotions as Ashleigh and I moved together.

So good.

But not enough.

Being careful to maintain our intimate connection, I rolled her beneath me. "I've missed you so much, Ashleigh baby."

Running my hands over her legs, I hooked my palms beneath her knees, bending them and opening her more to me. Lifting her hips, she gave me even more of herself, and I drove in all the way to my balls. "Ashleigh! Fuck!"

Trying not to lose myself before she came, I grabbed her ankles and placed them on my shoulders, her feet in those sexy heels ratcheting up my desire. I started rocking into her, increasing my rhythm, thrusting harder and harder until I was pounding against her.

Ashleigh's moans and whimpers, coupled with her nails digging into my thighs, told me she was right there with me. She sang my name as the hot velvet vise of her pussy rhythmically pulsed around me while she came. Her body drew up in a beautiful bow, her head thrown back against the pillows, her nipples straining to touch the ceiling, her belly taut as the strings on my guitar.

I continued to pound into her, my orgasm crescendoing to a song that with one final thrust burst into a thousand notes as I shouted her name in harmony with my perfect girl—Ashleigh.

When the final chords of our orgasms faded to soft sighs, I let her feet drop back down to the mattress so I could pillow my chest on her luscious breasts. My kiss on her full mouth was a lingering fadeaway of the perfect melody of making love with the love of my life.

Hours later, the ringing of my phone jarred us awake after it seemed we'd barely dropped off to sleep. Making love completely naked, completely vulnerable, completely open to another person who was all those things with me took the experience to an entirely new place. Nothing I'd ever done in the past, even with more than one girl at once, could compare to loving Ashleigh naked. To loving Ashleigh, period. So of course, I'd hardly let us rest all night.

The name on the screen shot my good mood at the way our reunion went all to hell.

"What do you want?" I growled into the phone.

"Good morning to you too, sunshine. In case you forgot, we fly out in an hour."

"Shit. What time is it?"

"Ten. You all said you wanted to fly out early so you could catch a little beach time. The rest of the band is waiting in the lobby."

"I'm not going to make it."

"What the hell, Blu?"

"Listen, have room service send my duffel over to the Magnolia Inn on Bee Street, room—" I looked over at Ashleigh, her hair tumbled in a gorgeous chestnut-colored mess around her head and shoulders, her sleepy eyes questioning me. "What's the number for the room, babe?"

"Two-fifteen."

"Room two-fifteen. Tell Dan to fly back to pick me up tomorrow morning." Smiling at Ashleigh, I added, "I've got something more interesting than the beach here."

"That took longer than I thought it would." The snark in his tone should have warned me.

"What?"

"You finding some groupie to hook up with. For a while there, I almost thought you deserved her." There was no sincerity in his laughter.

"Fuck you, Garrett. We pay you to be our manager, not our mom. Send my shit over here and let Dan know he's making some overtime on this tour."

I clicked off and tossed my phone onto the table beside the bed.

"What's wrong? Why are you so upset?"

"I had other plans for how we were going to wake each other up today, but we were going to have to talk about this eventually, so it might as well be now." I pushed up on my elbow and rested the side of my face in my palm so I could look her in the eyes.

Turning on her side, she mirrored me. "What are you talking about?"

"That night in Dallas. Garrett lied."

Ashleigh's eyes rounded. "Why would he do that?"

"Because Garrett has it bad for you, and beyond being polite to him, you didn't give him the time of day. Looks like he thought if I hurt you by bringing those women back to the hotel—to our suite—you'd run to him. He could comfort you and steal you away from me."

She gaped at me before she abruptly snapped her mouth shut and gave me a speculative look. "That explains a lot, actually."

"What do you mean?"

"He started coming on to me almost from the day you introduced me to everyone at your studio last summer. I didn't think much of it since Dakota made a run at me too."

My face must have given away my thoughts because she picked up my other hand, turned it over, and kissed my palm before placing it against her chest.

"Both of them were too late, Blu. By then I was already gone for you."

I relaxed a fraction. "Go on."

"Anyway, like you said, I didn't pay much attention to Garrett except when I interviewed him and he tried to make himself into some kind of hero for managing the band. By then, I already knew about Dakota's and your business acumen, so aside from day-to-day logistics and such, I realized Garrett is more of a glorified secretary than a manager."

"Maybe you should have mentioned that in the article," I grumbled.

Ashleigh laughed. "I didn't even mention him in the article, Blu."

I smirked. "Oh yeah, that's right. I knew that. Good call, by the way, babe."

Her smile evanesced as the implications of Garrett's duplicity fully registered with her. "So he set us up to split us up?"

"And he succeeded. Only you didn't run to him for comfort like you did in his fantasies," I said as I soothed myself by tracing patterns over her skin with my fingertips.

"I can't imagine why he thought I would go to him at all."

"Like I said, he was living in la-la land where you were concerned."

Ashleigh frowned at me. "You let him believe you're with someone else. Why?"

"Because when you and I step off our jet in Florida tomorrow, Garrett will have no doubt we're back together for good. I want him to stew, and then I want to burst his bubble all to hell."

Blinking her eyes wide, she drawled, "Blu Connolly, I had no idea you were so vindictive."

"Only toward someone I trusted to have my back before he stabbed me right between the shoulder blades."

"You—" She swallowed, started again. "You want me to come with you to Florida?"

"You got other plans?"

"No, but—"

"We're back together, Ashleigh." I rolled up on top of her. "For good. I want you to be with me wherever I am."

"But I have an assignment for the magazine."

"When?"

"Starting next week. I'm following the all-girl group Carnival as they begin their first headlining tour. I should be working on background material right now."

"Where does their tour begin?" I asked cautiously. I'd just reconnected with her and already the clock was ticking down on our time together.

"California."

"Son of a bitch! We're on the East Coast until April."

"Carnival is crisscrossing the country. Five dates in California and three dates in Texas before they start in Florida and follow you guys up the East Coast."

"We'll figure something out." Tangling my fingers in the silk of her hair, I said, "I'll send our jet for you or come to you when we have a day or two break. Somehow, we'll see each other while we're on tour."

"Yeah?"

"Yeah. Now come here. We shouldn't waste any of the time we have."

CHAPTER TWENTY-THREE

Ashleigh

I T WAS WEIRD yet beyond cool to be the only ones flying in Balefire's private jet. As we winged toward Miami, I'd nearly dozed off in the comfy captain's chair I reclined in when, with no warning whatsoever, Blu jumped out of his chair and grabbed my hand. Yanking me up, he said, "Jesus, Ashleigh. All right, already." The wicked gleam in his eye should have been a clue, but I was a little slow to catch on.

He all but dragged me out of my seat.

"What—?"

"Nag, nag, nag. I can see you're not going to let up until you have your chance." He kept talking as he pulled me along behind him until we stepped through the door at the back of the cabin.

"My chance for what?" I asked as my eyes settled on the wall-to-wall bed taking up the back room of the plane's cabin. Then our conversation from my first flight on Balefire's jet flashed through my head. Was he suggesting . . .?

Blu let go of me long enough to close and lock the door behind us before he started stripping off his clothes. "Ashleigh, stop messing around. I said I'd take care of helping you join the mile-high club, but you have to be naked." The teasing tone in his voice confirmed my suspicions.

He sighed dramatically as first his jeans then his boxers hit the floor, allowing his long, thick erection to spring free at the apex of his thighs. Next, he pulled his T-shirt over his head and dropped it on the pile of clothes at his feet. When he was completely naked, he launched himself backward onto the middle of the bed. Resting one hand behind his head, his pose deceptively nonchalant, he slowly jacked himself with the other hand. Watching him was so erotic I could feel myself creaming my panties.

"Come on, Ash. This was your big idea. It's a bit late for you to turn all shy."

The exasperated expression in his voice warred with the unholy mischief glittering in the golden-green depths of his eyes and with the naughty smile playing over his beautiful sculpted mouth.

Playing his game, I lifted an eyebrow. "Shoes on or off?"

"Off. Along with everything else."

I stripped off my blouse and wide-legged trousers, hanging them on a hook attached to the back of the door. My ivory lace bra and panty set along with my heels joined the pile of his clothes on the floor.

Starting at his feet, I crawled up his body until I straddled him. Still, he continued to jack himself, his knuckles brushing against my clit, making me even wetter. When I started rocking against his hand, all the playfulness vanished from his face, a deadly serious expression replacing it.

"Say it, Ash," he demanded.

"I want you, Blu."

"Yes, and?"

He gave me more of his hand before he rubbed the head of his cock along my seam.

"I thought we weren't saying that when we were having sex," I breathed, becoming lost in the sensations he drew from me.

"That was only the first time when we both needed to know our foundation is built on something more solid than sex. Now say it."

"I love you, Blu. So much."

"There it is." He positioned himself at my entrance, digging his fingers into my hips and guiding me down to sheath him completely.

I closed my eyes as he filled me full, my body pulsing with pleasure. Arching my back and angling my hips slightly, I pulled all of him inside me. He gripped my hips tightly, the lust-filled huskiness of his voice reverberating through my chest.

As he captured my eyes with his, his tone was solemn. "There is no one in the world like you, Ashleigh. I love you so much." He held me still, suspended, before his expression changed to a wicked smile. "Now, you gotta move on me, baby, before I go out of my damn mind."

I smiled back at him. My turn to tease and play.

"Like this?" I inquired innocently as I scored my nails over his chest and down his taut abs.

He sucked in air and warned me with his golden-green eyes, a warning I ignored.

"Or like this?"

I ran my hands up my belly to my breasts, which I cupped as I rolled my nipples between my thumbs and forefingers. The play caused my pussy to clench around him, and I discovered I had no choice but to wiggle my hips over him.

The next thing I knew, I was on my back, Blu on top of me and still inside me.

"For someone who wanted to join the mile-high club as badly as you did, you sure are taking your sweet-ass time about it, Ash," he joked.

"The mile-high club was always your big idea—"

He grinned and thrust deep.

When I recovered my breath, I said, "But I'm all on board with it." I grinned back at him as I clamped my inner muscles around him.

He started moving, and all thoughts of teasing and being teased and where we were flew out of my head. My body, my mind, my heart filled to the brim with Blu.

After we completely sated each other, we lay quietly, his chest pillowing my head, his arms cocooning me to his body.

I sensed his voice rumbling in his chest more than heard it, a deep, quiet confession that left me smiling all over. "I always wondered what it would feel like to make love while flying through space. Now I know it's fucking awesome."

Lifting my head so I could see his face, I asked, "Are you saying we just joined the mile-high club together?"

"Yeah."

"So that's why you gave in so easily when I insisted on joining it." I smiled mischievously up at him, playing along with his tale.

"Exactly. That and the fact that you're demanding. In case no one's pointed that out to you yet." He smirked at our new running joke.

"Uh-huh."

Interrupting our conversation, the pilot spoke over the intercom, "Mr. Connolly, we have a report to expect high winds and turbulence in about fifteen minutes. You may want to buckle up."

Blu burst out laughing.

"What's so funny?" I asked.

"The crew. Dakota warned all of us after he took a couple of girls for a flight."

"I'm still confused."

"They're letting us know that Cory, our flight steward, has discovered the main cabin empty and reported to the pilot. They're jealous."

It was as though my face caught fire even though Blu and I were safely alone. At some point, however, I'd have to return to the main cabin where Cory would be awaiting us, and I'd have to exit the plane where Dan the pilot always stood at the top of the stairs to wish us well. Ugh.

"Don't worry, Ashleigh. They all know you're my girl. They'd be more concerned if we didn't take advantage of the master bedroom when we were flying this bird alone," Blu said soothing me as he smoothed his hand up and down my side. "Still, we must be nearing our destination, so we should probably get dressed."

Blu

The look on Garrett's face was priceless when he arrived to pick me up at the airport. I made sure to exit the jet first, so when Ashleigh stepped out of the cabin behind me, she stood at the top of the stairs alone for a few seconds, giving Garrett a chance to see my "groupie." When I reached the bottom of the stairs, I turned to give Ash a hand, pulling her to me. "Welcome to Florida, Ashleigh Baker," I said with a smile before I leaned in and laid the mother of all kisses on her.

Of course, us being us, in a nanosecond the kiss deepened into something rivaling the Florida heat.

"You two about done there, 'cause we have sound checks in about an hour, Blu," Garrett sneered.

Not taking my eyes from her beautiful face I said, "I'll never be done with Ashleigh."

She smiled shyly up at me, and it was all I could do not to kiss her again. But Balefire had a show to do, and we'd cut it pretty close as it was. I guided my lady to the waiting town car and thanked Cory for stowing our bags in the trunk.

"Nice to see you again, Miss Baker. I speak for the entire crew when I say it's good to have you back with us." Cory gave her a little bow and walked away, Ashleigh's "thank you" trailing him on the breeze.

"Hey Garrett, why don't you ride up front, give Ashleigh and me some privacy, yeah?" I suggested as I pulled the door he'd opened from his hand.

Ashleigh slid into the back seat, and I slid in beside her, pulling the door closed behind me. Even through the smoked glass of the window, I caught Garrett's angry glare before he turned and opened the front door of the town car to ride up front with the driver, my actions and intent not lost on him. Idly, I wondered how he was going to excuse his behavior when we discussed it later. Then Ashleigh leaned her head on my shoulder, and I forgot all about Garrett Phillips.

♪

Playing a sold-out show always energized us, but tonight would be something special, and I couldn't remember a time, even when we played our first stadium show, when I'd been so nervous. Like I told Ashleigh months ago when I introduced her to Benson Strauss, the adrenaline rush from a little stage fright goes a long way toward helping a person give a kick-ass performance. Tonight's show, however, was far more than a performance. Tonight's show was about Ashleigh. She was back in my life, and I planned on keeping her in it forever.

She stood in the wings offstage, and I could sense her eyes on me as we gave the throng of people in the stadium the show they came to see. The lights, the fireworks, Jack's wild-ass drumming, Dakota's blistering guitar licks, Tron's thumping steady bass, and my voice pulling it all together combined into one giant rock 'n' roll extravaganza. Our shows sold out because we gave the people what they wanted. But tonight, the only person whose opinion mattered to me smiled at me every time I looked over at her, which I admit was several times a song.

Near the end of our set, we slowed down the show, playing "Missing You," Jack's love song to Clio, before I turned to Dakota and gave him the sign.

"By now you all know the backstory behind that last song you like so much. Turns out, Blu wrote a song for another special lady. We tried out an acoustic version at a small venue a couple of days ago and that went so well, we thought we'd try out the rock version for you. What do you say?"

The crowd roared its approval, of course.

Dakota continued. "The lady who inspired Blu to write this one is standing offstage. Hey Ashleigh, how 'bout you come on out here and join us?"

She stared at me, and I held my hand out to her, inviting her onstage with us. During all the lead-up to the moment, one of the roadies had placed a stool beside me, and when she hesitated too long, he walked over and put his hand on the small of her back, propelling her out to me.

"Hey babe," I said into her ear, "I want everyone to know that you're mine and I'm yours."

She never took her eyes from me as I strummed the opening riffs to "My Beauty." Her eyes widened into saucers as the rest of the band joined me, and I began to sing the words. Before the final chorus, we stopped playing like the guys and I had planned, and I dropped to one knee in front of her.

"I love you so much, Ashleigh Baker. Will you marry me?"

Grinning, Dakota stepped over to us and handed me the ring I'd found online while Ashleigh slept on the plane, the one I'd had a courier deliver to him to keep for me. I took it from him and slipped it on Ashleigh's finger, a big-ass Tiffany diamond that glittered under the stage lights. For several agonizing seconds she stared into my eyes. Finally, she nodded, and I stood and took her into my arms and kissed her. When our lips met, the crowd faded away. I might have continued to forget where we were if Jack and Tron hadn't started a thumping beat to remind me.

I let her go, and we finished the song to the roaring approval of the audience. After I walked Ashleigh back to the wings, I winked at her and strolled back out onto the stage to finish the show.

♪

Sweat streamed off me when I ran backstage before the encore. Ashleigh waited right inside the wings, and I put my hands on her shoulders to push her back farther from the stage. When I judged we were sufficiently out of sight of the audience, I leaned my forehead against hers.

"Did you mean it?"

"Did *you* mean it?" she parroted back.

"That wasn't a stunt out there, Ash."

She fisted her hands in my shirt, and her body softened against mine.

"I love you, Blu."

"Jesus, Ash. I can't wait to get you alone babe. Unfortunately, the fans need some additional entertainment. Later, the only word I want to hear you say is *yes*. You got me?"

Her eyes sparkled mischievously. "Yes. Blu."

"Smart-ass," I growled as I leaned in and covered that sexy mouth with my own.

"Hey you guys. Save it for your room," Dakota heckled as he stood nearby draining a water bottle over his head.

After we finished the show, the crew joined the band behind the stage, everyone congratulating Ashleigh and me. Everyone, that is, except for Garrett who stood to one side and glared at us. Raising a brow at him, I dared him to say anything that would damage the moment. Instead, he shrugged and wandered away. Smart man.

♪

I held Ashleigh tightly to my side as we walked through the doors to the hotel ballroom where the after-party pulsed to a salsa beat. Pressing a kiss to her temple, I whispered, "I see the monk and Clio over at the bar. What do you say we join them?"

Jack's fiancée, Clio Barnes, their daughter Angel, and Jack's mom Lori had flown out the day before to join the band for a few dates along the southeast coast during Clio's spring break from college.

While Lori babysat Angel, Clio joined the band for the show and the after-party.

"You okay, Ashleigh? You seemed a little shell-shocked out there on the stage," Jack drawled before he took a pull from his beer and winked at his fiancée.

"I'm fine. But I think from now on I'll leave the performing to you guys."

She smiled at me, and I squeezed her hand, the one with the big-ass rock on it.

"Congratulations, you two," Clio said as she leaned in to hug us simultaneously.

"Judging from the way the fans reacted to our little show, they're all right with another Balefire member out of circulation," Jack said with a smile.

"They don't have a choice." I dropped a hand on his shoulder. "When we were on our last tour, I didn't get it with you. Now I do."

Jack handed me a beer and we toasted each other, a look of understanding passing between us. The music, the shows, the guys in the band—all of that was still important, but the greatest happiness in my life stood in the circle of my arms. Jesus, the woman slayed me. Until I met Ashleigh Baker, I had no idea the best rock 'n' roll party in the world is the one you share with the person you know you'll love for the rest of your life.

"I love you," I whispered in her ear.

She looked up at me with shining eyes. "I love you too, Blu. Always."

Sing For Me Playlist:

"Rockstar"—Nickelback

"What Was I Thinking"—Theory of a Deadman

"Paralyzer"—Finger Eleven

"The Lucky One"—Alison Krauss

"Here We Are"—Breaking Benjamin

"Stars"—Sixx:A.M.

"Baby Come Home"—Bush

"Ashes of Eden"—Breaking Benjamin

"If Only For Now"—Pop Evil

"Don't Walk Away"—Sick Puppies

Thank you for reading *Sing For Me*.

Turn the page to read an excerpt from *Wild For Me*,
Book Three in the Balefire Series coming in November 2021.

CHAPTER ONE

Dakota

WHEN I STROLLED into the rehearsal for the monk's wedding, I was knocked flat on my ass. Metaphorically speaking. We didn't start the evening with a brawl. Kind of amazing considering how much grief my little joke caused Jack for a while. Now the joke was on me. The girl who haunted my dreams stood laughing with a couple of other women, oblivious to my presence. It left me with an ache in my chest so intense it threatened to choke me.

Last time I saw Annabelle, she tossed me a wave as she drove away in her sweet blacked-out Mustang. After checking another experience off her bucket list, an after-concert night of sex with a rock star, she drove right out of my life. Too bad she left all those incredible memories behind.

Closing my eyes, I could see her again, haltingly giving her first—and I hoped only—striptease. Then she climbed up my body where I lay on the bed, leaned in and kissed me so hot and deep and dark I almost came in my jeans. For the rest of the night, we torched my sheets to the point we could have set off the hotel fire alarms.

As the sun sneaked in under the drapes the morning after, she gathered her clothes like she assumed she was another one-night stand in a decade of one-night stands for me. Except in unguarded moments over the last two years, I'd caught myself thinking about her, dreaming about her. That girl gave me the best night ever—and the next morning she calmly walked away like banging a rock star was something she did every other day. No begging for a selfie to prove her night to her girlfriends. No slyly hinting I might want her number. No outright asking to join the band on tour. Maybe she did bang rock stars regularly. Hell, I didn't know. As I watched her with the monk's fiancée, for some reason the thought burned like acid in my gut.

Whether he planned it or not, Jack revenged me well, saddling me with his fiancée's friend MandMs for the wedding. The girl was so starstruck she could barely look at me let alone speak to me when Clio Barnes soon-to-be Whitehorse introduced us. Instead of taking my arm to walk down the aisle the way every other bridesmaid did at the wedding rehearsal, she let her fingers hover somewhere near my elbow and studiously watched the grass as we walked to the pretty arbor in the Whitehorse family's backyard. I was going to have to work on relaxing her, or she might fall flat on her face at the start of the ceremony the next day. What I would have rather been doing was talking Annabelle back into my bed.

As I stood beside our bass guitarist Adam Tron and lead singer Blu Connolly, the other members of Balefire, I knew I was supposed to be listening to the justice of the peace explain what all would be happening tomorrow afternoon during the ceremony. Instead, I couldn't help but remember my earlier encounter with the only girl who'd ever been more than a blip on my radar once I finally approached her.

"Annabelle."

"Dakota."

"You two know each other?" Blu had asked, looking from one of us to the other like a spectator at a ping-pong game.

As we stared at each other, I watched her eyes widen a fraction and felt my own mirror hers. Damn, she was cool.

"Not really," we said in unison.

"We met after the concert at Red Rocks," I said.

"The same night Jack and Clio managed the first of their reconciliations," Annabelle added with a little smile.

Blu tilted his head. "Huh. Wonder how I missed all that."

"It was a big night, playing in front of our home crowd and all. I think you were celebrating." I was addressing Blu but never took my eyes off Annabelle.

What whirred around in her pretty head? What did she truly think about the night we met?

Before I could pursue the topic any further, Lori Whitehorse, Jack's mom, interrupted us to let us know the JP had arrived and we were needed in the rehearsal.

Now, Blu hissing at me under his breath jerked me back into the present.

"You get that?"

"What?" I asked, confused.

"Where'd you go?"

I shrugged. What was I gonna say? That I was reliving moments with Annabelle since she'd unexpectedly walked back into my life?

"When the JP says, 'This is a union of love,' that's our cue to grab our guitars to play Jack's song to Clio. Pay attention, dude."

"Got it," I whispered back as I tried not to stare at Annabelle across the aisle.

That's when I caught her sneaking a look at me, and I couldn't help it. I grinned at her and winked. Of course I wanted her attention. What I really wanted was to know if she'd give me another night like that one magic night we spent together two years ago.

Annabelle

When we gathered at the back door to Jack's parents' house, Dakota Perri slipped behind me and whispered in my ear. "Annabelle, can I hope for another private striptease later?"

Since the man was a walking, talking ad for hot sex, I shouldn't have been surprised. I could hear laughter in his voice, but Clio saved me from answering when she interrupted to pair up the wedding party. I'd be walking in with Adam Tron, the bassist for Balefire. We'd walk ahead of Stacy Newhouse, our sorority sister and the maid of honor, and Colin Whitehorse, Jack's older brother and best man. I couldn't decide if I was relieved or disappointed about not walking in with Dakota.

Good thing I didn't have to answer his question. What could I say? I had no idea what he thought about what happened between us. I'd earned my reputation for wildness, but that strip show I'd given him the night we first met was a one-off. I couldn't decide if he was teasing me or actually wanted a repeat performance.

Even though I'd played it cool, I couldn't keep from shifting my gaze across the aisle to that man. Damn him and his bona fide rock star gorgeousness, those incredible sea blue eyes, that shock of sun-kissed brown hair, that lean muscular body decorated with tats in the most interesting places. It would help if I didn't remember every detail about him. When he grinned and winked at me, my heart jumped and I struggled not to lose my breath.

Yep, Dakota was definitely laughing at me.

But I remembered the way he groaned and shouted his pleasure during that one magical night I spent with him after a Balefire concert two years ago. Not only was the man a virtuoso guitar player, he was also a master at pleasuring a woman. My skin tingled, and my lady parts tightened and wept at the sound of his voice so deep and warm in my ear when we saw each other at the start of the rehearsal.

Since he'd undoubtedly had countless women over years of

touring with Balefire, I was under no illusions about him remembering much of what happened with me. After all, I'd been a junior in college, hardly a worldly woman when I slept with him. Certainly, my little strip show couldn't have been the first—or last—private show some woman had given him either.

Still, I never thought I'd actually see him again even after it came out that my best friend Clio's baby daddy was Jack Whitehorse, Balefire's drummer. Yet here we were, meeting again nearly two years after that incredible night following the Red Rocks concert.

From some distant place, the sounds of the string quartet playing and people moving jerked me back to the present. We filed down the aisle between the chairs Jack's army of brothers had set up in the Whitehorses's back yard. Adam Tron and I walked out ahead of Dakota and my sorority sister MandMs, who fluttered beside him, apparently starstruck. I understood the feeling, but for a different reason. The heat on my backside told me his gorgeous eyes were trained right there, and I couldn't wait for the rehearsal to end. The girls and I had planned one last single ladies' night with Clio, which meant I could escape Dakota Perri until I could process all the emotions skittering through me at seeing him in person again.

Too bad Dakota had other plans.

Cornering me away from the others, he asked, "Annabelle, you are planning to save me a dance after the ceremony tomorrow, aren't ya?"

"I think the entire wedding party is expected to dance together at least once."

"I meant a private dance."

When he deepened the timbre of his voice, dripping seduction into the delivery of the word *private,* I couldn't miss what he meant. But I pretended to anyway. "If you want to dance with me at the reception tomorrow, Dakota, just ask."

He moved closer to me, nearly but not quite touching me yet

stealing all the available air. "Last time, Annabelle, I didn't have to ask."

Since Dakota stood somewhere north of six feet while I topped out at five five, I had to lock up into his eyes. The desire I saw there tripped my pulse into overdrive. Maybe he remembered that night better than I thought.

Blu's fiancée, Ashleigh Baker, saved me from giving in to temptation and probably making a fool of myself.

"Hey, Annabelle, you riding with us?" she called.

Sliding awkwardly beneath his arm where he had me partially caged in beside the house, I mumbled, "Excuse me, Dakota. The girls and I are taking Clio out for one last fling. I think I'm holding up the show."

"I heard. Have a good time, Annabelle. I'll see you tomorrow."

The deep rumble of his voice, the promise in the word *tomorrow* sent shivers straight through me. I heard more than saw the smile on his face, and a little voice inside me screamed, "Run! Run for your heart!" But of course I didn't. I walked away with as much bravado as I could pretend and knew I'd spend the rest of the evening thinking even more than usual about Dakota Perri.

ACKNOWLEDGEMENTS

This last year has been a challenge for so many people and among the hardest hit were entertainers and musicians. As an avid rock concert enthusiast, I've truly missed supporting local, regional, national, and international acts by attending live shows. The energy that flows between artists and audiences connects us in ways that can't be replicated over a zoom call or a concert event played on the screen at a drive-in theater. During the pandemic, NIVA (National Independent Venue Association) formed in an effort to keep small stages and the personnel who support the live music industry afloat through #saveourstages. Though Congress included independent artists and venues in the last COVID relief bill, many musicians, roadies, technicians, drivers, promoters, and more still need help. NIVA continues to collect donations for these people, so if enjoying live music is important to you, please consider donating to this association.

Bri Brasher Weigel, thank you for reading the early drafts and for your input on cover designs, blurbs, tag lines—the list goes on. Your opinions have steered me in the right direction, and I appreciate that so much.

A big thank you to LindaRae Sande, K.J. Gillenwater, and Sara

Vinduska for all of your help and ideas for marketing this series. It's a good thing we snagged the bigger table in our favorite restaurant so I have more room to take notes. ;) Thanks also to the three of you and to Jacque Coburn for your comments, suggestions, and catches when I shared this story with you. Writing is a solitary endeavor, but it isn't lonely when I can share it with my writer buddies.

Nikki Busch, you truly are a rock star editor. I know I say this in every book, but I'm a better writer because of how you edit my work. Thank you.

While I've been waiting to enjoy live shows again, I've immersed myself in recreating them in the Balefire Series. Thank you for taking this ride with me. Reviews make a big difference in the life of an indie book (and author). If you enjoyed this story, please take a minute and leave a review on whichever platform works for you.

Interacting with readers is the best part of putting my books out into the world. You can find me on BookBub at Tam DeRudder Jackson, on Facebook at Tam DeRudder Jackson Reader Group, on Instagram @tamstales32, and on my website: *https://www.tamderud-derjackson.com*. Let's hang out and talk books, music, what we want for dinner . . . Did someone say chocolate?

ABOUT THE AUTHOR

Tam DeRudder Jackson is the author of the paranormal romance Talisman Series and the contemporary romance Balefire Series. Her favorite "room" in her house is her patio where she dreams up stories of romance and risk. When she's not writing her latest paranormal or contemporary romance, you can find her driving around in her convertible or carving turns on the slopes of the local ski hill. The mom of two grown sons, Tam likes to travel, attend rock concerts, watch football and soccer, and visit old car shows with her husband. She lives in the mountains of northwest Wyoming where she spends most of her free time trying to read all the books. Her TBR piles are threatening to take over her office, and she's fine with that.